1

This is a work of fiction that was inspired by my experiences as a driver for a summer camp a long
time ago.

Copyright January 17, 2017 by Richard D. Rotberg
No. 1-4353004351

ISBN-13:978-1975718497
ISBN-10:1975718496

For Lynne, Bart and in Remembrance of Betsy

Acknowledgments

I want to thank Elaine S. Fox J.D. for her help and encouragement in completing this work, and especially for her patience in editing my freshman efforts. I also want to thank my long time friend, Richard Manners for his input, artistic inspiration and especially his uncanny understanding of the entire effort.

Max Lewis: Road to Manhood

A Novel By Richard Rotberg

Prologue

It is the late 1950's. Max Lewis is a 19-year-old who lives with his parents, a lower- middle-class-family on the west side of Chicago. His parents, despite a lack of religious affiliation, have raised Max with a strong moral and ethical code of hard work, strict adherence to the law, and doing what's right at all times.

The decade of the '50's was a time in American history that was caught up with the "Cold War." A time when children practiced getting under their desks at school in case the Russians dropped atom bombs on our cities. Although America was the only legitimate superpower, it was also a time when the political right feared communists everywhere in society. The Sexual Revolution had not yet happened, and a puritanical approach to sex was the norm. It was a time of growing wealth, cars with big engines, fins like rockets, and a growing interest in Classical Freudian psychology.

In this setting we find Max Lewis learning about, and coming to grips with, the values of trust, honor, the politics of work, and increasingly complicated relationships with women.

CHAPTER I

A New Venture

Mickey Kamen and I stood on the Independence Avenue bridge overlooking the old Congress Street Expressway on the west side of Chicago. It was late. It was mid-May and a warm night. There was a sliver moon that gave us a little light. I planned to stop, kiss her, tell her that I liked her very much, and wanted her to go steady with me. I had my class ring ready and loose in my pocket. We had been dating for nearly six months.

Every time I was with her I felt like a world champion. My friends didn't like her. They said she was a phony, a dreamer, that I ought to do better. What I saw was an enchanting smile, a sparkle in dreamy eyes, and a physical presence that put me on an emotional elevator when we were together. I thought the Barbie Doll people had a hand in building Mickey's figure.

So I kissed her, let myself get dizzy on that special perfume she wore, and held her close. A few cars rolling by under the bridge blew their horns. A *victory fanfare*, I thought. This was the moment. I told her that I wanted to "go steady." This was what passed for commitment in 1959. I envisioned my ring on a gold chain around her neck. It was going to be everything I wanted.
She pulled away and gave me her wide smile. It gave me tingles.

"Max, you're special, but I don't think going steady is something I want right now. We're graduating soon, I have a lot of plans, and I know that you don't know what you'll do. It's really been fun, you're the neatest guy I've dated, but I think it's time to move along."

An argument stuck in my throat. The tingles turned to beads of sweat running down my back. It was the last thing I expected after all the good times we had. Negative comments from my friends about our relationship flooded my thoughts. I think I said I would walk her home, but she said maybe better that I should go. She would be okay. I muttered how much fun we'd had and that I wished things had gone different, words to that effect. The words bounced off her back as she was already walking away. Traffic rolled quietly by under the bridge, the celebration had been very brief. I watched while she crossed the rest of the bridge, and kept watching long after she was gone. She never looked back. Not once.

It was late on a Friday evening when this happened, just a month before our graduation from high school. I figured I probably wouldn't see her anymore, as we went to two different schools. I was four miles from home and started walking. Ordinarily I took the bus after seeing her home. I just wanted to walk and puzzle out what went wrong and what I had lost.

I got home just before midnight. My father was waiting up, wearing his old tattered wool robe and sitting on his favorite chair in the living room when I walked in. He shifted a cigar around in his mouth, took it out and dumped it in an overflowing ash tray.

"I waited up for you, Max".

"Yeah, dad, I see. Something wrong?"
" Nah, nothing's wrong. I just worry till you get home. Your sister called and wants you to call her tomorrow morning."

"Why, dad, what's Margie want?"

"She knows you don't have anything going for the summer. She said there's a possible summer job at her agency, at that camp they run. Nowatoma, I think it's called. Listen, Max, I know you want to go on to college and we don't really have enough to send you away. But you can go to the University of Illinois at the Pier, it's a good school. And you need to work and save as much as possible even to go there. The camp job would be a great one. They'll give you a place to live, three meals, and nowhere to spend your salary. Margie and I think it's a perfect idea for you. You'll get out of the city for the summer, meet people; lot of girls work at the camp. I think it would be good for you to see someone other than that kid you moon about. What's her name? Molly?"
"No, dad, it's Michelle, her nickname is Mickey. You don't have to worry about her, though. She just dumped me on the Independence Avenue bridge."

"She dumped you on a bridge? What's that supposed to mean?"

"Um, dad, I don't really want to go into it if that's ok, you know? I mean it just happened and I'm a little down."

" Oh, so you mean she dumped you. Max, that's great! I never liked that kid the one time I saw her. Neither did your mother, you know? We thought she was a phony."

"Yeah, dad, my friends thought so, too, but, you know, I really liked her."

I thought I was about to choke up, and I didn't want to cry in front of him. I told him that I needed to get some sleep and he reminded me to call my sister in the morning.

"Yeah, ok, dad, g'night. I'll call Margie first thing."

"Night, son. Listen," He put a fatherly arm around my shoulders, which was tough for him to do as I'm a foot taller than he is.

"I can see you're looking a little down, but you know, these things happen with the broads. You'll be fine. You're a neat kid and the broads will go for you now that you're finished with that girl. You're too young to get tangled up. You need to play the field, see other..."

"Yeah, thanks, dad. Listen, I really need some sleep, so good night, okay."

"It's always for the better, believe me. You'll be fine."

"Ok, dad, thanks. "Night."

"Night, Max."

I slept well given the evening I'd had, breaking up, having to be civil to my dad, and recognizing that maybe he, my mother and all my friends might just be right about Mickey. Oh, God, I loved her so hard it hurt. I thought she was it, the one I'd spend my life with. I slept okay; maybe it was the long sad walk, but I felt like hell the next morning.

Dad had already gone to work when I got to the kitchen for breakfast. Mom had some French toast in a pan and a sad look on her face. When she had that face she always talked slow, like she had a bad headache.

"Hi, Max. How're you feeling this morning?"
Very slow speech. Here we go, I thought.

"Dad told me about your break up. How could that little bitch do that to you? We never liked her. She's a phony, you'll see. Why not call that little Suzie Slater? She's really cute!"

"Mom! How do you even know who she is? You know what they call her? Her nickname is 'See ya' later, Suzie Slater!' You know why? Because she's a gossip and a liar. Mom, I'm really down, I don't want to talk about Mickey and me. I really liked her and I know she wasn't anyone's favorite, but she was special to me, okay? Let's just leave it. Can I have some of that French toast?"

"Sure, Max, coming right up. But you know, the one time we met her...."

"MA!"

"Okay, okay, I know, it's hard right now. What about that Henrietta Thompson? Now, she's really sweet."

"MA, enough, please!"

I had the French toast. It tasted like vinegar in my mouth. I soaked it in syrup, but it got no better.

After breakfast I called Margie at home. It was Saturday and I figured that's where she'd be, but my brother-in-law Phil answered. "Hey, Max, how's it going? You looking for Marge?"

"Yeah, hi, Phil, everything's fine. Is Margie there?"

"I heard that little broad you go with gave you a rough time last night."

Jesus, I thought, *was this a headline in The Daily News*?

"Um, yeah, Phil, um, yeah, we ended our thing. How did you know?"

"Well, your mom talked with Margie, and, you know, she...."

"Phil, just listen, I'm in a hurry. Can I talk to Margie?"

"Max, Marge is at the office. They have a lot going on, so everyone had to go in on the weekend to get some stuff ready for camp. Marge is the get- it- done member of the team. Call her. She really wants to talk to you."

I hung up and dialed Margie's number at work.

"Hello, this is Margaret Larson."

Hi, Margie, it's Max. Please don't say anything about Mickey. Please?"

Max, it's really busy down here and I don't have a lot of time. Did dad tell you there are some jobs at our summer camp?"

"Yep, let's hear."

"Fine, the camp runs from late June to near the end of summer. It's a social work camp and...."

"What's that mean?"

"Well, the primary focus is getting kids from different socioeconomic levels out to the country where they can get to know each other, learn to live and play together, learn respect for each other; it's a wonderful concept. So the camp recruits college students who are majoring in mostly group social work and trains them in our philosophy. Then they work as camp counselors."

"What's that got to do with me? I'm still in high school."

"Just listen a minute, will you? In addition to the counselor jobs are other positions called 'specialists.' There's a wide range of jobs, like Waterfront Director, but you need a WSI certificate for that. There's also Camp Craft Director and Arts and Crafts instructors, and they need drivers, people to teach canoeing, cooks and dishwashers, maintenance people. I think maybe you could get one of those jobs. They pay even more."

"Why's that, and what's a WSI?"

"Well, a WSI means Water Safety Instructor, like life-guards. And the college types want the experience for their careers, so they'll take less money. It also gets them used to the fact that no one earns anything in this field. The specialists sometimes have to put up with less interesting work, you know, like maintenance or dish-washing. Now, here's the thing, I thought we wouldn't be getting into the hiring till next week, but it's starting now for the specialists. The Camp Director does most of the counselor recruiting by visiting campuses, and he needs to start that pretty soon. So if you're going to get a job you need to come down right away. I already have an appointment set for you this morning. Can you get here by 9:30?"

"Yeah, I guess so if I hustle."

"Great, come down to my office at 120 Randolph, sec-ond floor. Bring a good pen, wear fresh clothes, and look sharp. You don't need a tie, but wear a good sport shirt and pressed pants. You'll be meeting first with our per-sonnel director, Moira Wallace. She'll screen you and probably send you on to talk with Larry Reznik, the As-sistant Director. If you get by him and get to see the Camp Director, you'll probably have a good shot at a position. I know the Director pretty well and already put in a word for you. He's a neat guy; you'll like him. Now, just a word about the others. Moira is a little overpower-ing and sort of flashy. So don't let her rattle you. She comes on really strong with guys she interviews. Play it strong and silent, you hearing me?"

Marge didn't wait for my answer. she was rushing the information.

"Larry is ——um, well, he's not terribly effective and likes to hear himself talk. Just listen, play it cool and get to Ken Greenman. He's the important guy, the Director. You see him and you'll be pretty much set. And, Max, one more thing; play it like you really want a job. Let them know that even if you don't want one there."

"Why would I do that, Marge?"

"Because it's better that you turn down an offer you don't want than be rejected. It's just good interviewing practice for the job you might want another time."

"Oh, so like batting practice?"

"Yes. Listen, I have to run. Good luck. Let me know how it goes."

I took the Lake Street "el" and got off at Randolph. It was only a couple of blocks to the building. It was an old office building with a heavy revolving door, small lobby, and a reception desk. The guy at the desk looked like they built the building around him. He was bald and dumpy, and was stooped over a racing newsletter with a package of Chesterfield cigarettes in one hand and a zippo lighter in the other. A cigarette dangled from his heavy lips, and smoke curled up his cheek into his right eye. Without looking up he said, "Yeah?"

I said, "Hi, I'm here for a job interview at Central Human Services."

He snickered, "The social workers, yeah, second floor, turn left out of the elevator, last door end of corridor."

I walked a short distance down a dirty hall featuring old newspapers and candy wrappers on the floor. One sign of life, a potted philodendron suffering from leprosy.
I got in the elevator, punched 2 and waited. Nothing. The reception guy yelled, "Press the 'close door button', kid."

"Got it, thanks!"
The elevator started moving, and the car jolted to a halt on two. I wasn't sure the door would open but it did, and I was in a hallway that was a bit cleaner. I saw a door down the hall that had "Central Human Services, Office of Camp Nowatoma" on it's frosted glass window. There was an open transom at the top with a crack in the glass. The door stuck; I gave it a push and was facing a large, old oak desk piled high with manila folders and a sign that said the woman behind the desk was Wilhelmina Kestenmier. She looked like an extra from a Ma and Pa Kettle movie.

"Ya?"

" Well, hi there. I'm here to see Moira Wallace about a job at the camp."

"Ya. You Max?" She didn't wait for my answer. "You need to fill out form. Application. Here."

She handed me a two page form on a clipboard and
pointed me to a wooden bench that was against the wall
in what remained of her tiny office.
"You heff pen?"

"Ya— uh, I mean, yes." She gave me a look.

"Venn you iss done, giff me zeh board, ya?"

"Yes ma'am."

Her hair was put up in some sort of bun with what
looked like knitting needles sticking out of it. She wore a
drab brown dress, no rings or jewelry that I could see,
and no makeup. She had a figure like a stack of used
tires. She was working on what I guessed were camper
files and was totaling fees on a 10 key calculator. She
looked dumpy, but her fingers flew on the calculator like
hummingbird wings.
I got down to work on the application. Usual stuff, name,
address, phone, next of kin to contact in case of emergency, education, degrees, work history, interests, hob-
bies, special skills, credentials, languages; it seemed
pretty complete to me even without much experience in
filling out forms. I didn't have my social security number
with me. I handed it back to Wilhelmina, who looked at it
and said, "You forget to fill in zeh zojial number."

"Yes, ma'm, I didn't have it with me. I can call it in if
that's okay."
"Zit".
"Zit?"
"By zeh bench, zo."

"Ah, yes, ma'am."
I zat zo zdill. While I waited, I mentally ran through how I would present myself in the interview, ran over everything Margie told me. Fifteen minutes went by, twenty, a half hour. Wilhelmina finally said, "She iss late running, Moira."

Just then the door opened, and swirling out came Miss Moira Wallace, Director of Personnel, like Loretta Young opening her half hour TV show. I wouldn't say she was a classic beauty, but she was for sure sexy, knew it, and put it out there to let you know who she was. Tall, big green eyes, auburn hair, shoulder length with a bit of over the eye Veronica Lake look. Blouse too open, skirt too tight, and heels too high. She jingled from a lot of bracelets, hula hoop earrings, and a sparkling necklace that ended in a medallion like a traffic sign at her cleavage. Given the drab office, she sparkled like diamonds set in a box of used plumbing parts.

She snapped her fingers at Wilhelmina a couple of times and impatiently asked for the clipboard. Wilhelmina handed it over. She waited till Moira turned her back, rolled her eyes, and went back to the calculator.

"Max?"

"Yes, ma'am."

I mean, who else was in the room?
She walked up too close as I was getting up, slipped the clipboard under her arm, and offered her hand. When I took it she covered my hand with her now unoc-

cupied left. Warm hands, I thought, *this is over the top.*
We were practically nose to nose. I felt the heat of her
body and the smell of a heavy perfume. I thought about
Margie's warning that Moira came on strong. She got
that right. I thought that Miss Wallace came on like General Patton's 3rd Army.

"Come with me, Max."

Yes, ma'am." And then I wondered why I kept calling her
'ma'm'. She didn't look all that much older than I was. I
guessed I was impressed by her title and the profes-
sional-looking outfit. We went through a door and down
a long hall. She was swinging her hips. Exaggerated.
Something told me she would turn to try and catch me
looking at her behind. I kept my eyes up, and when she
turned I gave her a very slight friendly smile, no teeth.
She returned it the same way. Tie, one all.

"Sit here, Max."
The chair was along the side of her desk, not across
from it. She said it made her feel closer to the people
she interviewed and she could get to know them better.
It also gave her a chance to show off her legs.
Her office was a little better put together than the outside
reception area. There was a window behind her desk
that looked out over Randolph Street. Some nice prints
on the wall. She had turned off the overhead fluores-
cent lights, and had a lamp on her desk with a much
warmer light. It gave the room a cozy feeling. The furni-
ture was a step up also. I noticed a framed diploma from
the University of Wisconsin on the wall, a Bachelor's of
Liberal Arts degree. The ink looked wet. Her desk was
very neat, nothing extraneous on it. A large green four

drawer file cabinet was in the corner. She put on horned-rim reading glasses and began reading my application. She straightened her back while she read so I could be sure to see how nicely put together she was.
I kept my eyes out the window or up on her framed prints while she read. I knew she would try to catch me ogling her boobs.

"Max, do you have a resume? I like to look at them also."

Damned if I didn't almost say, "I like to look at them also!"

"No, Miss Wallace, I don't have one, sorry. I didn't think one would be needed for the kind of jobs I'm here for."

"And what kind of jobs would those be, Max?" Said with a sly smile as though she was setting a trap.

"Well, I'm pretty sure that I would only qualify for something like a dishwasher or maybe maintenance if it's not too technical. I'm pretty handy with tools. I'm also a very good driver."

"So, Max, what's your driving experience like?" She made notes while I talked.

"My dad is a truck driver. He has a route sales business and I help him on the weekends, sometimes in the summer also. So he taught me to drive his truck. I can handle anything up to a large van. I've driven panel jobs, pickups, and of course a station wagon. I can do standard transmissions, three-on-a-tree, or floor shifts."

"I'll keep that in mind. We have a couple of drivers at the camp. We generally hire locals from the area because they know their way around. We'll see. You also need to be pretty strong to be a driver. They run errands, pick up equipment, take campers and canoes to their river trips. Requires a man with strength."
She looked up from the clipboard like a fox eying a chicken. "Are you strong, Max?"

I got flustered. It wasn't what she said, it was the way she said it.

"Yes, ma'am!" I said it too loud, "I lift weights!" I said it too dumb. I felt foolish. I don't brag like that.

"Oh, I love a man who works with weights! Tell me, what do you press?"

I didn't like where this was going. She was pushing me to look foolish. I should have kept my mouth shut about the weights.

"So?" she said.

"Well, on a good day I can bench about 250,10 reps." I think I looked down and then realized she might think I was looking at her legs, so I looked up to see a prim smile. She was toying with me. Two to one, visitors up, home team down. I was losing whatever cool I had. Marge said she would rattle me. I was rattled.

"Ok, Max, I'll put a notation on your file for driving and being *very strong!* Any thing else? Sports?"

"Well, yes, I'm on the wrestling team (that got a smile), and my dad sent me for private martial arts. He thinks everyone needs to know how to take care of themselves. And that's all."
She moved on, thankfully.

"Now, will you be available to work through the summer? That means as soon as you're out of school and right up to Labor Day or as close to then as possible."

"Yes, I can do that."

"Good, now, if we hire you there will be a physical required." She wrinkled her nose cutesy and said, "You'll need a doctor for that, I don't do that."

I said, "A pity." It froze her for a beat. I don't know why I said that- it was a mistake- but I guess I was irritated with her sexy routine and put-downs. She was what the guys in the locker room called a tease artist. So I made a mistake and let her get to me.

"Ok," she said, letting that pass, "I think I have what I need for now. Look, before you can be offered a job with the camp we'll have to get some references, do some checking. I know your sister works for the Executive Director, so I don't think that will be a problem. I want to walk you down to meet our Assistant Camp Director, Mr. Reznik. And then, if that goes well, maybe Ken Greenman will have some time to talk with you. He's the Camp Director and has the last word on all hires. Any questions?"

"No, that all sounds fine."

"Right, well, let's go meet Larry."

She got up and offered her hand. When I took it she moved very close to me and for a second I thought she was going to hug me. But then she squeezed my bicep and it flexed involuntarily.

"Ooo! You *do* lift weights, don't you?" I made a very slight move toward her, and she froze and moved back and was flustered. I just raised my hands and said, "Yep, I work out a lot." A look of panic flashed across her face, and then the composure was back. I thought there was something very strange about Miss Wallace.

"Come", she said, "we'll go see if Larry's in his office. This way."

She started down the hall. I walked next to her and she veered away as we walked. Seemed to me that Moira Wallace was either too close or too far and maybe had trouble with "just right." There was a corner and we turned it, and the second door down had a frosted glass window with *Lawrence K. Reznik, M.S.W.* and *Assistant Camp Director* in black letters. Miss Wallace knocked and walked right in.

"Hi, Larry. Whoops, sorry, didn't know you were on the phone!"

She barged in anyway. Reznik held up his hand like a traffic cop, made a couple of comments into the phone and hung up. He was a strange-looking duck. Short, chubby, a lot of coppery curls, thick glasses that hung on a small pinched nose and a pasty complexion. He didn't look like anyone who spent a lot of time camping. He smiled with crooked teeth and pushed the glasses up on his pinched little nose.

"Larry, this is Max Lewis. His sister is Marge upstairs in the executive suite who sent him our way. He's on your interviewing list and he's interested in a job with us this summer. We've already had our interview. Can you see him now?"

Reznik hefted himself out of his swivel chair and offered me his hand. "Thanks, Moira. Yes I'm ready to talk with him. Hello, Max, please, have a seat."

As soon as I was seated, Moira handed my application to Reznik, put two warm hands on my shoulders, and bent down and said, "Okay, Max, it was nice to meet you. Good luck." whispered In a soft bedtime tone. I was getting used to her on-and-off-stuff. She reminded me of a turn signal light- on, off, on, off. I looked up and thanked her and then she was gone.

Reznik said, "Okay, Max, tell me a little about yourself. I'm good friends with your sister. Very glad to meet you. I want to give you a bit of an overview about the camp. Do you know anything about our philosophy? Well, we're about 25 years old now, started up just before the war, and we're unique because we try to serve a very diverse population, kids from the poor neighborhoods side by side with the more affluent kids from the north shore. They learn from each other how to live together, understand each other and get along. The camp is be- coming well known for its efforts in bringing children from different socio-economic levels together and creat-

ing relationships and understanding that continues to
last even after the camping season is over.
I've written several papers on our philosophy and I'm
expecting at least one to be published. During the year
I'm an adjunct professor of group social work, so this is
really my whole career, you know, teaching, working with
kids and helping them with social relationships."

I was impressed that he could say all that in one breath.
Larry went on in this vein for another thirty minutes. Periodically he would ask me a question and then jump in
to talk about his career before I could get an answer out.
He must have adjusted his glasses forty times. I sat and
nodded and smiled when it seemed right to do that, and
tried to stay awake. I was afraid that I would nod off, so I
periodically chewed on the inside of my mouth and sur-
reptitiously dug fingernails into my thigh. Even at that,
my eyelids felt like they were lined with lead. This guy
was a cure for insomnia. Finally, his phone rang and he
got into a conversation with someone who was asking
him if he could meet to discuss equipment needs for the
camp in fifteen minutes. He ended the call, asked one
question and actually listened to my answer.

"So, Max, do you think you can work in a scullery and
treat kids well? Some are tough from ghetto life, others
are 'entitled' and from families of wealth. What do you
think?"

"What's a scullery, Mr. Reznik?"

"Oh, sorry. It's the part of the kitchen where the dishes
are washed. It's outfitted with stainless steel counters,
commercial dish washers, you know."

"Mr. Reznik, I'm sure I can wash dishes, do a great job, and I like all kinds of kids. I'd really like a shot at working with you."

I felt like puking but I did what Marge told me to do. I wanted to get as far from this jerk as I could. He twiddled with his pencil, pushed on his glasses and made some notes on the application and gave me what I guessed was his best professional serious look.

"Okay, Max, I like your candor and enjoyed our talk. Look, I think you should talk with Ken Greenman, our Director. I'm going into a meeting, but you can find him by going back down the hall to our reception desk. Wilhelmina will call him for you and send you up to his office. He's on four."

Reznik handed me the clipboard (complete with his notes as well as Miss Wallace's, that even I, with no experience in confidentiality, knew was a breach), got up and gave me a second limp handshake, thanked me for coming down and wished me well.

I went back to the reception office. No no one was there. I stood there for a couple of minutes trying to figure out what to do when Miss Wallace did her Loretta Young routine, stopped short and said, "Max, what are you doing back here? Are you done interviewing? Did you see Ken Greenman?"

I explained Reznik's instructions and pointed out that Wilhelmina was gone.

"Okay, Max, I'll take you up to four and introduce you to Ken." Then her eyes popped out and she said, "Hey, you're not supposed to have your application! It has our notes." I handed over the clipboard.

"Well, come on." She led the way down the hall without the hip swinging. Her heels clacked on the granite floor, short, quick, athletic steps, and she rang for the elevator, which I could hear creaking up to our floor.

"Get in, come on. I've got a lunch date."

I moved to get on. She was in such a hurry we bumped hips and did a "Three Stooge Routine" getting on the elevator. She pressed the door-close button pushed 4, and up we went. Getting off the elevator was done with an "after-you-Alphonse-and-Gaston" pantomime. No more sexy moves, at least.

Across the hall was an office with *Office of the Camp Director, Mr. Kenneth Greenman, MSW*" in black letters on the frosted glass window. Miss Wallace knocked softly on the door and opened it slowly, with much greater respect than she showed at Reznick's office. There was a secretary/receptionist desk but no one behind it. Miss Wallace walked past and knocked on what I figured was the office door of Mr. Greenman.

"Come on in." Miss Wallace opened the door and said, "Ken, I have Max Lewis here. He's interviewed with me and Larry. Have you time to see him?"

I didn't know what a camp director was supposed to look like, but whatever it was couldn't be further from what

Mr. Greenman was: Heavy-set, tawny skin, wearing a short-sleeved Hawaiian shirt and a St. Louis baseball cap on the back of his head. His somewhat-brown, somewhat- gray hair was combed-over and messy. His gray eyes had a look of intelligence that belied the rest of his appearance.

"Sit down, Max, make yourself comfy. Moira, I thought you had a lunch date. Go on, leave the clipboard."

"Thanks, Ken. Good luck, Max." And she was gone; no more hot hands on clenched shoulders or bedroom whispers in my ear this time. I figured it was proper-be-havior-time in front of the boss.

"So, you're Margie's kid brother. We all like Marge, she's a real powerhouse upstairs in the executive suite. How were your meetings with Moira and Larry?"

"Well, Mr. Greenman, I think things went well. Miss Wallace spent a little time with me kind of sorting out the jobs I might qualify for, and I heard a lot about the camp from Mr. Reznick."

"I'll bet you did. So, did Moira come on a little strong?"

I decided not to take the bait and said, "Well, she sure knows how the jobs get filled and who's a fit, that's for sure."
Mr. Greenman let me off the hook and asked what I'd learned about the camp from Reznick. From that point on we had a really good conversation about the camp philosophy and what it tried to accomplish. The interview was short, and he ended by telling me that decisions on

hiring for the specialist jobs would be made in the next week or so. But he had a problem in one area that came up every year, and he wanted to spell it out, like talking about it might give him some insight.

"Max, I can find plenty of social work students at colleges who really want the experience of working at our camp. But each year it's a problem to find certain specialists. In addition to the social work types who are the counselors, I have to find, screen and hire people with special skills. This year I need an Assistant Waterfront Director, an Assistant Camp Craft Director, a canoeing specialist and a few others. The people who've done those jobs the past couple of years have graduated and moved on. I've reached out to many former staff but I'm afraid they've outgrown these jobs."

As we talked about the various positions, I realized that I had several friends who could probably fit those jobs. I began telling him about Bruce Marshall, my oldest friend, who was an Eagle Scout and knew a hell of a lot about building campfires in the rain, tying knots and pitching tents in a gale. I told him about my friend Martha Kramer, who is an artist, potter, and weaver. She could teach little kids all sorts of skills. And I had others in mind as well.

Greenman said, "Listen, Max, I'll make a deal with you. If you can get these friends to call me I'll give you five bucks a piece, and if I hire them I'll give you another twenty. How's that sound?"

Well, that sounded pretty good to me. Mr. G. gave me a list of jobs with descriptions of duties and requirements. I figured if he trusted me that far I would have a good shot at a job with the camp also. And I could see that filling the jobs would put a lot of extra points in for me. We tied up the interview and I thanked him for the opportunity to work on recruiting for him.

I left the building without trying to see Marge. I knew she was busy if she was in on a Saturday, so I got back on the "el" and went home. It was a pretty productive morning.
No one was home when I got there. It was about noon and I was starving. I made a baloney sandwich on rye and took a scoop of leftover potato salad and a new dill pickle. I eyed a Blatz Beer in the fridge, but decided to drink coke instead. I was feeling pretty good about the morning interviews, especially my chance to make a few bucks while doing my friends a favor and maybe getting them summer jobs. Naturally, the phone rang as soon as I had my mouth filled with the sandwich. It was Marge. "Max, how did it go? Tell me!"

"Really great, Marge. Do you think I'll have a shot at a job there? I mean, I had a really neat meeting with Mr. Greenman." I told her about the deal we had and the extra cash I might make by sending people to fill open positions.

"Okay, Max, that sounds really good. The hiring letters won't go out for a while. We're waiting for Bob Wheeler to tell us who he's hired up at the camp. Bob's the all around maintenance man for the camp. Really, he's more than that; he practically runs all the operations. There will be a meeting later this afternoon of the camp staff, and we expect a call from Bob then. We'll know what our staff needs will be, and then we'll send letters. I think you'll have a good shot if Ken trusted you enough to look for some friends to work there. It looks great, Max!"

I got off the phone feeling pretty good about my chances. I took another bite of my baloney sandwich, and the phone rang.

"Hi, Maaaax! It's Suzy."

My heart sank, my stomach turned, and I forced down the bite of sandwich I had in my mouth. It was "See ya later, Suzy Slater." What could she possibly want? Did mom put her up to calling me?

"Hi, Suzy, what's happening?"

"Max, I heard about you and Mickey breaking up...."

I will kill my mother.

"And, you know, the Prom is only a few weeks off and I thought maybe we could go together. I know you don't want to miss the prom. After all, how many proms are there in a lifetime?"

One of the things about Suzy that made me grind my teeth was that she always told everyone how they were feeling, like she knew for sure. A regular psychic, the complete fortune teller, a total pain in the ass.

"Suze, how did you find out that Mickey and I were a done deal? I mean, that just happened like Twenty-four hours ago!"

"Oh, Max, it's all over, everyone knows. Mickey told Chicken, and you know, Chicken and I are *LIKE SIS-TERS!* And I know that Mickey's going to the prom with Michael Vandon."

Chicken was Julie Marie Cacciatore, another class nuisance on the Olympic Gossip team. Her nickname "Chicken," was a tag she couldn't shake — "Chicken Cacciatore." The guys thought it was hysterical. The guys didn't like her, and neither did I.

I thought, Michael Vandon, yet. The star quarterback of our high school football team, ace pitcher on the baseball team, center of the basketball team and captain of the debate team. The big man in the class. I bet the two of them will be King and Queen at the prom. But maybe not, I thought. After all Mickey went to another school. Maybe that would disqualify her. On such small things does hope cling. I wondered if Mickey had been two-timing me all along. After all, one minute we were together and the next, bingo, at the prom with the big guy.

"Suze, thanks for your offer, but you know, I'm sort of down about me and Mickey. I was thinking that I'd just forgo the prom. I'm really sorry. I know I'd just be a drag on your good time."

"Oh, Maaax, no! I know you're just saying that because the pain is so fresh. Think it over. We'd have a great

time. I know you would just pop right back if we went together."
I was thinking that I'd pop right back if I could strangle her in the back seat of my dad's Chevy.

"No, Suze, I just can't. I'm sorry. I have to get off now. I know you'll find someone to go with, and *I know you'll have a great time there.*"
I did it. I got her off the phone and me off the hook, and with a dose of her own medicine, no less!

I took another bite of the baloney sandwich. It was starting to taste like sawdust and salt. Okay, I needed to take charge. I got out my address book and looked up Bruce Marshall, my oldest friend and the Eagle Scout I told Mr. G. about.

"Hello?"

"Bruce, Max. You got a minute? I got something to tell you that might make your summer."

"Yeah, hi, Max. Go."

"Here's the deal. You know my sister works for a big social service agency...."

I spent a half-hour on the phone with Bruce, selling like crazy. Not only did I think he'd fit the job, I really wanted people I knew to share this summer experience. I had nothing to fear. Bruce loved the idea, took Mr. G's. number, and said he'd call as soon as we were off the phone. Five bucks in the kitty!

My next call went to Ted Wilson, not as close to me as Bruce, but a great fit for the assistant waterfront director job. Ted was older than I and had a year of college under his belt. Better, he was on the swim team and was an all around water buff. He could handle small sail boats and was experienced in camping and canoeing. Another half-hour explaining; ten bucks in the till.

I made another baloney sandwich and called Martha Kramer. Martha was a tall, slim, stoic girl who always struck me as sad and wistful. But she had a nice touch with kids and was a skilled artist, potter, arts-and-crafts person who came alive when doing an art project. Even better, adults always liked her style. Though a teenager, she could really hit it off with them. Another half-hour and another sale.

The only hitch was that Martha asked if I was going to the prom and I had to tell her that I didn't want to. She expressed real disappointment, and I realized that she liked me. I'd had no clue. Martha was a couple of inches taller than I, and while I always found her attractive, I never thought she had any interest. It was too late to show up at the prom with her, though. Once I gave my word on something, it was set in stone. Maybe something would happen at camp if Martha got there. Anyway, I was up fifteen bucks, and I hoped that I would have people I knew up at the camp.

It was then that I realized all my friends might be up there, but so far I didn't have a job myself! I spent the next few days studying for finals and checking the mail box. I let mom off the hook after learning that Suzy Slater got the word about me and Mickey from

''Chicken,'' who must have talked to Mickey directly. It made me sad and angry that Mickey was going around blabbing about our breakup and rubbing it in about Michael Vandon. Damn the torpedoes, I decided, I would survive!

Finally, on Thursday after the Saturday interviews, there was a large manilla envelope stuffed in the mail box. It was from the camp. I knew before I opened it that I had a job. It was thick, and I figured they wouldn't put that much paper into a rejection letter. There was a hiring letter with a one-page contract that said I would be earning $375 for the summer. It asked that I sign the contract and either send it to the main office on Randolph or bring it to the camp. There was a suggested list of items to bring and another application. I worked right away on the formal application that replicated a lot of stuff I'd already written, but went farther asking, for a lot more information on my health, a form for a doctor's physical, and a request for references. I was on my way.

Things sped up. Studying and taking finals, graduation. The prom came and went. I spent prom night with several guys playing poker. Some didn't want to go, some couldn't get a date (no one would go with Suzy), and some said it wasn't worth the expense. The poker game was okay but it wasn't as good as being at the prom with Mickey. I couldn't shake her from my mind.The next day I got a call from Bruce Marshall, who told me that the prom was a blast.

"Max, the prom was terrific. They had a band called Hal Metrick and the Metro-Gnomes, a bunch of guys who looked like real jerks but, man, they could really belt rock and roll."

"Yeah, sounds great, Bruce. Was Mickey there?"

"Man, can't you get that broad out of your head?"

"I'm trying!"

"Yeah, she was there with Michael Vandon. She was hanging on him like wallpaper. He had a handfull of her soon as the lights dimmed for the slow dancing. Looked like my mom kneading bread dough. I bet he got more off her on that dance floor than you would in her bed- room with her folks in the Bahamas."

A dagger in the heart, but I'd asked for it. I needed to change the subject. "Bruce, did you hear anything from the camp?"

"Yep, I talked to them yesterday, went down, had an in- terview with the personnel woman. Boy, she's weird, but what a body. Anyway, we talked about the Assistant Camp Craft job. She said I didn't have any experience for the director job, but I'd make a good assistant be- cause of my camping skills, and the scouting I've done. She liked that. So, I'll be up there. When do you leave?"

"This Sunday, how about you!"

"I'm going up a week or so later. My brother is getting married and I'll be in town for that. I'll see you up there. I bet it will be a great summer. Thanks again for setting me up. I have to get going."

"Okay, Bruce. Just one more thing, were Michael and Mickey the King and Queen."

"No, they picked Lois Morgan and Denny Carter. Lois is a real looker, and Denny is the smartest guy in the class. But somehow Mickey and Michael got more attention than the King and Queen. Everyone was buzzing about all the groping they were doing on the dance floor. I gotta run. See you next week."

I gritted my teeth as the dagger plunged again. Why couldn't I just let it go? It hurt to hear about Mickey, but I asked for it. All right, I thought, I have a plan, a place to be far away from her and I was confident that I'd even have some of my best buddies up there also.

A few days later I got a call from Mr. G's secretary (the one who was out of the office when I met him). I had made twenty-five bucks on calls to his office from friends who might be hired. I still had a few more bucks possible, as I'd convinced eight people to call about jobs. And if they started getting hired I would be wealthy!

Finally, the travel day arrived. I kissed my mom and shouldered a large duffel bag stuffed with everything on the suggested item list, plus a couple of 'who-done-its' by Raymond Chandler.

My dad drove me down to Union Station to take the train up to Walkerville, Wisconsin, the closest town to the camp that had a train stop. We got into his blue Chevy 210 (same as the fancier Bel Aire, he said, but cheaper). It always stank from cigars. The inside of the windshield was plastered with tiny bits of tobacco. He bit off the end of a new cigar every morning and spat it on the glass. The ashtray was always loaded with cigar butts; dead matches littered the floor. Papers, orders, maps and receipts were stuck in the seats.

"Dad, why don't you clean the car up once in a while. It's gross."

"What? Who cares? It's okay, your mother never complains. What's the big deal? So it's a little messy. Don't be such a fuss budget, for chrissake."

I should have known better. We drove in silence for a while. He took Madison Street east, right into the loop, turned south on Clinton to Adams, and got me to Union Station with plenty of time to spare. One thing dad could do was make a delivery. He pulled to the curb and shut off the engine.

"Listen, Max, I got some stuff for you to take up there." He handed over a new Wisconsin road map and a small military surplus compass.

"Dad, I'll be washing dishes. What's this for?"

"Max, you never know what you'll need. Take this stuff and maybe you'll get a shot at driving. Let me tell you something. Once you're on the road, even if you work for some son of a bitch, you're your own boss. The road is freedom. Here's a Buck pocket knife, and this little container has wood matches. It's waterproof. You need stuff like this in the woods. Now, here's a small box with some fishhooks and line in case...."

"Dad, it's a summer camp for kids, not a survival outing. I'll be fine."

"Take the stuff, Max, you'll thank me. You never know! Now, a couple more things. There's college girls up there and they're a little looser than the kids you hang with. I bet you never got your hand up that kid Molly's...."

"Dad, please!"

"Ok, I won't get graphic. But here's the deal. I don't mind you getting a little up there, but I think you're on the, um, inexperienced side. So, here, take this."

He handed me a small brown bag.
"What is it, dad?"

"It's, ah, what's the formal name, condo-mums?"

"What?"

"Rubbers."

"Oh, fer...."

"Look, Max, just take them, okay. Have fun, but don't make me a grandfather. I ain't ready, and your mother will have a canary."

"Okay, okay, dad. And thanks."

"Good bye, son Write, let us know how it's going, your
mother and me. We'll miss you. First Margie gets married and now my little one is going away for the
summer."

I never saw dad get so emotional. I didn't think he had it
in him. He was always even-tempered, and a little gruff.
He actually teared up, so we hugged as best we could in
a car seat and I got out.
I took my duffel bag off the back seat, stuffed in all the
"extras" he thought to bring and gave him a smile and a
wave.

As I walked away from the car, I got a lump in my throat
that surprised me. This was really the first time I was
going away from my family. It was my own adventure
and it was a little bit scary.

Chapter 2
Forward, Ho!

I went down the station stairs and followed the signs to
the ticket office. The camp instruction letter said to buy a
ticket to Walkerville, Wisconsin, the closest station to the
camp that was situated in northern Wisconsin near Cas-
tle Rock State Park and the Wisconsin River. After a lot
of stamping and calculating, I had my ticket. The agent

told me the train was on time, and that I should go to
track fifteen. He suggested that I buy something to eat
because the dining car wasn't scheduled for this run. I
thanked him and stopped at a sandwich shop, picked up
a tuna sandwich, some potato chips and an apple.

I found track fifteen and boarded the train, found a seat
with a wide window, and hoisted my duffel bag up on a
rack that ran down the center of the car. I liked trains. I
liked the way they cut through the big city, small towns,
woods, and ran along rivers. I found the swaying motion
of the cars very relaxing. I couldn't wait to get to the
camp! I was loaded with anticipation and ready for a different experience.

The trip went without any hitches. After a half-hour or
so, the city started to thin out, and soon we were headed
northwest through prairie and then rolling hills as we got
across the Wisconsin border.
The car I was in was nearly empty except for a few college age-kids, some sailors on leave, and a little old
lady who sat a few seats ahead of me. She was knitting
something pink that looked like a blanket for a baby. Periodically, the conductor came through to announce
stops along the way. We picked up more people,
dropped some, and kept rolling.

Around ten o'clock, I started to get hungry and ate the
sandwich and chips. I saved the apple for an emergency. I hadn't heard from any of my friends and hoped
that some would be up there or on their way. I was okay
with making new friends, but there's nothing better than
being with old ones.

It was nearly noon. I had dozed off while watching the countryside roll by. The conductor came through the car door behind me and shouted, "Walkerville, next! All off who want Walkerville!" It gave me a jolt, and I came right off the seat. I looked around, hoping no one saw me. The old lady was standing right at my seat looking at me.

"What's the matter, sonny, you got the shakes?"

"No, ma'am, sorry. I was asleep when the conductor called the stop and it startled me."

"Would you mind helping me with my suitcase? It's up on the rack where the conductor put it for me and I can't reach that high with my rheumatiz and all."

"Sure thing." I got her suitcase down and grabbed my duffel bag. The train was slowing up. We moved to the rear door of the car where the conductor was waiting. He pushed the door buttons, and I climbed down and turned around to get the old woman's suitcase. She clambered down pretty spry for her age.

"Thanks, sonny. You ain't from around here. I don't think I ever saw you in town."

"No, ma'm, I'm here for the first time. Working up at Camp Nowatoma."

"Oh, my, yes, the camp. You know, I used to work there myself. Course, that was about twenty years back. Worked in the kitchen. Cooked, baked, peeled potatoes, all-round kitchen stuff. Worked for several years till the rumatiz got my hands."

She kept chattering on.

"I didn't hold with them bringin' the black kids up though. Some of 'em were a handful. But the minister said they got to have a place in this world, too, and I reckon he's right. And those girls!"

"What girls, ma'am?"

"Why, the college girls! My stars, you get them out of the city or off the campus and they just go wild up here. The boys ain't no better, though."

"You mean the staff?"

"Yes, certainly, who else? Now during the day they all act fine, but once the campers went to bed it was carnival time. Heard about it from my nephew, Jonas. He used to be one of the kitchen boys. Still, I suppose, part of it was youth. You know all those hormone juices you have when you're young. Tell me, is Bob Wheeler still running the show up there? That man had more energy than a circus band. Could run rings around the kitchen boys, I'll tell ya."

"Yes, ma'am, he still works for the camp."

"Well, you tell him hello from Bessie Akers. He'll remember me, and my cherry pies, too."

A Cadillac pulled into the parking lot and a horn blew. The old lady turned, smiled, and waved. She had ill-fitting dentures.
"That's my granddaughter Kate, come to pick me up. You need a ride up ta the camp?"

"No, thank you, they're sending someone. It was very nice to meet you."

"Okay, son, thanks for helping me with the bag. I hope you'll have a nice summer."

Kate got out of the car. she was a tall woman with a blonde pony tail, wearing a red University of Wisconsin sweatshirt that was puffed out. She looked pregnant, and I wondered if the blanket Bessie was knitting was for that unborn great grand child. The sweatshirt had a cartoon of a feisty badger on it. An all-American girl type, fresh beauty. She hugged the old lady, there were brief introductions, and then they were gone in a cloud of dust.

It was getting warm. I pulled my duffel bag into the shade, sat on a bench outside the station, and ate my apple. About an hour went by and no one showed up. I dropped a nickel into the pay phone that was on the station wall and dialed operator.
"Number plea-uzz."

"Operator, can you connect me with Camp Nowatoma?"

"Do you know the number?"

"No, I'm sorry. There probably is only one Camp Nowatoma, though."

"One moment ple-uzz. That number, sir, is WA-415. Please make a note of it."

The phone rang about a dozen times, and I was about to hang up when a voice said, "This is camp. Can I help you?"

"Yes, hi, this is Max Lewis. I'm at the Walkerville train station, and someone from the camp was supposed to meet me at the train. I've been here for a while. Is anyone coming?"

"Hello, Max, this is Bob Wheeler. It's nice to meet you. Looking forward to getting to know you. You were supposed to be picked up by our camp driver. Look for a light green Chevy wagon. He should have been there by now."

"Okay, Mr. Wheeler. I've heard nice things about you too. Looking forward to working with you. Oh, and I have a hello from Bessie Akers."

"Oh, I love that old gal! Thanks. How did you ever meet her?"

"We got off the train together, and I helped her with her suitcase. We had a nice chat about the camp."

"Well, she's a favorite of mine. Listen, I have a lot of things going on right now. Look me up when you get here and we'll get to know each other."

"Thank you, sir."

"No need for the formality. We're all on first name basis, but it's nice to hear a "sir" now and then. See you short-ly."

He rang off, and I sat on my bench with my feet up on the duffel bag. Another twenty minutes went by, and a dusty light-green Chevy wagon pulled in, very fast. The driver jammed the brakes and blew the horn unneces-sarily. I was the only person around.

I walked over to the car and stuck my head in the pas-senger-side window. The car smelled of stale tobacco, and I thought I got a whiff of alcohol, too. The driver was a seedy, lanky fellow wearing overalls and a t-shirt. He sported a scraggly goatee, hair done by mixmaster, and a bad complexion. He wore aviator sun glasses and a leather wristband. A cigarette dangled from his lip. I thought he was a mixture of hip and dip.

The inside of the car was as dusty as the outside. Crumpled candy wrappers were tossed on the floor, the ashtray was open and filled with butts and ashes. There were a couple of empty beer cans, and a clipboard with notes and messages sat on the passenger seat.

"Hey, you Max? I'm "Crash" Kelly, the camp driver."

"Yeah, I'm Max. Nice to meet you, Crash."

"Toss the duffel in the back. I'm running late. I'm sup-posed to bring you in and give you an overview of the camp. This your first year? I've been working up here for four summers. Ain't seen you before that I can recall."

"Right. Looking forward to working here."

I heaved the duffel on the back seat and climbed in front, trying not to sit on the assortment of papers, old receipts and the clipboard. Crash popped a cigarette out of a pack and offered it to me. I declined.

"Not a smoker? You'll change that. Not much to do in the off hours. Everyone smokes. So, what are you gonna do up here?"

"Well, I guess I'm headed for the scullery and a lot of dirty dishes."

"Yeah, that's where a lot of new guys start. I did it my first year too. Got lucky to get this job. I'm free as the wind and I love driving the roads, making pickups, ferrying people back and forth, taking the kids into town when they really get sick or need their braces fixed. It's a lot of freedom."

"Sounds neat, I'd love a shot at that."

"All right, let's go! I'm running late this morning and have lots left to do."

And with that, Crash put the car in gear and floored it. He let the clutch in really fast, ground the gears, and laid rubber that was bad for the tires. We pulled out of the driveway just as a woman with a baby buggy was approaching it. Crash hit the horn and kept going with no thought about the woman or her child.

"So, Max, when we get to the camp I was asked to give you a quick tour and show you the high points. If you're hungry we can stop at the camp mess hall and get you a sandwich. Usually stuff available."

His driving was awful. He changed lanes for no apparent reason and was speeding. We were doing 75 in a 60-mile-an-hour-zone. His left arm rested on the windowsill and the other down at a six o'clock position on the steering wheel. My dad would kill me if I drove that way.

It didn't take long to get out of Walkerville, and we were soon out in the sticks. I watched the countryside go by. Lot of pine trees, thick vegetation, small farms, cows sitting around in pasture, horses nibbling grass. The sky was a clear blue with billowy white clouds that just hung up there with no motion. A lot of birds in flocks swirled high up. I put my window all the way down, and let the fresh country air flow through the wagon.

Crash droned on about his job and how important he was to the camp. After a while he started trashing the camp management and made fun of Larry Reznik, who he called an "asshole." He said worse things about Miss Wallace. So I asked what he thought about Bob Wheeler.

"Wheeler? Ah, man, he gets my goat. A real stickler, big shot ex-army guy all about rules. Gets his shorts up his ass if you make any mistakes. He makes my life miserable, but I just stay away and get stuff done. He doesn't know where I am most of the time anyway. A real prick."

So, that did it for me. Crash and I weren't destined to be friends. I figured I'd just let him blow steam and not have much to do with him.

"So, Crash, where do I stay out here?"

"Well, some of the kitchen boys, or ''scullery stumpers'' as I call them, stay in the camp. Some live close by, so they go home after work. There's a tent compound, four tents arranged in a circle around a fire pit. It ain't as bad as it sounds; the tents are all army surplus and they're up on wooden platforms. Keeps a lot of the bugs out. There's electricity; course it's only one light bulb hanging from the top horizontal pole support, but it's better than being in the dark. One thing, though, some of the kitchen boys are really lazy bastards. So if they have to piss in the middle of the night, they just pull up the side flap and piss out of the tent. Right from their beds. Easier than going to the bathhouse we use. Now, you might not think that sounds so bad, but, shit, when the sun comes up and we have a couple of really hot days, the stench is just awful!"

I didn't recall Miss Wallace or Mr. Reznik making mention of this during their charming descriptions of the camp. So, all of camp Nowatoma was not the "stuff of dreams," as Bogart would have said.

We turned off the main highway onto a spur road, and about two miles later we were in heavy pine forest. There were also oaks and birch along the road.

And then there it was! A sign across a gravel road held up by two high posts that said,"Camp Nowatoma." Crash slowed up just a little and swerved into the gravel road. The wagon fishtailed, but he expertly straightened it out.

We went in about a half block, and there was a low building on our right with a sign over the door that said "Office." The front of the building had a covered porch that ran its total length. There were six or seven people sitting on the porch. Two were playing guitars, and all were singing a popular song by the Weavers, "Go Tell it on the Mountain." The Weavers were my favorite folk singing group.

Crash said, "Well, there's some of the camp staff. Bunch of do-gooders. They'll bore you to death about saving trees and owls. Most of 'em never saw an owl before they came up here. But sure as hell they want to save 'em. We should stop here and check in. If you don't mind, I'll wait in the car for you. Can't stand those creeps."

I got out of the car and walked up three stairs to the porch. There were two guys about my age playing guitars and four others singing along. Sounded really neat. Three of the singers were girls about my age.

They stopped singing and started welcoming me, asking who I was and what I'd be doing at the camp. I think their interest waned a bit when I told them I would be working in the mess hall as a kitchen boy. So I complimented the music and excused myself. I walked into the office. Just inside the door was a long counter almost the width of the room. Behind it was a desk, and behind the desk was a short, homely overweight woman. She had frizzy hair and was wearing a paisley blouse with a 'Tiki' symbol on a leather loop around her neck. The sign on the desk said her name was Lee.

"Hi, there, and who might you be?"

"Hello, I'm Max Lewis. Nice to meet you. I just got here."

"Okay, Max. Yes, we've been expecting you. Bob Wheeler said that you should get an overview of the camp, get something to eat at the mess hall if you're hungry. Crash knows where you'll be bunking. You should find sheets, pillowcases, blankets and towels already on your bed. If they're not there, stop by Camp Craft and get whatever you need. Dinner is at six in the mess hall. After dinner tonight there will be a get-together of staff who have already arrived, so you'll get to know some of them. It's early, so most of us are specialists who get things in order. The counselors will be up soon, and then there will be a few days of orientation and training for them before the campers come up.

 If you need anything, just stop by the office here. You can drop off or pick up mail from or to home. We send Crash into Walkerville daily to pick up mail at the post office there. It's a lot faster than their delivery. Here's a form to fill out if you want to send your laundry out. We send it into town weekly and drop it off at a commercial laundry that's not too awful. Stuff comes back very clean, and it's mostly yours."

She went on giving me instructions in a sort of mechanical fashion, some written and verbal, for some time. I guessed that she'd done it so often it was like a recording. Lee struck me as very efficient, but not terribly happy. So I thanked her and went out to the car. A couple of the people on the porch waved. The two guys with the guitars were arguing about who was out of tune and didn't notice my departure.

Crash said, "Come on, let's get something to eat." We drove up to a large wooden building that I guessed was the mess hall. There was a flagpole in front; no flag was raised. Crash parked with an unneeded flourish, and we walked into a large cool dining room.

The ceiling was very high and beamed with timbers. Formica tables filled the room, chairs stacked on them. There were long serving tables with condiments, silverware trays, plastic glasses, napkins and so forth. There were beige Melmac dishes, the kind that are unbreakable.

Crash pointed to two large inside windows off to the side of the room on an inside wall. "Well, buddy, that's where you'll be stationed. Them's the scullery windows. Kids come up at the end of every meal and start dumping their plates, silver, and whatnot at you. You'll be on the other side grabbing the shit and scraping the garbage into a couple of big cans. Then you spray the dishes and stack 'em in racks and run 'em through the dishwasher. There's plenty of steam heat and scalding water. Stack 'em when they're dry, and then it's time to sweep up the dining area. You'll be amazed how the kids can crap the place up. But they're neat compared to the staff. Jesus, they're slobs!"

He led me through a door alongside of the windows, and we were in the kitchen. I'd never been in an industrial-size kitchen like this one. Large pots hung overhead. Long stainless steel tables and counters were every-where. At the back of the room there were two walk-in coolers. The room was well lit and functional. One of the tables held a tray with a loaf of bread, mustard, cold cuts and potato salad. A large steel container sat on the ta-ble. Crash said it was "bug juice," otherwise known as "Kool Aid." I opted for water which tasted like rotten eggs, so I reverted to the bug juice, which was only slightly better. We made some sandwiches and ate while Crash continued his spiel on the camp layout. I was beginning to take his comments with a grain of mustard. He walked me over to a wall where a large map showed the camp layout and started giving me an overview.

"Okay, so, this is the mess hall where you'll be working. The camp is laid out along this road, the one the wagon is parked on outside. You follow the road and you'll get to the Camp Craft building. That's where we keep all the stuff for camping out. Sometimes the canoe rack is there, sometimes it's over at the waterfront. It's a wheeled rack and we hook it to the trucks when we take canoe trips out. Farther along you'll get to "Arts and Crafts." All kinds of arty activities there; potter's wheels, jewelry-making, painting, and I don't know what all. A little further down the road forks. Go right, you get to the ball field, left leads to the lake, goes up a hill and then down. You'll see the beach, pier, some small boats and canoes, a hut for staff to store their stuff, papers, equipment and so on."

"Now, you'll see as we follow the road here and here, there are side paths that go off on the left and right. If you follow those paths they'll take you to the camper's cabins. All together there are eight clusters of cabins. Each cluster has four cabins where the kids sleep, eight or ten kids to the cabin. The counselors have a separate room in the cabin, so they can keep an eye on the little bastards at night. Now, keep in mind that as you go down the main road from here, the girl's cabins are to the left and the boys to the right. See, we keep them separated. The tent area where the kitchen boys stay is further down the main road. I'll show you when we go. The farther up each path, the older the kids are. I mean, the youngest kids are closest to the main road and the older kids are farther back. Got all that?"

"Yeah, makes sense. I get it."

"Okay, now, one last area. If you cross the ball field there are some woods on the far side. Take a right at the end of the ball field and you'll see a path that goes down a slope to a small bridge that goes over the stream that feeds our lake. Cross the bridge and you'll be at some cabins and a recreation center, a one-story building that has a large dining room that's also used for staff meetings. That's where the infirmary is, and also the staff social hall. The kids don't go there unless they're sick. We can't get there in the car, the bridge is too small and the path to it is too narrow. There's a road around to the other side but you have to leave the camp from the main entrance to access it."

"Why'd they set it up that way?"

"Because that land was not in the original property package. The camp bought it later from a guy who wanted to build a resort, but he went broke or nuts or something, I never really knew the story. But that's where the sick kids go. The Board members stay over there when they visit, and the 'ladies auxiliary' stays there. Boy, they're a bunch of fancy-dancey broads .

Okay, if you're finished with the sandwich, let's go and I'll drive you through, you'll get the lay of the land; it's not that complicated."

"I thought I'd get to meet Bob Wheeler here."

"Yeah, he's always on the move solving problems or throwing his weight around. You'll meet him, don't worry about that."

We got in the Chevy and Crash gave it the gun. I thought he drove too fast for a dirt road that wasn't all that wide. It was also the main path for pedestrians, not a highway. The layout he described was just as he said. I picked out the various cabin clusters back in the woods. We stopped at the Camp Craft and Arts and Crafts buildings, went down to the waterfront, and then went around the ball field down to the path that led to the bridge.

He called the area across the bridge the "other side." We got out of the car, crossed the bridge. Underneath it was a dam that moderated the flow of water out of the lake. Crash had everything right in his description, except that the water left the lake at this point. It was the dam that apparently made the lake. The waterfront was as he described it. We took a long ride out of the camp and toured the "other side" spending about an hour taking all of it in. I was now tired, the initial excitement of getting to the camp, seeing the sites, meeting some staff members and trying to keep all the information straight left me fatigued.

Crash took me to the tent area, and said, "Any bed that's not made is okay to take. Pick what you like and make it up. If you wanna sack out for a while, that's okay. Dinner's at six. You'll hear a big bell ring a few times, and then about ten minutes later a second one. The first is a "get ready' thing," the second means "eats are on." Just walk that way to get back to the mess hall. You really can't get lost here, even at night. You probably have a flash light, but once you learn you're way around, you'll find that there's enough light from the stars and moon to make your way. Okay, buddy, I'm going to bug out on you. Good luck with the dirty dishes, the garbage and the kids, 'specially those brats from the North Shore!"

I climbed into the tent nearest the road, picked a bed and fell in, clothes and all, and slept until I heard the bell ringing.

Chapter 3
Meeting the Clan

I sat up and found myself facing a stoic-looking character who sat stiffly erect on the bed across from me. He

half scared the wits out of me because of his posture and a far away look in his eyes, one of which wasn't quite focused where the other one was. He had straight coal-black hair parted in the middle that was almost shoulder length. He wore jeans with a tooled leather belt and a sort of fringed buckskin-looking shirt with painted designs on it, and a beaded necklace.
"Jesus, you scared the hell out of me. Who are you?"

"Me Billy Lightfoot, come to help paleface with dishes! Just kidding you. I'm Bill Lightfoot, one of
the kitchen boys. I just got here. I heard you got in earlier. They told me up at the office that you're Max. Nice to meet you."

He got up and reached over to shake hands. I stood, and found that he was a few inches taller than I, with a slim build. We shook hands.

"We Indians appear silently like the mist and leave without a trace."

"You're Indian?"

"Yeah, Menominee. I live a few miles from here with my folks in a trailer camp. For me this tent is home during the summer, and I get away again in September when I go back to school. I'm studying philosophy and pre-law at the University of Wisconsin, down at Madison. Well, come on, let's go stoke up on whatever the chef is cookin'. It smelled pretty good when I went past the mess hall just now. Figured I'd introduce myself since we're going to be bunk mates and all."

"Isn't philosophy a bit far out for an Indian? I'd figure someone who's Indian would study agriculture or natural sciences or something like that."

"Actually, my family thought I should study business. The tribe is working on some business ventures and they're helping my school expenses with a scholarship. But I told them my goal would be law, and they figured that would be a useful thing down the line. Let's get going. Once camp food is out and sitting for ten minutes it's a lot less appetizing."

We stepped off the tent platform and headed for the main road. Bill asked me what I did in the city. I told him I'd just graduated from high school and planned college, but wasn't sure what I wanted to study. He was a good listener and easy to be with. I'd never known any Indians, and all I knew about them was what you learned in cowboy movies, which turned out to be nothing at all. Bill was articulate and bright, and he had a subtle sense of humor. I felt comfortable with him right off.
So I asked, "Bill, do you know what 'Nowatoma' means in any Indian language?"

He looked at me and said, "You know, that's bothered me, too. I asked some of the elders about that name and they said they didn't know. So I consulted a higher authority."

He stopped short in the road and raised his arms high and wide. He got a faraway look in his eyes and then closed them and appeared to be in a trance.

He said, "Lightfoot enters the Wilderness! Chews sacred Peyote and drinks firewater, good stuff, 100 proof. Communes then with picture of Wild Turkey on bottle and asks, 'What means the name 'Nowatoma?' Great vision comes to Lightfoot. See Great White Squaw of Board speaking to Great White Executive Director of Agency. She recommends the name, 'Nowatoma'. Great White Executive Director laughs. Squaw passes certified check across table. Many numbers. No more laughing. Great White Director goes before Council of Elder Board People. Vision sparkles with diamond Rolex, pinky rings, Mount Blanc. Director speaks the name, 'Nowatoma.' Much laughter. Shows check of many numbers. Laughter stops."

Bill appeared to come out of his trance, looked at me and said, "Okay, you gett-um message from Spirit World?"

"Ugh, Me got-um." We laughed, and Bill put an arm around my shoulders. It seemed I'd made a good friend.

"Max, when we get to the mess hall, you should sit at a table with people and introduce yourself. I'll be talking with Bob Wheeler in the kitchen. Have you met him yet?"

"No, but I talked with him briefly on the telephone, and I'd really like to meet him first."

"Okay, then let's go into the kitchen, you can meet him and pick up some dinner before you sit down with the staff."

We arrived at the mess hall and Bill took me around to the back. We entered directly into the kitchen through a service door rather than through the main dining hall door. A wiry-looking man about mid-50's was scraping on a sizzling grill, flipping burgers. He moved like a cat, alternating between the burgers and working a deep-fat fryer loaded with French fried potatoes. He had sandy-colored curly hair, and a couple of day's growth on his face. His brow was beaded with sweat and he moved between stations, one minute flipping, the next slicing vegetables and shaking the fry basket. Without looking up he said, "Hi, Bill, and you must be Max. Nice to meet you. I'll be caught up in a minute and we'll talk." I didn't see him look at us so he either had great peripheral vision or eyes in back of his head. Finally, he eased up and came over to us. He offered his hand and had a strong grip.

"Well, Max, you look like a sturdy chap. I read your application. You have any accidents or tickets on your license?"

"No, sir."

"Love that 'no, sir', but you can call me Bob. Ok, Max, next question is about how handy you are. Said in the application you're good with tools."

So we talked a bit about my mechanical aptitude, driving record, and even my physical stamina. Bob said he needed a "swing man," someone to fill in on maintenance and maybe do some driving. One of the local boys he used came up with some contagious illness that put him in the hospital, and because he was contagious,

he wouldn't be allowed back in the camp for probably
most of the summer. Bob wasn't sure if they would find a
replacement, so I was to just learn all I could about the
kitchen. There might be other assignments as well. I
wondered why he just didn't promote Bill, but decided it
wasn't my business.

Despite what Crash Kelly said about Bob, my take was
instantly positive. I read him as a straightforward guy
who was smart and efficient, and I thought I'd get along
just fine with him. He knew what he wanted, and I
thought I could work with a man who gave straight orders. I liked to get things done, too.

"Okay, Max, pick up some dinner and go out and meet
some of the staff. When it's over, come on back here
and I'll give you a lesson on the scullery operation. You
can start earning your keep tonight. Bill will help me with
the rest of the meal and the three of us will clean the
place up later."

I got a plate and a hamburger bun, and Bob picked a
large juicy burger off the grill and put it on the bun.
"You want some grilled onions on that?"

I got some fries and walked into the main dining room.
There were a couple of tables filled with staff, about half
men and half women. Most looked to be no older than I
was. One of the tables was buzzing about something
philosophical, and others at the second table looked up
as I approached. One girl waved me over. She had been
on the porch with the folk singers.

"Hi, you're Max, right? We met on the porch. I'm Phyllis,
this is Sue, Marv, Patti...."

She continued around the table, rattling off names and positions, counselors, Unit Leaders, Assistant Unit Leaders and so forth. There was a tall, tanned guy wearing a sailor's cap named Al Swanson, who was wearing a sailor's cap and was introduced as the Waterfront Director. I wasn't sure if I would remember the names, but they were friendly and made space for me. They asked what I would be doing. I told them I was a kitchen boy, but might get a shot at driving and other possibilities. Everyone was in college, and after a while they resumed their conversation about classes, bad professors they'd had, grades, school costs, campus antics and the like, so I felt a bit out of my element.

I thought the burger was really good. I'd not eaten since I grabbed a sandwich with Crash, and realized how hungry I was. I just tucked into the food. Pretty soon people started getting up and bussing their own dishes. They were also making plans to meet later at the conference room at the lodge on the other side of camp. I didn't feel part of it so I finished up and went back into the kitchen area. Bob Wheeler and Bill were getting ready to do the cleanup routine.

Bob grabbed my arm and said, "Okay, Max, time for you to start earning your keep. I'm going to show you around the scullery. Right now, we have only around thirty-five staff up here, but in the next few days that's going to expand more than three times. We'll have about a hundred staff. After that the kids come in, and then we get to our full complement. We'll have a total group of close to four hundred, depending on the number of campers who signed up."

We went into the scullery, and he opened the shutters on the windows where the dishes would start to come in.

Bob said, "We scrape the dishes here, and then slide them on this table and keep pushing them down. At the other end is the dishwasher. We load these racks and slide them into the machine, and they come out the other end washed and steamed hot, so we let them dry for a short time and then rack them up for the next meal."

Bob showed me the switches for the dishwasher as well as the controls for the hot water and soap. It all seemed pretty well organized. There were two large garbage cans under the windows where we could scrape the food. Right then, people started walking up to the window and pushing trays of dirty dishes across. I started scraping, and things picked up quickly as one staff member after another came up to the window. I quickly saw that the small number of people would be manageable, but 400 campers and staff could be another story.

Bill was racking as I moved the scraped dishes down the heavy metal table. It was a regular factory line. As we worked, Bob spelled out the other duties we would be responsible for. After each meal the dishes would be done first, then came sweeping up the mess hall as best we could. After the supper meal we'd not only have to sweep up, but stack all the chairs and mop the floor. This would take well over an hour given the size of the room and the number of chairs to be hoisted. The chairs were heavy dense wood, oak and maple, providing a good workout for anyone. It was close to eight o'clock before we got everything done. So far Bill and I were the only two kitchen boys. There would be a couple more when we were fully staffed.

After we got everything in order, Bill went outside around the back of the hall and lit a cigarette. I decided to walk the main road. It had been a long day. The staff was going to the "other side" to party, but I decided to walk around and get to know the place better. I finally got back to my tent and fell into bed. It had been a heck of a day, and it started to flash by before I conked out. The car ride to the train, my father's concern, his bag of goodies, the train ride, Bessie Akers, who softly warned about the "girls" at camp, Crash Kelly and his negative attitude, and finally, the mix of college kids I would be working with. Would they accept me? Would I be able to find someone to take my mind off Mickey? My last thoughts were about me and Mickey on the bridge, the last time I saw her, the image etched there that I thought would never dull. I went under and slept as never before.

Chapter 4
A More Complicated Place Than You'd Guess

I have a sort of built-in clock, I don't know how it works, but after six hours of sleep, my mind starts talking or playing music and it wakes me. I never need an alarm clock. This time it didn't go off. Bill was shaking me.

"Hey, Max, get up! you slept right through both bells, breakfast is half done, and you gotta get to your station. Last night a lot of staff arrived, we're almost at full strength now, and we need you at the kitchen!"

He kept shaking me, and finally I came out of a really deep sleep.

"Yeah, okay, Bill, I'm up, stop shoving. Gimme a couple of minutes to get some clothes on and I'll jog down to the mess hall."

Bill left, and I hurried into jeans and a tee shirt, got my gym shoes on, and hustled down to the mess hall. I went into the back entrance and got to the scullery windows just as the staff was bussing the tables and bringing the dirty dishes up. There were some new staff, but mostly the people I'd already met. I spotted Martha Kramer, who I'd set up for the Arts and Crafts job, and thought I'd have an extra twenty in my pay check, all to the good.

I went to my station and saw another kitchen boy, so I introduced myself. His name was Michael Jenner, he was a local kid who was about my age and a senior at Walkerville High. We shook hands and then got down to business. There was definitely a higher volume of plates and leftovers to manage. I wondered how we would handle all four hundred kids and staff. Michael and I scraped and stacked, Bill was racking up the dishes and running them through the washer.

After we got things pretty well under control, I looked around and saw a very pretty girl sitting and peeling potatoes in the kitchen area. There was also an older woman who was thumbing through some papers on a clipboard. I went in and introduced myself to the girl.

"Hi, I'm Max Lewis, working here in the kitchen. This is my second day."

"Hi, Max, I'm Honey Swenson."

She was a blonde with light blue eyes that were almost gray. But there was no spark in them. She looked at me with no expression. "So, Honey, I didn't know there were 'kitchen girls' to go along with the kitchen boys." Nothing, only a soft smile. The older woman came over and said, "Max, I'm Frieda Bergstrom, the head cook. Come over here for a moment, will you?"

We walked into the dining room and Frieda said, "Max, Honey has some limitations. She's in a work program from her high school and she works in the kitchen summers. She's really sweet, but, you know, just has some special needs. We watch out for her and we want the kitchen boys to make sure no one takes advantage of her. You know what I mean?"

"Frieda, you mean like sexually?"

"Yep, exactly. You okay with that?"

"Yes, ma'am."

"Okay, Max, I think it's time to start sweeping up. We're getting ready for lunch. After you, Bill and Michael get things in order, you can help prepare the vegetables, or lug the heavy pots filled with boiling water. Always something around here to do. Just keep looking for it."

I got the brooms out of the janitor's closet along with the sweeping compound that helped keep dust off the floor and went to work. Bill was finishing up the dishes, and Michael was sitting and working on vegetables with Honey, who he seemed to know. She talked while he just listened and kept nodding his head.

After about an hour, Bob Wheeler came into the dining hall and said, "Max, can you handle a jeep?"

"I never did. What's the shift pattern on it?"

"It's engraved on the shift knob."

"Then I can handle it. What do you need?"

"Some of the units didn't get their pillowcases. There are packages of them in the jeep with the unit numbers on 'em. I'd deliver them myself but there's a meeting up at the front office. Geez, they have meetings for everything here. So, I'd like you to deliver this stuff. You think you know your way around well enough?"

"Sure thing. I've been exploring."

"Okay, take the jeep and get going. It should take you about an hour to get this done and bring the jeep back here, I have other things to do."

"Got it!"
I hopped into the jeep. It had no top, no doors. This was a real World War II army surplus model. The first thing I noticed was a small plaque on the dashboard that said, "Presented to Lt. Col. Robert A. Wheeler from the men

of the 27th Marines, who fought beside him at IWO JIMA, April, 1943." I thought, *Wow, I'd better be very careful with this thing, it must have a hell of a lot of meaning to Bob.* And now I understood why he brightened when I initially addressed him as 'sir.'

I didn't know much about Iwo Jima, except for the picture everyone knew of the Marines putting up the flag on Mount Suribachi. I thought I would ask him about the battle when I felt more comfortable with him.
I started the jeep and carefully, put it in first gear and let the clutch out. Off we went. Jeeps, I learned, are fun to drive; their short wheelbase and primitive suspension make for a jouncy ride. I decided to go down to the oldest girls' unit first and work my way back to the main road, cross over, and deliver to the boys' side last, then back to the mess hall.

It didn't take long to get over to the older camper unit on the girls' side. I pulled up to the fire circle that was between the four cabins, which were arranged in a wider circle around it. I called out, "Anyone home?"

"Over here," a girl's voice called. I walked up three shallow stairs and into the kid's cabin, a long room with beds on each wall and a center aisle, like a barracks. There was a counselor working on a bed at the end of the room who had her back to me and was tucking in a sheet. She had red pigtails and was wearing a sweatshirt and very tight Levis.

"Put 'em on the bed", she said, then she got up and turned around. She was tall and had green eyes and freckles; a real red head. A girlfriend at school who is a

redhead once told me that "redheads are either dyna-
mite or dogs." This one had "nitroglycerin" written all
over her.

"Hey, who are you?"

"Hi, I'm Max Lewis, kitchen boy and sometime camp driver. And you are…?"

She stuck out her hand and said, "Pleased to meetcha,
Max, I'm Cassiopeia Katz."

"Cass…"

"Cassiopeia," she said again. I tried it once more.

"Casey-o-…., Well, what do they call you for short,
Cass?

She looked up at the ceiling and raised her arms wide,
like Moses parting the Red Sea ,and said, "Thank you,
O Lord for sending your poor servant, Cassiopeia, yet
another male boob who needs education! Amen and
Amen."

"Okay, Max, let's make it simple for you. My friends call
me "Kitty." Can you get that?"

"Kitty Katz!" I said.

"Bingo!" she said, and gave me a big hug. "Listen, she
continued, "I have a lot of work to do here. Help me fold
this sheet. It's an extra large, and it's easier for two to
fold these things."

As we stretched out the sheet I asked, "How did you get that name?"
She said, "Well, my father is a physics professor and an amateur astronomer, and— say, do you even know what Cassiopeia is?"

To which I answered, "No clue."

"It's a cluster of stars more than a few blocks away. In the middle there's a supernova, a star that exploded a while back. When my dad saw me for the first time he said "I think we got a supernova here," and there it was!"

"So Kitty became your nickname because…."

"Yep, Cassiopeia is a mouthful. And dad some how got it right. I've been sort of an exploding star ever since. He wanted me to be a teacher. I'm a math/science major and I want to be in science or maybe physics. I minor in boys, too."

"Meaning what?" I said.

"I rattle 'em, make them nuts. Here, I'll show you."
We had the bed sheet stretched out the long way, and she gave me instructions.

"Okay, fold it in half the long way and pick up the bottom corner. Good, now turn it ninety degrees to the horizontal. Now walk toward me. When we meet we'll have it in half again. Got it?"

We walked toward each other holding the sheet corners at chest level. When we got close, I stopped, but Kitty kept coming and dropped her hands. She walked her breasts right into my fists.

I said, "Oh, gee, I'm sorry!" And she said, "Firm, huh?"

This made me very anxious, and I stepped back. My left heel caught on a bed frame and I went backwards down on the bed.

Kitty said, "Whoa, you okay, Max?" She flopped down on top of me and planted a kiss on my mouth. I could feel her hot breath and when she broke off the kiss she said, "What's a matter, cat got your tongue? Kitty didn't get any." I could feel my face getting hot; I was blushing and flustered. Kitty pushed up, got off me, and started laughing. "See?", she said, "I rattled you pretty good! Okay, Max, you're a good sport. Let me give you a hand up. No more funny stuff, ok?"

Without thinking, I gave her my hand, and she pulled me off the bed with a lot more strength than I would have credited her. I was without words. I didn't know what to make of this girl, so I straightened myself out and foolishly said, "Well, Kitty, it was nice to meet you, but I have to finish delivering the pillowcases."

And at that she started to laugh and couldn't stop. "He's got to deliver pillowcases! Hahahahah!"

Laughter, they say, is contagious, and I started to laugh too. "I got to go!" As I ran out of the cabin she was still laughing and called after me, "Max, there's a staff party tonight on the other side. Even kitchen boys who are sometimes 'pillowcase delivery boys' can come. Hope to see you!"

I got in the jeep and took off as fast as I could, feeling mortified even while I laughed at how ridiculous the whole episode was. Somehow I got around to the other cabins, dropped off the packages, and then went back to the mess hall. Bob Wheeler was standing in front looking at his watch. I realized that I had been gone a lot longer than he said the whole job should have taken. I pulled up and turned off the engine.

Bob said, "Max, where the hell have you been? You should have been back here at least thirty minutes ago."

Gee, I'm sorry, Mr. Wheeler…"

"Bob."

"Bob, I, um, I met someone and we, well, we got to talking…"

"Max, you didn't meet that crazy Katz kid back in the older girls' unit, did you?"

"Well, I…." He started to laugh.

"You know they keep bringing her back every year and they swear they never had anyone who could relate to the teenage campers like she can. I think she's a real crackpot, but the professionals up at the front office tell me she's a genius. But boy, when it comes to the male staff, I think her elevator doesn't get up to the top floor.

Okay, no need to fumble for excuses, and I don't want to know what happened, but when I send you on an errand I expect it done well and on time." And then he started to laugh, and I blushed again. It made him double over and made me feel like a real dummy.

Bob got in the jeep and left. I went over to a bench alongside of the mess hall and tried to sort out just what had happened to me. Did I know that little about girls? Should I have somehow been quicker to control a situation like that? Was Kitty Katz really nuts or did she like me, and was the rest of it was just talk? No, I thought, no one could like me that fast; she had to be a real nut case. But one thing was for sure; she'd said she rattled the boys and she sure as hell rattled me.

The rest of the morning went quickly. Preparing for lunch, cleaning up again; there was a real structure to the day built in around meals. After lunch I took a long walk around camp, found a quiet place off the ball field, stretched out and got some sun and a nap. I heard the bell for dinner and set out for the mess hall.

I met Bill Lightfoot walking up the road.

"Max, it's good you're here. Most of the staff came in this afternoon, and we're going to have at least a hundred in the mess hall for dinner. And remember, after dinner we'll have to not only clean up, but we have to stack the chairs, sweep up, and then mop the place before we can get off. Oh, yeah, and there's a staff party tonight on the other side. The kids are coming up in a few days, so it's party time tonight; a lot of orientation and get-ready work for everyone, and then things really get going."

Michael Jenner, the other kitchen boy, showed up and we went into the kitchen. Frieda and Honey Swenson were already there, pots were boiling, vegetables were getting diced and sliced, and another very heavy-set woman was working on a large pot with pasta boiling in it. Later we were introduced. She was a local person named Wanda who came in part-time for the dinner meals. Wanda was one of those quiet, homely but sweet people who most of us don't pay much attention to. She, Frieda and Honey were a very effective team in that kitchen, and I grew to admire how they worked together in such harmony. Individually they didn't look like much, but together they were as effective as the New York Yankees in a playoff game. Bill, Michael and I pitched in to get things going.

The mess hall was filling up with staff, and the talking out there was increasing in volume. Ken Greenman and Reznik showed up and quieted the staff down. Reznik had a hard time getting everyone's attention, but then Ken asked for quiet and he got it right away. Each of them made a welcome speech and started talking about expectations for the season, the question of safety for the campers, and reminding the staff how important their role was.

I tuned the rest of it out and focused on meal preparation, helping with the heavy pots and a million other things that get a meal on the table. One advantage of being in the kitchen was that you could get the best of the food first, and we were working and eating the whole time. Honey and Wanda started into the dining room, pushing wheeled carts with the food in serving dishes. I stayed with the kitchen staff, and pretty soon the meal was over and the cleanup routine began.

My shift was on the dishwasher this time. It was funny to watch all the dirty dishes and leftover food coming through the window. At one point Bill dumped a plate of pasta into the garbage can while Michael was bent over shoving down the stuff already in it. Michael came up with a hurt expression and a hairdo of limp noodles, and griped, "What the hell did you do that for?" We all laughed, Frieda the hardest, and even Honey giggled.

It was about seven pm when the dinner crowd broke up and left. It took almost another hour to finish cleaning and straightening out the mess hall which was for sure a real mess.

While Bill and I were mopping up, he asked if I was going to the staff party.
"Sure, Bill. Why're you asking?"

"Michael and I are going off the camp to get a couple of beers, and wanted to know if you want to join us."

"You don't want to go to the staff party?"

"Max, the kitchen boys don't really fit in. The staff are all college kids."

"So what? You are too."

"Max, believe me, I don't fit in, been there. Try it for yourself; maybe it can work for you. Local guys just don't fit."

"Okay, Bill. I want to see what's going on there, maybe meet some friends of mine who I think got jobs. I saw one I know, but if everyone's here now, I don't want to miss them at a party."

"Got it. Well, you're welcome to join us next time, just so you know."

We finished up, and they took off. Bill had an old Plymouth coupe in the parking area. It was dark by the time we were done, and I had worked up a real sweat. I sat down on the bench outside the mess hall again and thought more about the day I'd had, the people I'd met, and especially the crazy episode with Kitty Katz. I found myself worrying about her. I figured that one day she was going to pick on a guy she thought she could rattle, and instead of a puppy like me, he would turn out to be a Doberman. So, why did I care? I didn't know. I wasn't especially attracted to her, it might be something about being protective of women. I thought about Mickey again.

I was always thinking about her. I think there was some need I had to protect her. When she dumped me it was a real blow to my feeling like a man who takes care of those he loves. I wondered about Martha and whether she and I might get together. After a while I got tired of thinking in circles and decided I just didn't know the how's and why's of me and women.

Chapter 5
You Never Know What's Around the Corner

I wanted to go to that party. I needed someone to date up here and maybe to take care of.

 I went back to the tent, got a fresh change of clothes, and took a hot shower in the bathhouse near the tent compound. It was 8:30 pm by the time I walked across the ball field, down the path to the bridge. Halfway over it I heard my name being called. I turned around and it was Kitty.

"Max, wait up!"

 She was jogging down the path and she looked pretty good. Her thick red hair was out of the pigtails, and it was full and very attractive. I put my hands up and said, "No funny business, Kitty. I'm ready for you."

She laughed, "All right, Max, not now."

"Kitty, I was thinking about you. I think you might get yourself into something you can't manage with this "boy rattling business."

"Thank you very much, dad, I can take care of myself."

"No, wait, I want to…"
And with that she walked off with attitude. I followed, giving her plenty of space. I had touched a nerve, and felt that I hadn't handled my attempt to help her very much. Okay, so I had a lot more to learn about girls. Lesson

one: don't be so helpful; it causes more trouble than the trouble you're trying to avoid. Lesson two: maybe help isn't something girls want. And maybe lesson three: stay off bridges with women; it never seems to work out well. I thought maybe I was bridge cursed or something.

I entered the large meeting hall. The place was very crowded, had very low light and a lot of cigarette smoke in the air. Or maybe better, there was a little air in the cigarette smoke. The room was about twice as long as it was wide. There were couches along one wall to my left and a guy, who I later learned was Jack Ryan the Camp Craft Director, was sitting on a couch playing a guitar. This was a guy I'd heard a lot about. He had climbed in the Alps, trekked deserts and knew his way around the jungle. He was also something to look at, and, if I was a girl, I would find him some hunk of a man. He had a dark complexion, wavy black hair, and unusually grey eyes with long lashes that any girl would kill for. He also had a kind of presence or magnetism that got him the attention of the staff's real lookers. One on each side and two sitting at his feet, enraptured at the bluesy song he was singing. I might not be the sharpest thinker when it came to women, but I knew I had no chance to edge my way into that group.

I looked around and saw Martha talking to a disheveled artsy-looking guy, so I eased my way through a lot of animated talkers and said hello to her. She gave me a hug and thanked me for helping her get a shot at the camp job, then introduced me to the schleppy-looking guy she was talking to, Harvey Jacobs, who was her boss at Arts and Crafts. He was cordial, but I could tell that I'd interrupted a conversation about arts or maybe crafts, and sensed they wanted to get back to it, so I excused myself and told Martha that I'd catch up with her.

There was a noisy bunch of fellas at the other end of the room. They were in a sort of semicircle, laughing, yelling, pushing each other and altogether seemed to be an obnoxious group. I realized that they were competing for attention from a girl whom I could barely see between the low light, the smoke, and the screen they made around her. I started to turn away, and just then one of them pushed another, a gap opened and my god, there was Mickey!

She was laughing and flirting and pushing back on them. I was nailed to the floor, wishing that a hole would open beneath me so I could drop into it and disappear. I felt hot and sweaty, and started to choke from the smoke-filled air. I turned again and headed for the door.

"Max!" It was Mickey calling me. I kept walking; I bumped someone and almost knocked a girl over. Mickey caught me as I got to the back entrance.

"Max, wait! Why are you running away? Max, stop, I have to talk to you."

I stopped, but didn't say anything. I couldn't believe that she was here, and I realized the great summer I'd hoped for was roadkill.

"Max, I have to talk to you. It's important. Please, let's get out of here."

"Okay, Mickey, I can't breathe the air in here. Let's go outside." We went out of the meeting room and walked up the path. There was no one on the bridge, so we stopped there and I said, "Mickey, what are you doing here?"

"Max, listen, I need your help. I'm a counselor."

"What? A counselor? You? How could you be a counselor here, Mickey? They only hire people who are social work majors. You have zero college and no experience! How could you get a counselor job here?"

"All right, Max. Please, just listen. I got here, but I didn't do it exactly the way you're supposed to do it. I just sort of figured a way, okay?"

"Okay? What do you mean, okay? You figured out a way? What the hell does that mean? You need my help? For what? You got here without it."

"Max, please, don't be angry with me. And I don't want you to tell anyone here that you know me from home, okay? It's important."

"Mickey, I think you'd better tell me what's going on. I don't lie, and you know it. How did you get a job here?" She thought for a moment, looking down at her shoes. "Okay," she said at last, "I'll tell you how I got here. I was dating a guy..."

"Who, Michael Vandon, I suppose?" I shouldn't have said that. I realized how jealous and hurt I sounded. I didn't want to reveal that.

"Michael? I just went to your prom with him. No, another guy. Listen, it doesn't matter who. He was studying at the Chicago Teacher's College up north. He told me that they were having interviews for camp jobs, and I thought it would be good work for the summer. I have a friend who works part time in the Dean's Office, so I called her and she gave me the dates they were going to interview. I asked her as a favor to put my name down."

"She's either a really good friend or really dumb. You don't even go to that school."

"Well, not exactly. I did apply there for the fall semester, so I had their catalogue. Anyway, if you want to know how I got here, stop interrupting. So, I came for the interview…"

"Yeah, but you would have interviewed with the Executive Director. I met him, and he would never hire you. He'd see right through you."

"Max, please! Shut up and stop interrupting! He didn't do the interviews that day. He had some kind of emergency board meeting and sent that guy Reznik. He wasn't so hard to get past. He talked the whole time, and I played up to him like he was Frank Sinatra and I was the president of his fan club."

"Yeah, but what about the application and references and meeting with that personnel woman, Wallace?"

"Max, just shut up and I'll tell you, okay? *God!*"

She was very frustrated with me because I kept interrupting. I couldn't help it. I was very angry. I took a deep
breath, and she studied her shoes some more. I wondered if she was really going to tell me the truth, or if I
was in for yet another snow job.

"Okay," she said, "I filled out the application I got at the
interview, and my friend, Chicken…"

Oh, boy, I thought, *Chicken again, this is getting really
crazy.*

".… was doing filing in the Dean's Office, so I talked her
into getting me some of the school's stationery and
some envelopes. I picked a couple of psychology professors out of the school catalogue and wrote glowing
references over their names, and mailed the package.
The interview with Miss Wallace was nothing to get past.
When I arrived, she had a bunch of guys sitting and
waiting to see her. She floated into the reception area,
took one look at the guys and waved me in. She asked
like two questions, and I just repeated the stuff on the
application. Then she said, 'Okay it looks all in order.
We'll let you know.' And she got me out of there in five
minutes!"

I couldn't believe it. I worried my ass off to get a job
washing dishes, and she waltzes in with phony references and bullshits her way past the assistant director
and the personnel woman. She really was a fake, just
like everyone told me, and I was too dumb to see it. She
studied her shoes some more, and I couldn't tell if it was
guilt she was feeling, or remorse that I was there and a
threat to her job.

"Max, please, don't tell anyone. Don't even admit that we know each other, please, Max."

She threw her arms around my waist and hugged me. And worse, she flashed the dreamy eyes that melted me, and then put her head down on my chest.

"Please?"

"Yeah, ah, yeah, okay, Mickey. I can do that much, I guess."

"For old time's sake?"

"Yeah, sure. Yeah, okay."

"Thanks, Max, you're a doll."

She hugged me tighter. I thought, no, I'm no doll. I'm a class-A jerk. Mickey got what she wanted out of me. She thanked me again, patted my shoulder once and walked back to the meeting room. For the second time that night, I watched a girl leave me and walk off that bridge. So, my bad bridge curse-tally included twice with Mickey on two different bridges and once with Kitty. *Three times and you're out*, goes the saying. Or was it, '*Three on a match and you're dead?*' There was something about bridges that didn't work for me. I went back to the tent and tried to sleep. As I dozed off I heard an owl somewhere in a tree call, "Whoo?" And I answered him, "Who, What, Why and How?" I didn't have a clue to his Whoo or much else.

It was morning, and I wasn't yet used to sleeping in a tent, even an army surplus model that at least had a light bulb. Mornings at camp were cool, and when you're used to living in a house you don't realize how the morning dew and dampness creeps in and makes it uncomfortable to get up and going. I took a hot shower and cleaned up. It was early; the first bell for breakfast was at least a half hour away. I decided to go down to the mess hall and see if anyone had started coffee. I was on the main road, the sand close packed and still damp. The shrubbery was heavy with dew. It was very quiet here in the early morning. I wondered how it would sound with 300 campers and a hundred staff all yelling.

I heard footsteps crunching behind me, turned and saw Bruce Marshall, my friend from Chicago, coming up. "Hey, Max, wait up!"
I was really glad to see him. "Hi, Bruce! Hey you got here! When did you get in? What job did you get?"

"Yeah, I came up last night and got lost. No one came to get me at the train, and I wandered around town for a while before I found a cab. So, I got to the party late. They said you'd already left. You know, Mickey is here! Man, I was surprised to see her. You see her at the party room? She's the one who told me you'd already gone. She didn't look happy to see me and wanted to get away, seemed like. What's going on? How'd she wind up here? You didn't tell her about this place, did you?"

I looked around to see if anyone was in earshot and said, "Listen, I can't talk about how she got here, okay. She doesn't want anyone to know that I know her, and probably she doesn't want anything to do with any of us. Leave it at that."

Bruce looked puzzled, but there were other things to discuss.

"Did you know Fat Freddy Ginzberg is up here?" he asked.

"No, I didn't. Really?"

"You didn't know? I thought you called him about jobs here."

"Yeah, he was the last guy I called, and he said he planned to spend the summer at Farwell Beach eating hot dogs and chasing girls."

"He told me the same thing. But his parents raised a fuss and told him to find a job. So he called Moira Wallace, the contact you gave him, and went for an interview. He figured he wouldn't be offered anything and he'd be off the hook with his dad.

"So?"

"Well, he got to the interview and asked about the kitchen boy jobs, but they were all filled, so Wallace asked him if he had any interest in food! Well, boy, that started a great conversation, he said. You know, Freddy knows more about food than anything else. He started telling her about his knowledge of food, nutrition, and his cooking skill, and guess what. She hired him for Camp Craft! He'll be working for me."

"I don't get it. Doing what?"

"Well, the Camp Craft department sends campers out on overnight camping trips, canoe trips, long hikes and all that. So someone is needed to provision the groups. You know, to make sure they have all the food and supplies, cooking gear, pup tents, that stuff. And Freddy and Moira hit it off; he loved the idea of being around all that food."

"I can't believe this! Did you see Ted? Did he come up?"

"Yep, he's going to be working as the Assistant Waterfront Director. Man, you got all of us jobs, Max."

I thought, *Wow, that's about eighty bucks plus five each for the calls. A hundred!*

"Max, listen, do you know a tall pretty redhead, freckles, reminds me of Katherine Hepburn? I saw her at the party last night and she was flirting with some guys, so I didn't get a chance to meet her. You know who I mean?"

"Yeah, her name is Katz. I met her. She's a bit odd." I filled him in on my encounter with her, and we stopped walking when I got to the folding bed sheet routine. His eyes widened. We started walking again, and he said,

"So, if I get a chance to fold sheets with her I should definitely keep my palms facing forward with my pinkies up so she'll think I'm innocent, right? So fill me in. Her boobs are..."

"Bruce, you're drooling." We were laughing at this point and I started to feel the presence of someone close behind us on the road. "Bruce, you should also know her name is Cassiopeia, but she goes by 'Kitty'."

I felt a tap on the shoulder, turned, and, *oh shit,* it was Kitty. I didn't know how long she had been behind us or how much she heard. "Oh! Hey there! Hi, Kitty, we were just talking about you."

"Uh-huh, Max, I got the drift. Who's this?"

" Oh, right, ah, Kitty, this is a good friend of mine from Chicago, Bruce Marshall. He's the Assistant Camp Craft Director, his first year. Bruce, meet Kitty Katz, who's a special person!" I said all that with too much energy and embarrassment, but Kitty was cool about it. She said hello to Bruce, and the three of us started walking to the mess hall again.

Kitty said, "Bruce, so you'll be working with Jack Ryan, right? I think *he's* quite a guy."
Bruce was calm; he's always calm, one of those guys you want to have around when there's an emergency. He was going to study pre-med next year and was always in control.

"Jack's a good guy. I'm just getting to know him, Kitty. Do you know him well?"

"Oh, sure, we've worked up here together for the last couple of years, but I'd sure like to know him MUCH better. *He's so cool.*"

I couldn't tell if she was praising Jack to make me jealous or to put me down, or if she was just angry about what I'd told Bruce about her. But whatever her reason, I felt embarrassed. And she just kept sticking it to me. And then she put an arm around Bruce and gave him a kiss on the cheek. "Nice to meet you Brucey. Got to go back to my cabin for a sweater. And, looking right at me, said, "It's *very* chilly this morning. 'Bye, Max." No kiss. I figured maybe a kiss-off.

We got to the mess hall, and Bruce said, "Woof, she's hot!"

"Or nuts, I haven't figured her out at all."

"Who needs to figure anything?" he said. "Max, there's something I want to kick around with you about Jack."

"What's that?"

"I think he's a hotshot who isn't all he says he is. We've been getting to know each other, and, you know, he's got this reputation of being a great outdoorsman. He told me that he's going to give a demonstration of rappelling after lunch. You know what that is?"

I didn't, so Bruce gave me a quick explanation. I said, "Okay, so he's going to do that where?"

"He said he talked to Reznick and got permission to rappel down the side of the mess hall. Between you and me, I think it's a crazy idea and that he only wants to show off in front of the girls. Reznick told him he had to do it before the kids come up, so they wouldn't get any crazy ideas. Jack told him that it would be good for the staff to know about this technique, but I think it's too dangerous for the staff, and not good for small kids. And also, I think he's a show off. More sure of himself than he should be."

"Why's that?"

"Well, he started to show me how he plans to do the stunt and how he would tie his knots, work his ropes, like that. I don't think he's all that skilled."

"So, did you say anything?

"Yeah, sure, I tried. The guy doesn't listen, he doesn't have to; he knows everything. Max, I've done this sport; it's tricky. And going down the side of a building isn't the same as a hill. Hills have slant, stuff to dig your feet into, brush to hold onto. So I asked him if he ever did this down a building and he said, 'No, but it's all the same idea.' It isn't, and I think he could really get hurt."

"Well, you tried, and I don't see what else you can do unless you went to Reznick and told him what you think."

"Yeah, I thought of that. And then spend the summer with a boss I've undercut."

"That's a point," I had to admit.

We were at the mess hall and it was time to work. I told Bruce we'd just have to hope for the best, and I went in to start the shift. The morning went quickly. We finished breakfast, went through the cleanup routine, and I had some time until lunch.

As I walked through the camp, I saw groups of counselors with their supervisors sitting in circles on the ground. Everyone had a clipboard, and they were getting instructions on the camp philosophy, scheduling and safety issues. I saw Mickey, but when she saw me she shifted her position so we wouldn't make eye contact. I saw Kitty in another group, and she looked away. I was starting to feel like the guy in the deodorant ad on TV who everyone shunned.

There were now a lot of people in the camp, and it was starting to have a different feel. No longer an empty, quiet woodland, it was something more alive and exciting. The buzz about the 'campers coming' was everywhere. I was starting to feel the excitement myself, even though I didn't think I'd have much to do with them.

Around a quarter to twelve, I walked back to the mess hall for the lunch shift. Everyone was gathered around the flagpole, and Reznick was talking to the assembly.

"This afternoon, right after lunch, we're going to have a demonstration of rappelling by Jack Ryan." There was a murmur from the crowd, especially the girls.

"Jack feels that this is a good outdoor sport to know about and he thinks you may want to learn more. So, people, let's all assemble here directly after lunch to watch the demonstration. That's all; see you then."

Everyone filed in for lunch. I got mine in the kitchen with the other kitchen staff. The meal was egg salad, tuna salad, and macaroni. I thought it was pretty good, but I heard complaints coming in from the dining hall. So what did they expect at a camp, prime rib? Cornish Hen with Hollandaise sauce, maybe?

Lunch finished, the kitchen boys wanted to watch Jack Ryan do his thing, so we promised Frieda we'd come right back in to clean up.
I walked out to the front and found Bruce standing behind the group where he could get a better angle on the event. I followed his gaze, and then I saw Ryan up on the roof of the mess hall. He was tying ropes around the base of a large pulley that was on the peak of the mess hall's roof.

He waved to the crowd. He was wearing military fatigues, aviator sunglass, and heavy boots. He had a Marine Corps hat on and looked like a real hero up there. I thought maybe Bruce was a bit jealous; the guy looked like he could be in the movies. There were a few flashbulbs popped as some of the girls took snapshots with their Brownie cameras. He waved and blew a kiss to the cuties that were around him the previous night. Then he wrapped the ropes around his wrist, swung around and stepped off the roof.

He planted his feet against the wall of the Mess Hall and made a test pull on the ropes. Something about that bothered me, and I heard Bruce gasp, but before I could ask him about it, I heard a loud wrenching noise, like a creaky door hinge in a horror movie. I realized the anchors that held the pulley to the roof were coming loose!

It came forward a few inches, and as it did, Jack dropped a bit and then his feet slipped off the wall. He dangled there with his legs working to get traction back on the wall, but the pulley dropped another couple of inches maybe because of his dead weight.

Bruce grabbed my arm, "Jesus! He's going to fall!"

And just then, the frame and pulley came all the way out of their moorings, and Jack dropped like a rock. There was a lot of screaming as he flailed away trying to climb a rope that could no longer support his weight. He fell and landed on his back with a horrifying noise, and the ground actually shook from the impact. The rope and the pulley followed him down and landed on his chest. The crowd froze. Bruce and I ran around them and got to Jack, who was trying to breathe, but couldn't seem to grab any air. Bruce tried some artificial respiration, and a woman who I later learned was Victoria Morrow, the camp nurse whom I had not yet met, got to us. She was British or South African or Australian or something.

She said, "Hey, careful with that artificial respiration bit, love. He could have a collapsed lung from 'is looks." She kneeled down, looked him over and said, "Ere, E's in shock. It looks like the pulley may have broken some ribs and maybe punctured 'is lungs! We need to get 'im to a 'ospital." She turned around and yelled, "Someone fetch a blanket!"

Strangely, with all that was going on I remembered thinking, *Boy, is she cute!*

Larry Reznick came running up, and the nurse gave him a quick assessment.

"Larry, E's hurt bad, we need an ambulance, 'E needs a 'ospital."

Larry was wringing his hands. He said, "We just had our safety unit this morning! This is terrible, what will Ken say? My God, I don't know what to do!"

"Larry," the nurse said, "Someone needs to call an ambulance, NOW!"

Just then, Bob Wheeler came jogging up and pushed his way through the group around Jack.
"What the hell is going on? Oh, Jesus, what happened to Jack?"
Bruce and Victoria brought Bob up to speed. He looked up at the mess hall roof, and with no hesitation started giving orders. He grabbed Michael Jenner by the arm and said, "Michael, run up to the office and tell Lee to call the Walkerville Clinic. Tell them what we got here and to get ready to help when we show up." He looked around and called to Crash to bring the big truck.

"Max, you and Bruce go behind the mess hall. There's a lumber pile there and some sheets of plywood. Go get one." He looked around and told two of the male counselors to bring the ladder that was leaning against the wall of the mess hall over. It must have been how Jack got up to the roof. It was a long extension model. Everyone started moving.

When we got the plywood, Bob told us to set it down next to Jack. Then we carefully slid him onto it by holding his feet together and getting our hands under his armpits. Jack gave a groan, but we got him onto it. I couldn't figure what Bob wanted the ladder for, but as soon as the truck was backed up as close as it could safely get, he told Bruce and me to get on one side of the plywood, then he and Crash got on the foot side. He had the ladder parallel to the board.

"Okay, fellas, when I give the word, I want you to slide the plywood onto the ladder. Ready, on three; one, two...." And just like that we had Jack and his plywood bed on the ladder.

"Now comes the tricky part. Victoria, hold his head; Larry, get his feet. Okay, the four of us lift the ladder onto the truck bed, and for Christ's sake keep it *level*." In a moment we had Jack resting on the truck. Victoria climbed up and covered him with another blanket.

Bob said, "Crash, where are the keys?" They were in the ignition. We put the tailgate up and secured it. Bob jumped in the cab and started the truck. He said to Larry, "We're going to the Walkerville Clinic. They'll look him over and figure out what he needs. You better tell Ken what's going on."

And with Victoria keeping an eye on Jack, Bob took off, avoiding potholes in the road and making a very gentle left turn onto the highway. They were gone, and we stood still for a few moments.

Then Bruce said, very calmly, "I think Jack has some very severe damage. I hope he makes it."
He looked at his hands, and they had a lot of blood on them.

"Bruce, your hands!"

He said, "Nothing to worry about; it's my blood. I got a rough corner on the plywood. I'll go over to the infirmary and fix it up."

I looked around, the group started to buzz; everyone had been frozen while the action was going on. The "Camp Cuties," as I began to think of them, were in a tight group, talking excitedly. Not so much from the "Macho Males," who were eying the Cuties like foxes looking into the hen house.

One man's misfortune was another's jackpot, I figured. It bothered me, but then I reasoned that I was always worrying about the underdog. I didn't like Jack all that much. I didn't even know him, really, but I couldn't help thinking that he might die just because he wanted to show off for a bunch of girls. I also didn't think much of Larry. He okayed the stunt. To me it showed poor judgment for a man who had his level of responsibility.

I saw Mickey at the edge of the crowd. When she saw me look in her direction, she turned away and started to read her clipboard. A couple of the porch singers came over and asked if I was okay. They asked if Jack would make it, how bad was he hurt, and so on. I told them I didn't know. Kitty had been right behind me through the whole business. She put a hand on my shoulder and said, "Max, you look pale. You doing okay?"

"Thanks, Kitty, yeah. I'm okay. I never saw anyone take a fall like that. Bruce said he's not in good shape. I hope he makes it."

Larry called everyone together and announced that there would be a mandatory additional safety training session scheduled in the next day or so. And then he asked that people get back to their orientation meetings. People started to flow into their training groups. The kitchen boys went in and started their cleanup routine. We were quiet as we worked. The sight of Jack's fall stayed with us, and no one wanted to talk about it.

Chapter 6
Now for Some Real Action

The next few days went by in a settled routine. The counselors continued to meet in their orientation groups; the kitchen team routine became finely honed. I didn't see much of Ken Greenman. He seemed to be holed up in the main office with Larry a lot of the time, and I wondered if Larry was going to get the heave-ho. I thought he sure deserved it. We had started referring to Ken as Mr. G. I really liked him and wanted to continue the great talk we had in his office back in Chicago, but I knew he had a lot to manage and little time for one kitchen boy.

The staff was developing a team mentality. The counselors continued being drilled and receiving instructions on everything from meal schedules to water safety. A botanist from the University of Wisconsin at Madison came up and gave a lecture on insects and plants, how to spot poison ivy, which kind of spiders to watch out for, what to do about hornet stings; really good stuff, I thought. They let me sit in on that one.

Ted Wilson, my friend from Chicago (and another $25, thank you,) hit it off with Al Swanson, the Waterfront Director. Some of the staff went to the Arts and Crafts building and painted a sign that said, "Wilson & Swanson, Waterfront, Inc." My friend Fat Freddy was working in Camp Craft, and, because of the injuries sustained by Jack Ryan, Bruce was promoted to his position (with a minor raise since he had no experience, but with full responsibility). I was learning a lot about non-profit management.

People kept asking me about Jack Ryan, but I knew as much as they did. Then one morning I was dropping off my laundry at the front office when a call came through that Lee picked up. I hung around the mailboxes in front to eavesdrop. From what I heard of the conversation, Jack was going to make it. When Lee got off the phone, she said, "Max, come here. As long as you're listening in anyway, I have some good news and some bad news. Jack will make it, but he has a lot of healing to do. They found four busted ribs, a perforation of one lung, two broken ankles, a concussion, and maybe a disc problem in his back. The emergency room people said he looked like he was run over by a train. They also said that whoever helped to get him to the hospital saved his life."

She said that Bob getting him to the Walkerville Clinic was crucial. The clinic staff took one look at Jack, stabilized him the best they could, and got him in an ambulance to Port Edwards, the closest hospital.

Lee said, "That business about getting him on a makeshift stretcher, they said that was brilliant thinking. He has some sort of back problem and moving him carelessly might have made him a cripple for life."

"Well, Lee, all praise to Bob. He told me after the accident that he learned to improvise in all kinds of ways in battle. He'd done stuff like that before." She said not to tell anyone about the call. She would tell Mr. G. and was sure he'd want to make an announcement to the whole staff so there would be no rumors.

That same afternoon, as everyone assembled for lunch, Mr. G. called for attention and said he had some important announcements.

"Okay, everyone, listen up. I have some 'housekeeping' announcements and other news to share. First and most important is that we've heard from the hospital, and Jack Ryan will be okay."
There was applause and a few cheers. Mr. G. held up his hands for silence.

"Okay," he said, "That's the good part. Jack needs a long time for recuperation and rehab. He has several broken bones, a concussion and other injuries, so he won't be back with us this summer."

I looked out of my scullery window, and the "Camp Cuties" looked crestfallen. The "Macho Males" looked relaxed. One of them actually blew air out of his mouth with relief.

"Now, one other thing about any sort of demonstrations you may think of or want to do. They will all have to get my personal approval. I hope that's understood."
Well, I thought, there's a knock on Larry's power, smart and deserved.

"Here's some other news," Ken went on. "Bruce Marshall has been promoted to Camp Craft Director. While he's new to our camp, Bruce is an Eagle Scout with years of experience in camping, hiking, tent set up, fire-building and many other skills. He and Fred Ginzberg will provide solid assistance for your overnight campouts and canoe trips, and will be happy to provide training in any area of camping, rope use, fire-building and safety that you may require. Bruce, Freddy, stand up and let them see you." A round of applause erupted as they took a bow. Fred was enjoying the attention and actually took a little bow. Bruce was calm as always.

"Thanks, fellows. All right, I know everyone is anticipating the arrival of the campers, and I can tell you that they're on the way. In a few hours we will see two large vans coming up the camp road. That will be the campers' luggage. The specialists, maintenance staff and kitchen boys will stay after lunch to receive their instructions for making sure the luggage gets unloaded and sent to the correct camper units. And tomorrow, folks, the campers will be boarding trains early on in Chicago and should get here by noon!"

A cheer went up. I thought, *Wow, good morale. He has the right people here.* I couldn't help but steal a look at Mickey. She had her head down, studiously reading something on her clipboard. Kitty was bright-eyed and bushy-tailed as a squirrel. It started me thinking about who was who, or what, maybe.

Ken said, "Okay, that's about it for now. Any questions?"

A hand went up from one of the folk-singer girls, "Mr. G., how do the kids get here from the train?"

"Oh, good catch, Phyllis. Okay, the unit leaders will go into town to meet the train. When the kids get off, we'll separate them by units and get the kids on buses. Now, we've contracted with the same bus company that serves Walkerville High School, so they're used to bus-ing a large number of kids. They'll drive right into the cir-cle outside the mess hall here, and counselors will get their kids together and take them down to their cabins. There will be a preliminary sorting at the train station; the campers will have tags with their unit numbers on them, I hope! (A lot of laughter.) Get them settled in, and by then it will almost be time for dinner.

Okay, I think that's it. Anything else? No? Okay, see you tomorrow morning and everyone get a good night's sleep. No schnoogling in the bushes tonight." Mr. G. ob-viously knew what went on in his camp.

There was another hearty round of laughter at that, and I heard my dad say in my ear, "Are ya gettin' any, Max?" I shook that off. The crowd filed out of the Mess Hall

except for the kitchen boys, specialists, and the maintenance staff. Bob Wheeler gathered everyone around to
give his instructions.
"Men," he started, then chuckled to himself. "Okay,
everyone, here's how we're going to manage the luggage." And with that he reeled off instructions. We listened intently; nobody wanted to disappoint Bob. And
then we were off for the night.

The luggage effort happened just like we were told it
would. Next morning around noon, two large vans rolled
into the camp and parked in front of the mess hall. We
were assigned in pairs. I got stuck with Crash Kelly.

We spent the better part of the afternoon sorting luggage by tags, pink for the girls and blue for the boys.
After that we sorted by unit number. The big pile shrank,
and small piles were everywhere. I found it interesting
that you could look at a suitcase or a duffel bag and
know whether the owner came from a poor neighbor-
hood or a wealthy suburb. I got hold of one trunk with a
pink-tagged that I could barely lift. The thing came from
Glencoe, and the tag said "Rosalie Finkelstein, Dad's
Princess." But it wasn't only the Jewish kid that had
good stuff. A matched set of suitcases came from Kenilworth, and the names on them stated "Lorelei van
Mater." Some of the bags were clearly from very poor
families. And there were several beat up cardboard boxes held together by string, tape, rope or sometimes just
a prayer. I felt really sad picking up those boxes, and I
treated them with a lot of respect.

It wasn't much fun working with Crash. He shirked,
avoided the heavy bags and complained the whole time.

He found time to ask questions about the tag information, said he couldn't read the writing, needed several cigarette breaks, had to pee about four times in a couple of hours, and it took him forever to get back. I decided to keep quiet about all of his goldbricking, but it made me angry. The tension between us was building the whole afternoon, and I was glad when we got everything sorted and delivered. By the end of it he knew I was angry, but we didn't discuss it. He tried to make things right when we were done.

"Well, Babe, nice work we did. You wanna go into town, have a beer?" I just shook my head and walked away, and heard him mutter, "Asshole." I turned around and said, "What was that?" But he just waved it off and walked away. We were done being on civil terms, but I didn't care.

There was a lot of tension the next morning. Breakfast was all a-buzz from the staff as the time drew near when the campers would arrive. After breakfast, counselors hung around the mess hall, checking their watches. The two guys who played guitar organized a folk-sing to break the tension. There was intense activity inside the kitchen. Frieda, Wanda, Honey and the kitchen boys, now up to four with the recent addition of a guy named Leon Kozinski, were getting ready for our first meal that would serve a full four hundred people.

Bill Lightfoot introduced me to Leon, who was a lineman on the Walkerville High Football team and stood about six-five, weighing in at around 250 pounds.

"Nice to meet you, Leon, where were you when I was trying to lift Rosalie Finkelstein's trunk?"

Leon didn't get the joke, but everyone else had a good laugh, and I clued him in. He had a great sense of humor and came back with, "Geez, sorry about that, Max. I only bench three hundred pounds, though, so I wouldn't have helped you much."

I was feeling good about the kitchen crew. We were growing to be friends and an efficient team. We all looked up to Bob Wheeler and wanted to get things done really well for him. Then, from outside there was a loud cheer, and I heard the roar of buses coming up the road and rolling into the circle in front of the mess hall. The campers!

We walked out to see the show. The buses circled around, and the doors opened, and out came a mixed bunch of kids you wouldn't see in any other place. Well-dressed girls and boys from suburban families, good looking, self-assured and happy. And pouring out of the same buses were black kids, Hispanic kids and white kids, but not so well-dressed or happy. I guessed that they were stressed about this new experience. I felt for them. I also was new at being away for the first time, and I also came from a less-than-flush home. Just like the poor kids, I was learning how to fit in with college boys and girls who seemed a lot more sophisticated than I or anyone I knew.

The counselors went into action, calling names from their clipboard lists, rounding up the kids, and getting them into groups, and greeting them. I looked around for

Mickey to see how she was managing, but couldn't see her in the crowd. Some of the kids were as tall as she was.

I watched Kitty. She sparkled as she gathered up and greeted the older girls. She looked terrific, her red hair flowing, her eyes flashing at the kids, and a wide beautiful smile of welcome for each. I felt a twinge, and wondered if maybe I had screwed up a chance for a relationship that might just be better for me than any I'd known.

I was knocked out of my reverie by someone hugging my leg. I looked down, and there was a really cute little black girl. She had a lot of tiny pigtails and was looking up at me. "Missuh? I'ze los'."

I said, "Okay, sweetie, let me look at your name tag. I'll help you get found." I looked at the little pink tag that was around her wrist. It said, "Unit 2, Cabin 1. Miss M. Kamen." Just my luck, she belonged to Mickey. I thought of Bogart's line in Casablanca, "Of all the gin joints in the world, this kid had to pick mine," or something of that sort. After all, the kid was cute, but wasn't Ingrid Bergman by a long shot.

"I"m Ginny Jones," she said. "Okay, Ginny, let's go look for your counselor." I took her by the hand and we sort of needled our way through the crowd. I edged over to the girls' side of the main road, and it was easy to pick Mickey out with her group of younger girls.

"Mickey, I got one of your campers, Ginny Jones here."

"Thank you, Max. Hello, Ginny, I'm miss Kamen, your counselor, let's go meet the others." She took the kid by the hand and walked away. I thought, *Boy, that was chilly. To me and the kid.*

Chapter 7
Troubles by the Dozen, Heartaches by the Score

The camp environment changed a lot with the addition of the three hundred or so kids that were now part of the place. The quiet forest was filled with the shouts of kids' play and counselors bellowing themselves hoarse trying to keep control over the campers, who had endless energy to run, play and test limits. At night, there was the noise of campers getting ready for bed, the slamming of cabin doors, trips to the bath house, screeching with delight at every incident, lights on in every cabin, and again, the counselors hollering for order and even making threats if the kids didn't listen.

There was one counselor who took his boys out for daily workouts on the ball field. This guy was a dedicated baseball player who didn't quite get it that not everyone wanted four hours of baseball practice a day. One night I passed his cabin while he was trying to get his kids to bed and heard him yell, "Okay, you guys, if you don't quiet down there will be no baseball tomorrow!" This was followed by a mighty cheer of 'YAAAAY!!'"

As for the kitchen routine, things went well. To my surprise, our small crew was up to the task of managing all four hundred people, staff and kids. The dishwasher

held up and our crew learned to work with maximum efficiency. It wasn't a lot of fun to work on really hot days,
however. The steam from the dishwasher made for a
really uncomfortable couple of hours. I enjoyed the work
anyway and found that if I watched how much food I
packed away, my weight went up, not from fat, but rather
with muscle. The cleanup routine in the dining room was
a great workout. I was putting on muscle and was in the
best shape ever. I was also enjoying the camaraderie of
the other kitchen boys as well as the cooks. We became
much like a second family away from home.

I had some good talks with Bob Wheeler and asked him
how he came up with the stretcher idea when Jack Ryan
fell. He told me that he had been an officer on the land-
ing assault at Iwo Jima. He said that the battle was the
most vicious thing he had experienced during the war,
and that the careful planning done for the battle was
pretty much garbage after the Marines hit the beach.
Survival was a matter of quick thinking, luck and impro-
visation. He didn't want to go into it much more, but
mentioned that infantry battles had nothing to do with
who was right or wrong, only who was left when it was
finished.

Social life among the counselors and the specialists
slowed down quite a bit. During the first week of the
session there was a lot of learning how to put into practice everything that was taught during the orientation
week. Things picked up after a while, though. You can't
keep young people down for long.

One evening after work, I went back to my tent and noticed that my laundry bag was getting pretty full. I was

tired and only wanted to fall into bed, but decided I ought to get it down to the front office, as the pickup by the laundry company was usually early in the morning. I heaved the bag over my shoulder, and, looking like a woodsman's version of Santa, walked down the main road to the office. It was a dark night; there were scudding clouds that blocked the stars. The moon was just a sliver, but by this time I was familiar with the road.

I got to the office and dumped my laundry bag in the large canvas basket on the porch. On the way back to my tent I passed by the mess hall. Camp vehicles were parked in back for the night, and I thought I saw some movement in the Chevy wagon. I walked over to investigate, and when I got about twenty feet away I saw two people in the back seat. I just figured some late night necking was going on and started to walk away, but then I heard a muffled scream, and the car started rocking harder. I froze. I didn't want to butt in on something like this, but on the other hand, what if someone was in trouble? A second scream settled it; I dashed back to the car and knocked on the window. It was so dark I couldn't see who was inside. There was a dark form on the back seat, and when I peered in closer I recognized Crash Kelly, lying on top of a girl. The girl screamed again; this time it was piercing, and I wrenched the door open.

"Hey, what's going on?" Crash turned around; he had scratches on his face as well as some lipstick. "Get outta here, Max, this is none of your goddamn business!" I called to the girl, "You okay there?"
Crash said, "Max, if you don't get the fuck out of here, I'm going to beat the shit out of you!"

The girl cried, "Max, help!" Crash fumbled in a pocket and I heard a click. And then I saw it was Mickey under him and she shrieked, 'Watch out! He's got a knife!"

"Crash grated, "I told you twice, asshole, get out of here!" and with that he came up off the seat and out of the car, charging at me with a knife in his right hand. He jabbed with the knife and I tried to block it with my left arm, but it caught my shirtsleeve and I felt a hot burn on my forearm. I gritted my teeth and tried to tie up his knife arm, and stepped into him. I swung my right fist as hard as I could and caught him with a grazing shot off the jaw that slowed him up. He staggered back a step. I needed to get close again so he couldn't thrust the knife. I shifted my feet and was able to get my left hand around his right wrist, and got another shot with my right.
This time I had better balance as well as my feet planted, and I gave him an over hand jab to the nose with everything I had. I felt it break, blood spurted out and his head snapped back, but he wasn't done. I twisted his wrist and he dropped the knife, trying to knee me in the crotch.

I blocked him, shifted my weight, and said, "Stop it, Crash, you're hurt and I don't want to hurt you more". He gave a snarling guttural noise that sounded like something from a zoo animal, and came at me again. This time he tried to strangle me, and I knew then the fight was about over. I shot both arms up between his and wrenched them apart, gave him two short jabs, a left and a right, and he went down.

I picked up the knife. It was a switchblade. I threw it into the bushes behind the mess hall. I was breathing pretty hard, and the adrenaline had me keyed up to a high pitch. I looked into the car and saw Mickey pulling up her jeans and yanking her sweatshirt down. She was pale and very frightened. I rolled Crash over onto his back; he was almost out and moaning. Blood was all over his shirt and on mine as well, from him and the gash he'd given me.

I was embarrassed for Mickey. If she'd gotten herself in that back seat, it was probably with consent. I figured things had gotten out of hand. I smelled alcohol in the wagon, on her and Crash. She wouldn't go for me, but she'd play games with a jerk like Crash. I was angry with her, Crash and myself, and I felt ashamed that I had lost out to such a loser. And yet, part of my mind was calling me a jerk for holding on to a girl who had done nothing but reject me at every turn. I thought of the old cliche about winning the fight and losing the battle and, boy, was that ever me.

I gave Mickey my hand and pulled her out of the car. "You want me to walk you back to your cabin?" She said, " No, but Max, you're bleeding. And what about Crash, is he...."

"I think I broke his nose. He'll be okay. I'll stay with him and make sure he's all right. I can get him over to the infirmary if he wants, or into the Walkerville Clinic, maybe. You sure you're okay?"

She said yes, and thanked me for helping. She said they'd had a few drinks in town, and she'd flirted too much with him, and that he just kept coming on and things gotten wild. I felt disgusted, but kept it to myself.

She left. I got some water from the mess hall and splashed it over Crash. He came to, but there was no fight left in him. I asked if he wanted me to get him some help. He just called me a few names.

"This isn't over, asshole. You won this fight, but watch your ass." He went over to his own car, got in and drove off. I went over to the infirmary, and Victoria was still up. She asked what had happened. I said I was trying to fix something in the tent and a knife slipped. She didn't buy it. "How dumb do I look to you, luv?"

She said the gash looked like it needed a couple of stitches and asked if I'd had a tetanus shot recently. She was a good egg and didn't push the issue. She finally thought that a compression bandage might work, and told me that if it bled through I'd have to get sewn up.

The morning came and went, and after the lunch meal I was finishing up in the dining hall when Bob Wheeler came up and said he'd like to talk with me as soon as I was done. He told me to meet him in the small office he used in the back of the mess hall. I replied that I was almost done and would be in soon. I knew that I was in trouble.

"So, Max," he said, "Sit down, let's talk."
I took a seat across from his desk, and true to his character, he got right down to cases.

"Max, I've heard from Crash that the two of you fought last night. He blamed you for attacking him over a girl. I got a report this morning from the Walkerville Clinic that

he had a broken nose, a sprained wrist, and a concussion when he came in last night. He asked them to send
me a written report."

I thought, oh, boy, I'm in deep *do* here.

Bob went on, "All right, I've heard his story, I want to
hear yours. No bullshit, okay?"

I didn't want to implicate Mickey and I didn't want to lie,
so I decided to tell it the best way I could and keep her
out of it.

"Okay, Bob. I dropped my laundry up at the office and
was walking back to my tent. The camp wagon was
parked behind the mess hall, and as I passed it I noticed
it was sort of rocking. I figured someone was using it to
do some necking and kept walking. But then I heard a
muffled cry, went over to look, and saw Crash wrestling
with a girl."
I went on and filled him in with Crash's attack on me and
showed him the bandage on my arm. He was thoughtful
about that.

"Yeah," he said, "Vicky was in here this morning and she
told me about fixing you up last night. She said she
didn't buy your story and she thought something else
was going on."

"Well, I didn't want to cause a lot of trouble for Crash. I
knew I hurt him and I offered to take him to the clinic, but
he threatened me and left on his own. But, Bob, I didn't
start it. He came at me with a knife. It was self-defense."

"Max, can you prove that?"

I said I could, and told him that I threw the knife in the bushes behind the mess hall. We went out and poked around for a while. Bob said he had other things to do and told me to keep at it.

It took me another half-hour until I found the knife. It still had my blood on it. I went back into the mess hall and got some paper towels to wrap the knife. I wasn't sure if anyone would look for finger prints, but I guessed both mine and Crash's and mine would be on it.

I went back to Bob's office and saw through the window in his door that he was talking to Mickey. So, someone had opened the thing up wider. When he saw me he came to the door and said he would be tied up for a bit and that I should hang around for a while. I went out and sat on the bench outside the mess hall. I was thinking that while I tried to keep Mickey out of this thing she might be in there putting a second knife in my back. I was a threat to her secret and by confirming Crash's story she would cook my goose for sure. I felt my stock was sinking fast. I didn't trust Mickey anymore, and the summer looked like it was heading for a bad end.

It seemed like forever before Mickey came out of the mess hall and said, "Max, he wants you to come back to his office." That was all she said, no indication or hint that she was helping me. I went in to face the music.

Bob said, "Max, we need to go up to the front office. Ken wants to talk to us."

So now I knew it was curtains, and I steeled myself for getting fired, making a fool of myself before the whole camp, embarrassing my sister at her place of work and shaming my parents. All because I tried to help Mickey. I think I was angrier with myself for getting into this mess than I was at Mickey. I even felt sorry for Crash. I didn't want to hurt him. The whole thing was none of my business, and I kicked myself for ever getting involved.

We walked up to the front office, and Lee told us to go right back to Ken's room. Her posture was stiff, and I guessed she knew there was trouble.

When we sat down, Ken said, "Max, I know you've been through a rough time. We had to hear everyone's story to figure out who was to blame about last night. One thing that's not clear is who started the actual fight. Mickey told Bob that Crash had a knife, and Crash said she was wrong, that it was yours; and when the two of you fought he got the knife away from you, and it's now safe at his house."

In my worries I had forgotten about the knife! It was in my pocket, still wrapped in the paper towel.
"No, sir, I took the knife from Crash and I told Bob I would find it where I threw it. Here, look, I have it and it still has blood on the blade!"

I got the knife out and put it on Ken's desk. He opened the towel and peered at the knife like it was evidence in a murder. Bob used a corner of the towel to pick it up and look closely at it. "Ken," he said, "There are initials carved in the handle: 'CK'."

Ken said, "Crash's knife, looks like. Well, that ties it pretty good." He and Bob looked at each other and Bob gave a slight nod.

"Max, you think you can handle the driver's job full time?"

"Yes SIR!" Again I was overdoing it, the tension and anxiety making me nervous. But I felt reprieved or vindicated or whatever you feel when found innocent! And they laughed. I guessed everyone had some tension.

"Okay, Max, look, we've had problems with Crash before, and I don't want to get into it with you. This time we can't overlook his behavior, and I will terminate his employment at the camp. But I don't want the real story coming out. Let's just say that he's had an accident and won't be back. I'll make an announcement at dinner and we'll get this thing tied up. Bob will be your supervisor. Oh, and I think we can work out a small raise, too. Okay, that's it. Remember, keep all this to yourself. I don't want all kinds of rumors going on here. We have the Women's Auxiliary coming up in a few days to see how things are going here."

Bob said, "And Ken, don't forget Dr. Linzer. He's due before the Auxiliary, and that old coot doesn't miss anything."

"Um, if you don't think it's none of my business, who is this doctor fella?"

Ken said, "Dr. Linzer is a psychoanalyst who is on the Board of Directors. He comes up to camp once or twice a summer to see how things are going with the staff, reviews any problems we might be having with kids or sometimes staff. There's lots of stress for some of them. He's a sharp guy and we value his opinion. He has a private practice in Chicago and teaches at several colleges and one medical school. Oh, and, just so you are aware, the Women's Auxiliary is also part of the Board. They do a LOT of fundraising for the camp. *We take very good care of them*, you get my drift? Okay, anything else?"

Bob and I said no and got up to leave. Ken asked me to stay for another few minutes. We reviewed Dr. Linzer's schedule, and I was told when to pick him up at the Walkerville train station. He also told me that I would get some additional assignments from the front office on occasion in addition to those I got from Bob, and that if I had any questions or problems to check with him as well. He handed me a clipboard with some current jobs that Crash was supposed to have done and told me to see Lee every morning in case there were more items. I thanked him, we shook hands, and he wished me all success. I felt like a million bucks and wanted to find Mickey and thank her for making things right. I nearly bounced out of Ken's office, and Lee smiled at me when I left. I figured that Bob had spelled out what happened.

I walked down the main road past the mess hall and further into the camp area. I felt great and had a new spring in my step. I was heading back to my tent to dig the Wisconsin road map and the compass dad gave me out of the duffel bag when I ran into Phyllis, the girl from the office porch, and a bunch of little campers. I did a second take when I spotted little Ginny Jones, the black girl I'd helped. She was in Mickey's cabin. I waved to Phyllis, "Hey, Phyllis, isn't this Mickey's group? What are you doing with them?"

"Hi, Max. Yes, it's Mickey's kids. I'm the Assistant Unit Leader, and I relieve counselors when they take a day off. Mickey said she got a ride with one of the other counselors and was going to spend the day with him."

I had by this time lost count of the daggers Mickey's behavior had stuck in my heart. My head kept telling me to forget her and my heart kept upsetting the plan.

"Oh, okay, Phyllis, thanks!" *For what?* I thought? I got to the tent, and some of the kitchen boys were around the compound. Leon Kozinski, the huge kitchen boy, was dozing in his bed and I sort of woke him while poking around in my duffel bag.

"Max?"

"Yeah, Leon, sorry to bother you."

"Listen, Max, I heard about what happened between you and Crash."

I wondered how he heard anything because Ken had just said we should keep it a secret. For a half-second I wondered if Chicken, the Olympic gossip, was in camp and I hadn't seen her yet.

"Leon, what did you hear? Who told you?"

"I know Crash from around here. He was a couple of years ahead of me at Walkerville High. Anyway, I saw him around town. Man, he looked like he went through a meat grinder. He said that you jumped him and sucker-punched him, and he said he would get even. So, I just want you to know that. But I told him anything happened to you, I'd kick the shit out of him."

"Well, gee, thanks, Leon. Why would you back me like that? We just started working together, you know?"

"Max, when I was a freshman, I wasn't as big as I am now. Crash was always a bad ass guy and he used to push smaller kids around. He's a bully, and you have to watch your back when he's around. Anyway, somehow I stayed out of his way, but I saw how he'd push others around, and I thought one day I'd like to pay him back for some of the stuff he did to my friends. So here's my chance. Watch out for him, but he knows I'll come after him if he bothers you. You're a good guy, that's it."

"Thanks, Leon, I really appreciate that. Gee, I don't know how to thank you. Anything I can do for you, please let me know, okay?"

"Yeah, no problem."

He turned over and went back to sleep. First time I had a guy who'd stick up for me. Felt good.

Chapter 8
Let the Fun and Games Begin

I worked the regular kitchen boy shift for the rest of that day, and then after dinner Ken made the announcement that Crash had "an accident" and wouldn't be back for the summer. He told everyone that I would now be the regular camp driver.

There was a murmur from the staff. This was the second "accident," and the first camp session was less than a week old. People were talking and suspicious that maybe something else happened to Crash. I wondered if Mickey had been blabbing. A few people congratulated me and I got some good-natured ribbing from the other kitchen boys about brown-nosing my way up the camp career ladder. That night after work, I went over to the other side to see if my new position would increase my status with the girls. Mickey wasn't there. I talked with Phyllis for a while and found her to be very sweet, but there were no sparks between us.

There was a counselor named Tori who was very attractive, and a lot of the male staff was always around her. She was a dance major at a school in Boston. She was tall, had wavy black hair, large dark eyes, and legs that never ended. She used to walk around camp in a leotard and tights that left the guys gawking. I didn't stand a chance.

Kitty Katz blew in the door, saw me, said "Congrats, Max," and kept moving. I guess she wanted to find new rattling targets. I left after a half hour. Just couldn't seem to find the right entry point to make it in this group.

Next morning I was up and out of the tent early. I went down to the mess hall, got some coffee and chatted with Bob, who was always there first thing.
I now had a clipboard of my own with a lot of tasks and errands to do. There were a number of trips into to Walkerville to pick up and drop off items. Among them were trips to the Walkerville Locker, a huge refrigerated building where people stored perishables. The camp used it to store meat, perishables and government surplus butter. I was supposed to go there periodically to get boxes of various items for upcoming meals.

I didn't mind putting on the heavy parkas they kept on pegs by the door to keep people from freezing while they were getting the stuff they needed. I proved to myself that walking in and out of temperatures ranging from ninety degrees to below freezing didn't give you a cold as my mother believed. I told her a million times that colds came from germs, but she was hard to convince. I was unnerved, however, because the locker partitions and walls were narrow slats, and occasionally I found myself eye to eye with the head of a dead moose or a bear. There were a lot of hunters in the area.

One morning I walked into the front office, and Lee told me to meet the 11:00 am train in Walkerville to pick up Dr. Linzer.

Lee said, "Max, Dr. L. is coming up a couple of days before the 'All- Camp Program'. You need to meet the train and drive him in."

"Okay, Lee. What's an all-camp program?"

"Oh, it's a program that all the campers take part of. It's educational, and there's a theme that teaches about, you know, the environment and how to take care of it, or it might be a program on listening and learning from others. The kids put on skits around whatever the theme is, and there's special meals or a picnic outside. All sorts of possibilities. The up-coming program will be on farming and how we get our food. Ken, Larry and the unit leaders have been meeting on that one for the last few days. It's almost planned."

I looked at my watch and figured the time I'd need in order to meet the train. It wasn't all that far to Walkerville, so I could leave now and make the drive leisurely.

I reached the station a bit early, so I decided to clean a lot of the junk out of the wagon. There were a couple of trash barrels outside the station, and I emptied ash trays, tossed a lot of old paper along with empty cigarette packages and a box of stuff that looked like it was from the "lost and found" of 1947. I used some rags to wipe down the inside of the windows and get the dust off the dashboard. The wagon was going to be a place where I would spend a lot of time, and I like a neat work environment.

The train pulled in about fifteen minutes late, and I watched people getting off. Lee told me that I could not miss Dr. Linzer. She said he was a spry old fellow, had a white beard and wore a black beret in every kind of weather. He also had a cigar in his mouth nearly all the time. Nearly everyone was off the train, and I started to worry that either I'd missed him or he didn't make the trip. Then I saw the conductor come down, turn, and help a man with the right description down the stairs. Another conductor came down with a large suitcase and a briefcase. I got out of the wagon and walked over, "Dr. Linzer?"

"Yep!"

"I'm Max Lewis, from the camp."

"Yep! Okay!"

He didn't seem very articulate for a guy with his credentials.

"Okay, Max, good to meet you. You're new. What happened to that adolescent bully they always sent?"

Well, I thought, *he doesn't pull punches.*
"He had an accident," I said, keeping to the company line.

"More'n likely someone finally beat the shit out of him. Okay, can you manage the bag? I'll keep the briefcase with me."

We got in the car and I started it up. We headed for the camp, and he said, "So, Max, tell me something about yourself. I like to get to know the camp staff."

I started to speak; I guess I was feeling a bit lonely. I hadn't really had much opportunity to talk about myself the past week or so. I just began telling him about how I graduated from high school, got the job at camp, how I was trying to fit in, and then without realizing it, began telling him about Mickey and my episode with Kitty. I really had a need to talk, and it just slipped out of me. Somehow the guy listened to me in a way that I'd never experienced before. I'd have told him anything he wanted to know.

So I kept on talking about all that had happened since I got to the camp, and he said, "Hey, Max, there's a great little coffee shop I know. Let's stop. They got pastries like you wouldn't believe. See that intersection up there? Take a right and go about a hundred yards. You'll see it on the left side."

I said, "Dr. Linzer, we'll be late to camp, they're expecting us."

"Ach, we won't be late. The *train*, it was late! And, Max, please just call me 'professor,' works better for me than the doctor title."

I took the right and followed his direction, and soon enough we got to a little country store. I pulled into the lot; it was empty. The "Professor," as I now called him, got out of the car, and I followed him into the shop. At the door he yelled, "Hey, Fritz, Magda, I'm back!"

A very large man and woman practically galloped out of the room behind a long counter, and it was "old home week," with hugs and kisses and slaps on the back. Half the yakking was in German; I caught a little of it from the

three years of German I had in school from a teacher
with the unlikely name of "Herr O'Malley".

"Zo, Professor, you are visiting up at camp another
year? Zo good to zee you. Magda, caffee und ztrudel for
zeh Professor. Und who is zis?"

I told Fritz my name was Max. We shook hands; his was
the size of a catcher's mitt. After a lot of friendly hello's,
backslapping and updating, the Professor and I sat at a
small table and had coffee with some very good strudel.
He said that it was homemade by Fritz, who was a fabulous baker. He said he'd fill me in later about how he
knew him, but wanted to finish our talk.

So I told him all the rest of the story about Mickey,
Crash, how we fought, and how I became the camp dri-
ver. I even told him about my encounter with Kitty. The
Professor listened and never said a word.

When I finished up, he scratched his jaw and said, "Max,
you got a couple of maturational problems. If we were in
Chicago, you would come to my office and lay on a
couch three times a week for a couple of years at a
hundred and fifty bucks an hour, and at the end of that
time you would know what I'm going to tell you right now
without a fee, and I'll even pick up the tab for the
strudel."

I thought that sounded interesting and scary. I started to
fidget with my coffee cup, stirring and adding sugar just
to have something to do with my hands.
 He went right on.

"First of all, this Mickey. You erotized her!"

"No, sir! I might have felt her up a little once when we were necking, but…."

He held his hand up for silence.

"Wait, Max, you don't understand. Let's start this again, I'll use different words."

I added a little more sugar to the coffee.

" When you met Mickey you had powerful feelings of love for her, even without knowing her well, is that correct?"

"Yes, I guess it happened like that."

"Okay, and you also felt that you had to protect her, right?"

"Yes."

"And with the Katz kid, she startled you with her 'rattling the boys routine', yes?"

"Yes."

"Okay, so there are two issues."

I added a little more sugar.

"The first is when you meet women who attract you, there are real sparks that fly. And the second is that you have rescue fantasies."

I started to protest but he held up a hand and said, "Max, I think you're a pretty strong fellow psychologically and I'm giving you a lot to process, ah, to figure out, very fast. So just relax and let me walk you through a few things."

I took a sip of coffee but it was so sweet I couldn't drink it, so I added a little more sugar and then some salt and pepper for good measure; you know, just to even out the sugar.

"You said that even though Mickey dumped you on a bridge, and, by the way, that came out of you so smoothly I had the feeling that you've either said it or imagined those words so often they are engraved on your brain."

It was getting scary; it felt like he could read my mind. My hand was starting to tremble. I didn't know where he was headed. My hands started to shake, and I put them below the table so he wouldn't see how anxious I was.

"So even though Mickey dumped you, ignored you, pleaded for your help so she wouldn't get into trouble for scamming her way into the camp job and so on, when she was in trouble you protected her in a fight with a really nasty guy who came at you with a knife. And your thank you was that she told the truth about the fight and then went off with another guy, yes?"

"Um, well, I, ah, yeah. Um, Professor, I'm not getting Mickey in trouble telling you this, am I? I mean, I told her I wouldn't...."

"Nah, it's all confidential stuff." He went on without a breath.
"Okay, listen, you ever read 'Prince Valiant,' the cartoon strip?"

"No, Professor, I haven't."

"How about 'Rocky the Flying Squirrel,' that TV program?"

"Well, sure, it's really fun to watch."

"So, as I recall, there's a few different characters beside the squirrel and an elk."

"Yes," I said, "It's a moose, Bullwinkle." I was starting to think the professor was maybe a little off the wall.

"So, Max, there's a couple of other segments; one is a kid with a time machine and a talking dog, and another, a knock-off of the old Nelson Eddy and Jeanette Mac-Donald movies, I think it's called Dudley Do-Right and the Mounties, or something like that. You know it?"

Yeah, I thought, he's gone around the bend. I couldn't figure out what my relationship with women had to do with Dudley Do-Right and the Mounties. But, my folks said to always respect elders. The Professor got out a cigar and lit up. I slipped a little more sugar into my coffee.

"Yes, sir, I know it."

"So, in every episode Nell, Dudley's boss's daughter, gets herself in some kind of trouble and Dudley saves her, correct?"

"Yes."

"And for his trouble, she remains indifferent to him, yet he's always there for her. Correct?"

"Yes."

"Max, this is YOU! You are trying to save this girl and she isn't having anything to do with it. You have a rescue fantasy!"

"Gee, Professor, with all due respect, I don't see how you can come to a conclusion like that. You mean I'm trying to save women I like or the ones who like me?"

"Bingo! Look, Max, let's go back to the incident with the other girl, Kitty. She tells you she rattles boys as a hob-by, and she bumps her boobs into you. You step back, trip and fall on a bed, and she flops down on you and kisses you, fer cryin' out loud! Is this right? I have it right, yes?"

I gulped some coffee and nodded. It now tasted like pepper and candy.

"And then she says, if I remember what you said in the car, 'Cat must have your tongue 'cause Kitty isn't getting any', right?"

He was really getting me anxious, but I nodded.

"So, the next time you see her is on this bridge, and what do you do? You give her a speech that she shouldn't try to rattle boys because it might get out of hand, correct?"

I nodded and looked at the coffee, but I couldn't drink any more. I felt he was moving in for the kill. Somehow I knew where he was going, even if I couldn't quite get there myself.

"So, her response to you is 'Thanks, dad,' and she stalks off. She is experiencing you as her father, not as some-one to whom she is attracted. Did you ever see her 'rat-tle' anyone else?"

I thought about it, and shared the experience on the main road with Bruce.

"To make you jealous, I am suggesting. The girl likes you, and on the first occasion you get a shot at her, you freeze up. Tell me, would Romeo, Casanova, or Don Juan fall into bed with a woman like Kitty and become a statue? She is sending messages—sending messages? My god, it should only happen to me— and you are talk-ing to her like you're her old man!"

I got it. And 'it' hit me in the stomach like the pulley that fell on Jack Ryan. I felt like a total idiot.
"Well, I guess I've really screwed up my relationship with her. I've been trying to find someone to go with up here, and all I've done is...." I couldn't find the words. Too

much to think about. The Professor patted me on the shoulder.

"Max, listen, think all this over, and if it fits you can use it to your advantage with the girls. If you want relationships with women, god gave you two ears and one mouth. Use them in that proportion and you'll do a lot better.

Just one more thing," He took the cigar out of his mouth and poked it at me like it was a blackboard pointer. "One day you'll run into a woman who really does want you to rescue her. Be careful; it's a lot more trouble with that kind than the ones you're trying to help when they're not having any of it."

He stubbed out the cigar. I pretended to drink the last of the coffee and wolfed the strudel. I sat with my head spinning.

Meanwhile, the Professor got into a big to-do with Fritz about paying the bill. Fritz didn't want to take the Professor's money. So, while I stood by trying to make sense of all this, the Professor put a twenty on the table and said it was a tip. It was enough to cover the bill twice over plus the tip. We got in the wagon and headed for the camp.

The Professor said, "Max, you okay? You look a little pale. I think I gave you too much of a dose of help."

"I'm okay, Professor, I'm trying to get everything you said in some kind of order."

We drove back to the camp in relative quiet. My head was buzzing. I just wanted to find a quiet place to think things over. The Professor said that he usually stayed with Ken, who had a house across the road from the front office, deep back in the woods. I took him up as close as I could get, got his bag out of the back of the wagon. We went down a path, up a couple of steps, and knocked on the door.

Mrs. Greenman answered the door and welcomed the professor warmly. It was the first time I'd met her. She was a tall woman, a bit on the plump side, with a charming smile. She wore heavy horned-rimmed glasses hanging on a cord around her neck. She was holding what looked like a textbook and was wearing a dress which I thought a bit odd for a camp setting.

"Hello, Professor, how wonderful to see you! And you must be Max; I've heard all about you from Ken. Let me just say that he thinks you did a great job finding all those people he's hired. But, Professor, you must be tired! Please come in and I'll make some tea."

I brought the Professor's bag in, and Mrs. Greenman told me to set it in the hall. I thanked her for her kind words and left. I pulled the wagon out of their drive and parked it in front of the main office and sat down on a lawn chair on the porch. It was past midday, and while I'd missed lunch, I wasn't hungry because of the strudel and coffee. Between the caffein and the sugar, I was wired and jumpy. All I wanted was a little quiet time to think things over. It was tranquil on the porch, however my usual luck prevailed and Lee came out to see me.

"Hey, Max, where've you been? I have an errand for you."

"Hi, Lee. I just got the Professor from the train and it was a bit late." Even a simple lie like that bothered me. I was too worn down to care. And Lee didn't seem to care much either.

"Okay, listen. You have an important errand to run right now. Are you familiar with the 'Hollywood Dairy Farm' yet? You have to make a pick up there before three. It's for the 'All-Camp Program' tomorrow."

"Yeah, ok. What is it, some dairy products?"

"No, not exactly. It's a cow."

"*A COW?* Are you kidding me? How'm I supposed to pick up a cow, for Pete's sake? What do I do, stuff it in the glove compartment?"

"Oh, don't be silly. It's not a big cow, it's a small one. A calf, they said. Don't be so jumpy! what's wrong with you? You're always so even-tempered. Bob made the deal with the guy who owns the dairy; they're friends. His name is Titus Akers. Oh, and the cow is named Marilyn Monroe."

"Lee, are you kidding me or what, here?"

"Max, no joke. Bob said this guy names his cows after movie stars with big...."
She trailed off, too embarrassed to say it.

"Okay, I get it."

She got a look of relief and giggled. "He's got a whole herd with names like Jane Russell, Marlene Dietrich, even an old cow named Mae West." We both started laughing.

"He told Bob that he hopes the names would ensure the cows give a lot of milk."

"I'll bet! Should be great at the box office, too." We had a good chuckle at that.

"So, Bob said that the calf would fit inside the wagon, if you just put the seats down. He'll drop the thing off at the farm after the program. He said the kids would love seeing a calf, being able to pet it, and learning about how they get milk. Well, what are you waiting for? It's two already."

"Okay, okay. How do I get to this place?"

"Oh, right." She went back into the office and came out with a couple of sheets of paper.
"Here's directions; Bob's original and a copy. I typed it because no one can read his writing except me. And here's a map he sketched. It's not hard. Just take 54 west till you get to County Road Q. It's all there. So move it!"

I moved it; back into the wagon that was starting to feel like home, and out of the camp main entrance. I got onto Route 54 and headed west, watching for County Road Q. Along the way, I wondered if this Titus Akers was any relation to Bessie, the old woman I'd met on the train. It was a nice afternoon, not too hot or humid, not much traffic on the road. The Chevy hummed along, its six cylinders all firing nice and smooth. I liked the wagon. It had some road feel in the wheel, reasonably good suspension, and it got good mileage from what I could tell so far.

It felt good to be away from the camp, out of the scullery, and on my own. I remembered what dad had said about the freedom of the road even if you had a bastard for a boss. I had some really good bosses. I liked Ken, and liked Bob even better. I wasn't so sure about the Professor. The guy rattled me more than Kitty did, and he wasn't half as pretty.

As I drove along, I saw some Burma Shave signs. I loved reading them; they were really corny, but they gave me a laugh. One read, "He struck a match to check the tank/ that's why they call him/ 'Hairless Frank'/ Burma Shave." Corny to most, hysterical to me.

There were big black crows or maybe ravens flying along parallel to me. I guessed they were looking for a cornfield to check out. And then there it was. I slowed for County Q, made my turn and looked for the Hollywood Dairy Farm signs. It came up a bit farther than the hundred yards on my instructions, maybe a few city blocks. I figured that Bob was so used to the place it seemed closer. I pulled into a sandy road and drove slowly. Up ahead was a white farm house, and I could see some people on the front porch. Behind the house was a large barn and some other low buildings. An old woman came off the porch waving a handkerchief. Darned if it wasn't

Bessie Akers, the old gal from the train. I stopped, cut the engine, put the car in first gear, and pulled the emergency brake.

"Oh, I thought that Crash character would be here," she said. "You're the young man I met on the train. Manny."

"Max, Miss Akers. Yes, I got the driver's job!" She was all smiles and looked very happy, even with the ill-fitting dentures. I noticed her granddaughter's Cadillac parked off the road.

"Titus," she cried out, "the driver from the camp is here. Max, he'll be out in a minute. So nice that you came up. I know you'll take good care of Marilyn. She's our favorite, and so cute! The kids will adore her. Come into the house, won't you? I made one of my cherry pies. It's almost cool, and I'll give you the first slice."

"Oh, I'd love that, but I'm on a schedule and really have to get back. Next time for sure."
The screen door opened. An elderly gent who I guessed was Titus came down the stairs and waved, hollering that he'd get the calf and be right back. He had a nicely trimmed white beard and wore Oshkosh, By Gosh overalls, a red-checkered shirt and black leather boots. On his head perched a straw hat, and clenched a corncob pipe between his teeth. I chatted with Bessie, and a few minutes later Titus came walking up with a small calf on a tether.

"You're Max, right?"

"Yes, sir."

"Okay, Max," he said. Then he took the pipe out of his mouth and declared, "Wait a sec, let me get my Missouri Meerschaum going." He struck a kitchen match on his belt buckle and started working on firing up the pipe.

"Max, this here's Marilyn Monroe. She's the youngest calf on the farm. Now, Marilyn's a bit skittish, so you have to gentle her down once't in a while. I do it like this."

He leaned over and softly talked to the calf while he stroked her head, "Youse is a good calf, yes you is, darlin'...." This went on for a few moments, and then the calf said, "Maaaah."

"Okay, son. You got the idee?"

"Yes, sir."

"Kids love Marilyn. She's special."

Darned if the calf didn't rub her head against his leg at that.

"Yes, sir," I said, "She is pretty cute. Never been this close to a calf before."

"Open the back of the wagon. I see you got the seats down. Can you put her in? My back ain't what it was." He bent and demonstrated how to lift the calf. I'd never lifted anything like this, but I figured I could do it. I got low, wrapped my arms around Marilyn Monroe, one under her behind and the other under her neck, and lifted her up onto the wagon's tailgate. Easy. Marilyn skittered around a bit and said, "Maaaaah."

"She'll do just fine, son. Drive easy and take care around turns. I see the bed of that wagon is plastic, so she might slip around a bit."

I gave Mr. Akers the envelope Lee had given me. It had a check for renting the cow and a was sort of insurance in case something happened to her. Mr. Akers and I shook hands, and I reassured Bessie about having pie next time around. I got in the wagon, started it up, and waved. Mr. Akers yelled, "Now drive 'er easy, boy!" And I was off.

I drove slowly down their driveway and got onto County Q. I could feel Marilyn unease in the back of the wagon, and I thought maybe I should have asked for some feed or something to keep her busy. I was kind of nervous. *Look on the bright side*, I thought, *so far so good*.

When I reached US 54, I turned east back to the camp. The traffic had picked up quite a bit; there were a lot of commercial vehicles, pickups, and some motorcycle groups on the road. I was going slowly so the calf wouldn't get nervous, but I was cut off a couple of times and every time I braked or adjusted my direction, Marilyn would slide around or hit the back of my seat. Each time she said, "Maaaah," and I would try to reach around and say, "Good girl, youse is a real sweetie, yes, you is!" I felt dumb talking to a calf, but I was worried she would get upset. I felt her breath on my neck, and suddenly she was nibbling my shirt collar and licking my hair. I got an arm around to pat her, and just then a huge semi-trailer roared past from behind. He came up parallel to me and gave a blast of his Buell Air Horns, those big silver trumpets you see on the semis. They went, 'Booowaaahp!" That did it for Marilyn Monroe. I heard a plopping noise, a rush of liquid. My nose gave me confirmation that Marilyn had an accident back there. "Maaaah!"

"Augh, youse ain't such a good girl," I said. "Maaaah" she answered. The wagon filled with an awful stench. I rolled my window down, but couldn't reach any of the others. Well, we weren't far from the camp, and there was nothing I could do. I'd just get there the best I could. I thought, *Boy, wait till I tell everyone back home that Marilyn Monroe took a dump in my car!* And with that I started to laugh and couldn't stop. I howled so hard I had tears running down my face. "Maaaah!" I guffawed till I got an air bubble caught in my chest that hurt like hell. I still couldn't stop cracking up.

I finally got hold of myself and realized that my "over the top" laughter was a release of all the tension I'd had since I got to camp. Staying polite with everyone, seeing Mickey, fighting with Crash, fearing I would get fired, learning a new job, living in a tent, the crazy first meeting with Kitty, and finally, how much the professor shook me up.

All of a sudden I had a flood of understanding! The Professor's thinking was close, not perfect. What he did do was open something much deeper. I thought that maybe I was afraid of women, that I kept them at a distance, and that I picked out girls who would not let me get close. Then when Kitty jumped on me it scared me half to death. Maybe that's why I didn't respond to her. I was all right with protecting and saving; not so brave at loving, intimacy, or going the distance in a relationship. I made a promise right there: *no more rescuing!* I was going to let it fly the next time I had a chance! *Max Lewis,* I thought, *is a real man,* and I was going to prove it!

Marilyn Monroe and I got to the camp with no further problems, except I had a car that smelled like halftime at a Bear's game in the men's restroom at Wrigley Field.

I drove very slowly into camp, past the front office, and figured I would check in with Lee after I got the calf settled. I noticed that there were now three folksingers on the porch; the two with guitars, and a third guy who had a long-neck banjo like Pete Seeger plays. It looked like they were all arguing about who was in tune. I didn't have time for that deal.

I was supposed to bring the calf to the Camp Craft Building. Bruce and Fat Freddy were putting the finishing touches on a little pen for her. They had set up a square of tent poles and stretched chicken wire around them. It looked rickety to me.

I pulled up and said, "Howdy, boys, ah'm back from the roundup." Fred came over to the wagon and said, "Jesus, it smells like shit in here!"

"Correction, my friend, it smells not LIKE shit, but rather FROM shit in here!" Fred started laughing, and even the calm Bruce chuckled.

"Well," he said, "Let's get the thing out of the wagon and into the pen."

Fred had thought to put a gourmet cow meal together, taking care of Marilyn's every epicurean need. He had also thoughtfully provided a trough with fresh water. We got Marilyn out of the wagon and into the pen with no further problems.

I got back into the car and pulled it around to the back of the mess hall. There was a janitor's closet in the building where we kept mops, brooms, rags, buckets and various cleaning compounds. I exited the wagon and started to go into the building. Someone called my name. It was Ken, and he was running along the main road from the office.

"Max! Where the hell have you been? I have to meet the four o'clock train in Walkerville. I need the wagon!"

"Gee, Ken, I'm sorry. I didn't know there was even a late train there."

"Yeah, they run afternoon trains for commuters. Gimme the keys; I'm running late. The Executive Committee of the Women's Auxiliary is coming up. Mrs. Van Lauder, the President, our Treasurer, Mrs. Silverman, and the Secretary, Mrs. Dinwiddy; these are important people, and they're coming to see the 'All-Camp Program'. They raise a lot of money for the camp, and I need to get to Walkerville before that train. The keys!"

"Yeah, but Ken, there's been a problem, and I need to…."

"MAX! The keys now! I gotta go!"

What could I do? I handed over the keys, and Ken jumped into the wagon and took off in a cloud of dust. He never even looked at the back. I thought, *He must have a sinus condition or a congested nose for sure.*

I walked over to the office and took a seat on the porch. The three guys with the instruments had finally resolved their tuning differences and were singing, *"Go down, Moses, way down in Egypt land, let my people go." How appropriate,* I thought, *I was about to be let go myself.*

I sat pondering my situation. There was no way I'd survive this one. When those Board ladies got into that wagon, I would be a dead duck. The banjo player broke a string while trying to do the banjo introduction to a folk song called "Darling Corey;" it was a Pete Seeger special.
They decided to call off the concert and leave. Lee came out of the office, and I told her what happened. She cackled and kept saying, "No, Max, you're making all this up!"

"I wish." About an hour went by, and then I saw the wagon turning into the camp road. All the windows were down, and what looked like a collie wearing a flowery dress and a large floppy summer hat was leaning out of the front passenger side window with her mouth gaping open. Two other women had their heads hanging out of the back. Ken must have flipped up the seats before the ladies got into the car in order to hide the worst of things, but there would have been nothing he could have done about the stench in the hot car.

He pulled up in front of the office, and I heard him say, "Ladies, perhaps you would like to freshen up at my house before we go over to your rooms on the other side."
He was so smooth. How I admired his ability to say just the right thing.

They started across the road and up the path toward his house. Ken came running over to the porch, his face red as a beet. " Jesus, Max, what the hell is in the back of the wagon? It smells like cow shit."

"Ken, that's what I was trying to tell you. I had to pick up a calf for...."

"Take the wagon and clean it, goddammit, and get it back here as fast as you can! And then stick around; I'll need your help to get them to the other side and unload their overnight bags. Some of them weigh more than a Steinway piano!"

I took the wagon back to the mess hall and went to the janitor's closet. Bob Wheeler came out of his office snorting with laughter. "Max, I just got a call from Lee, and she told me what was going on. Come on, I have some stuff you'll need to clean up that mess."

I hooked up a hose to the kitchen sink and got some hot water in a bucket. Bob brought a scoop and some rags, and between us we were able to clean up the mess. He also had some stuff that freshened the inside, and in short order the wagon was in better shape than it had been since it was new. I took it back to the Director's place, and soon the ladies were back in their seats.

Ken was driving, and I got put into the back seat with Mrs. Silverman on my left and Mrs. Dinwiddy on the right. Mrs. Van Lauder, the President of the Women's Auxiliary, sat in front with Ken. She really did look like a collie; same hair and a long nose. She was no beauty but, at least her tongue didn't hang out.

Mrs. Silverman said, "Hey, Max, the wagon smells pretty good. Who stank it up?" I saw Ken's shoulders tighten and his head scrunch down like he was expecting a blow.

Without thinking I said, "Marilyn Monroe." Mrs. Silverman gave me a push on the shoulder and said, "Go on! Who're you joshing?"

"No, really, Mrs. Silverman," and I launched into the whole story about going out to the farm and picking up the calf, mimicking the way Titus Akers taught me to calm the calf down, the whole story about how they named the cows. Mrs. Van Lauder started to chuckle up front, and when I got to how Marilyn had slid around in back and took her dump everyone was cracking up, even Ken. Mrs. Silverman said, "Ken, you got to give this kid a raise! He's funnier than half the comics in the Borscht Belt!"

Eventually we got to the other side, and I helped get everyone settled with their luggage, ran some errands to get some bedding that was missing in the cabins, and pretty soon we were all friendly. I hoped maybe I would get out of the mess with my job.

After everyone got settled, Ken came out of the cabin complex and told me to get behind the wheel. He said he wanted to see how I handled the back roads. I thought maybe there was another reason, that he wanted to chew me out and could do it better when he didn't have to concentrate on driving. We got in the wagon, and I looked over at him. He looked sort of pale. I thought, *Well, here it comes.*

"Max, that story you gave the ladies made their day. I was pretty upset with you, but we'll let it go. I know you couldn't have done anything about the calf. I also want to ask you a personal question, nothing to do with work, okay, and you don't have to answer it."

"Okay, Ken," I thought, *What's coming now?*

"Mrs. Silverman asked if you were Jewish, and I told her I didn't know. You don't have to answer. I want to make that clear."

"Do you know why she wants to know?" I asked. I was always very uncomfortable in dealing with this question.

"Yes, she has a daughter and she thought the two of you might hit it off."

"Gee, I don't know, Ken. I mean, Mrs. Silverman looks like she's pretty well fixed. I don't know if I'd be comfortable with her daughter. It's like she's from a different world. You know anything about her?"

"Yeah, it probably is a different world. Her daughter's name is Shoshana. She's about your age. I met her several times at fundraising events for the camp. She's a real beauty, Max, and in addition, she's very talented, speaks French and Italian and is right now in London having a lesson with Yehudi Menuhin. You know who he is?"

"Yeah, isn't he a violinist?"

"More than that; he's one of the best in the world. And Shoshana has had lessons with him before. Barbara, that's Mrs. Silverman, told me that she dates some guys who she thinks are very spoiled and entitled. She likes your style. Listen, if you're uncomfortable about this, we don't have to...."

I cut him off. "Ken, I am uncomfortable, but probably not why you think. My dad is Jewish and my mother is Catholic. Neither of them practices any religion. My grandfather came from Poland, or maybe Russia. He lived in a small town on the border, and the country changed with every war. He studied at a small Yeshiva, you familiar with that?"

Ken nodded. "Studying to be a rabbi?"

"Yes, but one Friday night after the sun was down-- he was 'dovening'— praying, and went out for a breath of fresh air. He saw two of the rabbis smoking out back, a forbidden act on the Sabbath. He decided that they were a bunch of hypocrites and quit. His other formative experience was that he was beaten by a group of Cossacks when they rode through the town. Left him with a real distaste of not only religion, but anything military. Anyway, he came to this country because of these experiences. My dad never received any religious training. When he asked if he would have a bar mitzvah, grandpa said 'no' and that was the end of it. Funny thing is that when my dad married a non-Jew he was very upset. Go figure. Oh, and when my dad went to high school, he joined the R.O.T.C. and came home with a uniform and a rifle. Grandpa threw him right out of the house and my uncle Dave had to intercede with him and convince him that dad wasn't studying to be a Cossack.

So, technically, I'm not Jewish, or maybe I am by way of my friends. I hang out with mostly Jewish guys and even go to services on some holidays. It just feels right. But, Ken, I don't think I'd be a good fit for a girl like this one. She's way out of my class."

"Yeah, I see your point. The Silvermans are pretty well fixed. Her husband is a successful orthopedic surgeon and they live in the Electra."

"Wow, I know that building. It's near the Powhattan, the big Art Deco building on south Lake Shore Drive. Must cost a ton to have a place there!"

"All depends. Barbara told me once that they got a very good deal on the penthouse because her father owns the building and a couple of others as well."

"So Shoshana probably plays one of those expensive violins, too? What, a Stradivarius?"

"Actually, Barbara told me that she plays a Guarnieri Del Jesu, probably worth thirty thousand dollars in today's market."

"Ken, I can't see this going anywhere."

"What should I tell Barbara?"

"I'm okay with the truth.", I said, and left it at that.

"She insisted about this, Max. She says Shoshana needs to find someone with real character and she likes yours."

"Geez, Ken, I'm from a poor west side family. We have no degrees, my sister is a secretary for your agency, my dad has a small, route sales business, and my mom works part time in a clothing store. That's it. We don't belong anywhere religiously, we don't write checks to charities, and I'll be lucky to save enough to go to school at Navy Pier this September. How can that be any kind of a match for a girl who runs to London for a violin lesson? Please, just tell Mrs. Silverman that I have a girlfriend. That should be enough."

"Who's that Max? Anyone up here?"

Ach, I thought, another trap. I couldn't tell him about Mickey, and I didn't want to mention Kitty. That would be a real stretch for sure. I thought maybe I could use Susie Slater's name, but before I could say anything, I looked over and saw that Ken was looking even more pale and was sweating even though it wasn't a warm day. He was rubbing his chest and starting to breathe more heavily.

"Hey, Ken, are you okay? You don't look so good."

"Max, take me to the Walkerville Clinic, okay? Not feeling right— have— chest pain."

He grunted. I got the wagon off the back road and turned onto Highway 54 to Walkerville. I thought Ken was having a heart attack. I put the accelerator down, and we were doing about 85 when I saw a State Trooper with his red flasher light coming up fast. He pulled alongside and motioned for me to pull over. He pulled up and off the road in front of me and came back to the wagon.
 He was a big, sharp-looking guy with one of those Smoky the Bear hats and sunglasses. He leaned on my door, motioned for me to wind the window down, bent down and put big hands on the windowsill like he wanted to make sure I wouldn't drive away. A patch on his shirt said his name was 'MacDonald.'

"Where's the fire, buddy?" He looked in the window and saw Ken.

"Mr. Greenman?"

"Yeah, that's me, he said. "Not— feeling too good."

I said, "Officer, I think he's having a heart attack, I was trying to get to the Walkerville Clinic."

The trooper said, "Okay, put on your headlights and follow me. I'll get you there. Let's go!

We took off at a breathtaking rate of speed. The trooper
had his flashing lights and siren going, and we got to
the Clinic in a flash. I pulled up at the main entrance and
saw people coming out of the building to assist us. I
guessed that the siren gave them some warning, or
maybe the officer radioed ahead.
They got Ken in a wheelchair and took him right in. He
had told me to go back to the camp and tell Lee what
was going on, and for her to tell his wife and Larry
Reznik. I thought, *Oh, boy, Larry might be running the
show!* I thanked the trooper and took off for the camp.

Back at the office, I scrambled up the front steps and
brought Lee up to date. She said she would notify Mrs.
Greenman and Larry. I didn't know what else to do. It
was now late afternoon and I had finished my chores, so
I went over to the Camp Craft Building and found Bruce
Marshall. I told him what was going on, and we agreed
that it would be best to keep it to ourselves and hope
that Ken would be okay. We thought that Larry would
wreck the show if he'd be running it. Bruce told me that
there was an all-staff meeting tonight on the other side.

I had been running since early this morning and had one
heck of a day. I was tired and hungry. I had been on a
roller coaster, chasing around with Titus Akers, Marilyn
Monroe, the Women's Auxiliary, and now running back
to the Walkerville Clinic with Ken.

I went over to the mess hall and helped myself to a king
sized cold cuts special sandwich with some great beef-
steak tomatoes and a slice of sweet onion, some potato
chips, and a bottle of Coke. I wished it had been a cold
beer. I went outside on that same bench, ate, and

thought about all that had gone on. I finished eating, walked back to the main office, and asked Lee if she'd heard anything from the clinic.

She said, "They checked Ken's heart and think it's okay. They think he's had a gall bladder attack, and they want to keep him overnight to make sure it's not going to get worse. Maybe just some gall stones. A lot better than a heart attack, though. Say, with all your running around today, did you hear that there's an all-staff meeting on the other side tonight?"

"Bruce just told me about it. I guess Larry will run it. Say, how does the whole staff go? Who watches the kids?"

"Oh, we always have a night-watch person in each unit. One of the counselors stays with the kids."

"So that person misses out?"

"Depends on how you look at it. Staff that have been here before volunteer to stay back. It's a 'motivational meeting,' one of Larry's ideas. He brings in speakers to motivate the staff. It gets really boring, but you better be there. He never remembers who *is* there, but, he *always* remembers who doesn't show!"

"Okay, I'm going to sack out for a while. See you over there. Save me a seat in the back!"

Just as I said that, her phone rang. She picked up, listened for a moment, and said, "Yes, he's here." She waved at me to stay and said, "Yes, okay, I'll tell him. Max, that nap will have to wait. That was Kitty. One of her campers has a problem, and I have to call the Walkerville Clinic. Oh, I hope I can catch him!"

"Catch who, Lee?"

"Doctor Harris. He's an orthodontist, and he comes to Walkerville on Tuesdays. One of Kitty's campers broke her braces and is very upset. Let me call and see if I can get her in before he leaves! If you want to wait on the porch, I'll let you know if I get him. You'll have to run the girl into Walkerville."

Well, that wasn't what I really wanted to hear after the day I'd had. Also, I had been to Walkerville only a few hours earlier. I went out and sat on the porch, hoping the good doctor had packed it in for the day. I really wanted that nap.

I saw Kitty walking up the road to the office with her arm around one of her campers. She was a tall girl who seemed familiar. As they got closer, I could see wires sticking out of her mouth and she looked near tears. She also had some sort of contraption; another wire that looked like it was wrapped around her head, and seemed to be sort of cockeyed. She had enough antenna arrayed to pick up WGN TV in Chicago. She was a pretty little girl. Oval face with high cheekbones framed by long black hair, dark eyes.

Kitty said brightly, "Hi, Max, this is my very best camper; meet Rosalie Finkelstein. Rosalie, this is Max, our camp driver, and I bet he's going to get things going right for you. Okay, honey?"

I remembered her now. She was the kid from Glencoe, the one with the hundred-pound suitcase and the tag that said, "Daddy's little Princess", or something like that. I said, "Hi, there, Rosalie. How'd you get into so much trouble with those braces?"

She said, "One of the girls got a 'care package' from home and it had a lot of candy, and I ate some peanut brittle! It was SO good, but I'm not supposed to eat that stuff!"

"Gee, kid, you look like you were shot out of a cannon and into a barbed wire fence face first!"

The attempt at humor didn't go too well. Her face crumpled into an awful expression and she started bawling. Kitty looked at me with eyes that declared murder. Just then Lee came out onto the porch and beckoned me into the office.

She grabbed my arm and was whispering in a hoarse voice, "Max, I got to Doctor Harris and he said he'd stay but you have to hurry. Also, you know who that kid is?"

"Well, um, yeah, it's…"

"Shh, listen a minute. That's Rosalie Finkelstein. Her father is on the Board of Directors and a big contributor to the camp. I heard your crack about her braces. She's a bright, sensitive kid. She's a natural poet and a musician. We don't need her griping. You have to be more sensitive!"

Well, I had put my foot in my mouth once more. Or maybe worse; in Rosalie's mouth. Looking back on it, I realize how insensitive I'd been back then. I didn't mean to hurt the kid, though. I was just kidding her.

I went back onto the porch. Kitty and Rosalie were sitting on a lounge chair, and Kitty had an arm around her, trying to console her.

I knelt down and looked up at Rosalie and said, "Rosalie, I'm going to take you to a dentist who will fix your braces. And then, you know what? I'm going to take you for a very special treat, one that they don't have even in Glencoe! But you'll have to buck up and wipe the tears first, okay?"

It got her attention. A treat not even available in GLENCOE!

"What is it?"

"Oh, no, it's a surprise. Very special, okay? But we won't get it unless you and I can get going now."

She nodded once and looked at Kitty. "Kitty, come with, please!"

"I can't, honey. Max will take good care of you. Go now, okay? You'll be fine soon."

We piled in the wagon and were off to Walkerville.

"Are those wires hurting you, Rosalie?"

"It's okay unless I try to open my mouth wide. Something's sticking me. I have blisters in my cheek. What's the special treat?"

"I can't tell you. It's a surprise, remember? But I bet you'll like it."

We chatted a bit as I drove. After a while, she got quiet and then said, "Braces aren't my big problem."

"No? What's bothering you, sweetie?"

"I'm afraid my mom and dad are going to get a divorce."

"Oh, that's a big one all right, but how do you know? Are they arguing a lot, or what? You know, parents have arguments all the time. It's normal. Maybe that's all it is."

"No. Max. If I tell you will you keep it a secret?"

"I sure will, Rosalie, anything you tell me. Just between us."

"My dad has a boat. A big one. My mom doesn't like to go on it. She gets seasick. They argue about it all the time in the summer. So, my dad takes me to the boat and we have a daddy and daughter day once in a while. We cruise up and down the lakefront. One day I was on the boat down below; we were still tied up at the pier. It's a cabin cruiser and it's big, okay? So, I was changing into my swimsuit when I hear dad talking to a woman. They start arguing about the date she was supposed to meet him. I looked out the porthole and saw her standing on the pier. She was a hooker!"

"Oh, Rosalie, how could you know that? Maybe she was just a friend or someone from work."

"Max, get real. Someone from work wouldn't scream that he's not the only big shot she's banging, okay? My dad's a banker. His people from work don't wear short shorts, high heels, low-cut peasant blouses and no bras."

I wondered how twelve-year-old kids knew more about how the world worked than I did. Was I that naive?

"You won't tell anyone, will you, Max? I'm scared."

"No, Rosie, I won't." She was quiet for a time, and then said, "What's the special surprise?"

I thought she was pretty needy and that the surprise wouldn't be enough to fix her fears. Then we were at the clinic. I parked the wagon and we got out, and went in. I held Rosie's hand as we walked up to the reception desk.

"Rosalie Finkelstein to see Doctor Harris."

"Oh, yes, she can come right in; he's waiting. She's his last patient."

Rosalie walked around the desk, and the receptionist took her hand, and they went to the rear office. I turned around and my heart stopped. Crash Kelly sat against the far wall in a chair and he looked at me with hatred blazing from eyes that were still bruised from the broken nose I'd given him.

Hello, asshole. Enjoying the job you screwed me out of?"

"Listen, Crash, what did you expect me to do when you tried to stab me, buy you a beer? I didn't start the trouble."

"Yeah, well, you can bet your trouble ain't over. One day you'll know it. And don't think Leon can protect your ass. I know you set him up for protection and to keep an eye on me. Don't bet on it. I'm a lot smarter than that dumb ox."

I was getting hot under the collar. He started to get up. It looked like we were going to get into it right there. Crash reached into his pocket. I thought, *Oh, hell another knife?* The door opened and an old man wearing a straw hat and overalls came in. He was bent over and walked with a cane. Right behind him was a state trooper; a great big familiar-looking guy. I had to look twice. It was officer MacDonald, the state trooper who got Ken and me to the Walkerville Clinic just a few hours earlier.

He said, "Dad, take a seat and I'll tell the receptionist we're here. Then he saw us and looked at Crash. "Well, well, Mr. Kelly. And how are we today?"

Crash slowly eased his hand out of his pocket and sat down. His face was working to hide his emotions. I think he liked officer MacDonald no more than he liked me. He nodded, grunted a hello, and took up a magazine. I realized I'd been holding my breath, so I gulped air and said, "Hi, officer, I didn't recognize you at first. Is that your dad there?

He said, "Yes, that's dad, all right. Max, isn't it? How's Mr. Greenman doing?"

"We don't know anything yet; too early."

We chatted for a while. He told me his father was retired and was suffering from Parkinson's disease. It had been hard for him to make the adjustment to his physical limitations because he'd worked hard on a farm his whole life. A nurse came and called for "Mr. Kelly" and Crash got up and followed her to the back of the clinic. I started to relax. Just talking to that big trooper made everything better. He quietly told me that Crash had been in a lot more troubles lately, and just shook his head. He started to say something about being careful around Crash, but just then Rosalie came walking out to the reception room and he stopped. I shook hands with the officer and said good bye. Rosalie and I went out to the parking lot.

"So, Rosie, how're you doing? Feeling better?"
"I'm fine, Max. Oh, god, I'm so much better! And now, c'mon! WHAT'S the SURPRISE?"

"Coming right up!"

We scrambled into the wagon, and I pulled around and parked on the square in front of Niedermeir's Drug Store and Fountain. We went in and took a couple of stools at their soda fountain. I ordered two root beer sodas with pineapple ice cream. Rosalie looked a little unsure until she tried it. Her dark eyes went wide at the first taste.

After finishing half she said, "Max, this is so good, but I bet I could order this in Glencoe."

"Maybe, Rosie, but without me to tell you about it you would never have known."

We finished up and went back to the wagon. I could tell Rosalie was feeling better. As we got on the highway, I was thinking about my near run-in with Crash.

"Max, is something wrong? You got awfully quiet."

Rosalie had tuned in to my mood. She was indeed sensitive. I didn't want to tell her about the problem with Crash, so I came up with something else.

"I'm fine, Rosie. While you were in the office getting your braces fixed, an old, sick man came in with his son to get some treatment. I know his son; he's a state trooper named MacDonald, and he told me his dad was having a tough time because he got sick and couldn't do his farming." I thought that would cover things.

Rosalie was quiet for a moment, and she then sang, "Old MacDonald was infirm! Come on, Max do your part!"

To which I sang, "E-I-E-I-O!"

"And in his firm he caught a germ!"

"E-I-E-I-O!"

"With a cough, cough here, and a cough, cough there…"

And together we sang, "Here a cough, there a cough, everywhere a cough, cough...."

And then we burst into laughter. Rosalie added verse after verse, and we kept giggling all the way back to camp. When we got out of the wagon, Rosalie gave me a hug and thanked me for a great day. Years later, I learned that she'd gotten a degree from Brandeis University and had become a top creative director with J. Walter Thompson, no less. It didn't surprise me.

It was now too late to take that nap, so I just cleaned up a bit and walked across the ball field to the other side. I thought about the current list of girls I knew or met at the camp, but who I hadn't impressed. I was up to five: Mickey, who didn't want anything to do with me; Kitty, ditto; Tori, who really attracted me and didn't know I was alive; Phyllis, nice, no sparks; and Shoshana, who I thought would be the greatest long shot in my short history of chasing girls. Zero for five. I bet myself that I'd have a better shot at Mrs. Silverman. She was the only one who thought I was okay.

The meeting was called for eight o'clock, and I got there just as it was starting. Lee was sitting in the back and had saved a chair for me. There were only two chairs left, and Tori the dancer came in and took the one next to me. I felt a trickle of sweat roll down my back. I looked straight ahead, my mind racing. I had no idea in hell how to make a connection with her. *So much for 'Max the Man'*, I thought. She was chatting with Phyllis, who sat in front of her.

The room was set up auditorium-style with rows of folding chairs about eight across and nine or so deep. It was overcrowded, and with all the staff and no air conditioning, it was also warm. At least no one was smoking. There was a table across the front of the room with camp posters on the wall behind it, along with U.S. and Wisconsin state flags in the front corners. The table had three chairs behind it facing the group. Larry came in and held his hand up for our attention. The staff was buzzing and kept it up. Larry cleared his throat and began knocking on the table.

"People.... Everyone, please, your attention...." Nothing.
"People, I have some news about Ken. He is ill."
A hush fell on the group.

"Thank you. I am sorry to announce that Ken had what they think is a gallbladder attack this afternoon. Mrs. G. will be driving him back to Chicago, where he will see his personal physician and probably take some tests. We all wish him well and believe that he will be back soon."

There was a lot of murmuring among the staff. I leaned over to Lee and whispered, "I wonder why he took the wagon to pick up the ladies from the Auxiliary instead of his own car."

She whispered back, "He has a Plymouth two-door coupe. That's why he needed the wagon."
"Ah."

Tori put a hand on my leg and my heart gave a wild thump. It felt like an electric shock. I bet it would have cleared a clogged artery.

"Oh, isn't that awful?" she murmured. "He's such a nice man. Do you think that this Larry can carry the mail? I'm Tori Williams, by the way. Aren't you the driver? I see you in that wagon all the time."

Her mouth was very close to my ear; her low voice flooded me with emotion. She was so open, natural and pleasant that I couldn't believe it. I had imagined that she would be haughty and above all the guys. I mumbled back, "I think he'll be okay. I took him to the clinic in town because I thought he was having a heart attack. I'm sure he'll be back soon."

She nodded and asked softly, "Were you frightened when you had to rush him there so quickly?"

I had a chance to play hero and tell her how I can leap into action in an emergency like Clark Kent turning into Superman, but I muffed it and said, "Boy, was I ever!" Then thought to myself, "*YOU DUMMY!*" I consoled myself by thinking, *'Well at least I'm an honest dummy'.* Didn't go real far.

Larry went on because he had reasonable attention. Droning on for at least twenty minutes, he launched into his usual speech about the philosophy of the camp. At that point the door opened and a large man wearing a high collar and a double-breasted suit that looked like it was cut and sold during the Harding administration walked into the room and took a seat at the front table.

Larry introduced him as "the Right Reverend Thurston MacKenzie the Fourth, Pastor of the Heart of the Lamb Church in Walkerville." One of the macho counselors sitting in front of me said to his buddy, "You mean there were three more of those guys?" His friend whispered back, "I wish his church was the 'chop of the lamb.' I'd become a member for sure!" There was some snickering, elbowing, and jostling at that in the back row that fortunately didn't carry.

Larry said that he had asked the reverend to bestow blessings on our staff, a ritual the camp has had at the inception of every new camping season. He turned the floor over to the Reverend, who stood and cleared his throat for several moments till someone brought him a glass of water. He looked like President Roosevelt in those old pictures just before his stroke. He had a large head and a prominent nose with tiny glasses perched on it. His eyes were sunken and hollow with large dark patches under them.

After a lot of posturing, throat clearing, and water sipping, he began speaking in what some might have called a profound dramatic manner. His voice was deep and rumbling, and he really got attention from the group. He started by saying that his remarks would be brief. I didn't understand a lot of what he said, but it had to do with our responsibility for the campers and our being '*in loco parentis.*' Lee told me this was Latin and meant that we were the kids' parents as long as they were at camp. After forty minutes of brevity, he ended with, "And in conclusion, I want to make a benediction of motivation for the staff, counselors, specialists, and even those who tend to cleaning toilets."

Everyone but the kitchen boys, I thought.

"My prayer of motivation is from the Prophet Zechariah, 11:17.
'Oh, the worthless shepherd
Who abandons the flock!
Let a sword descend upon his arm
And upon his right eye!
His arm shall shrivel up;
His right eye shall go blind.'

Thank you all for your attention this evening."

There was a small smattering of applause and much more eye rolling, generally with the right eye, I thought. I leaned over to Lee and said, "Geez, where did they get this guy?" She said, "Larry visits the local churches to tell them about the good work of the camp. He finds these guys, and if they impress him, he invites them to address the staff. You know, there's a rumor about his son, Thurston Mackenzie the fifth."

"Really? What is it?"

"Well, by day he's a teller at Walkerville National Bank. But sometimes he rides the roads on a Harley motorcycle wearing a black mask, cape and a sombrero, cuts people off and gives them the 'finger.' They call him 'El Dédo.'"

"Super. Well, Larry is easily impressed. I'm going to bed. Enough for one day."

The group was breaking up, and several guys came over to talk to Tori. I wanted to talk to her as well. I walked toward her, but the 'Macho Men' shunted me aside like a sheep herded by a platoon of German Shepherds.

Morning would bring the 'All-Camp Program," and I figured I'd need a good night's sleep. Many of the staff stayed to party a bit. The male staff started stacking the folding chairs, and the girls brought cookies and coffee from the kitchen.

I saw Mickey and Kitty cutting up cakes and piling the cookies on a platter. Tori the dancer went into the kitchen and started making coffee. She was something to look at. I thought she would look good wearing overalls and changing the oil on the wagon. Lee was at the refrigerator getting milk and cream for the coffee. I suddenly felt out of place and decided to go back to the tent and get a good night's sleep. It was 10:30 by the time I got back to the tents. The other guys were already sleeping, so I got ready as quietly as I could and was asleep before I got the covers on.

Chapter 9
At Last, the All Camp Program and the Longest Day!

Morning dawned bright, cool and sunny. Up early, as usual, I went down to the mess hall before the first bell. There was a lot of activity in the kitchen, as "special meals" were the order of the day during an All-Camp Program. In addition to the breakfast and supper meals, there was a special outdoor barbecue for lunch. This took a lot of logistics and planning by the entire kitchen and specialist staff.

Excitement bubbled over, as the area around the mess hall filled up with campers and staff. Kids were rehearsing their skits in small clusters. Counselors herded their groups into the mess hall, and Larry Reznik skittered around waving his arms and giving directions. He was largely ignored.

My clipboard was loaded with a lot of "around-camp-delivery" items. At the top was a note in red from Lee that I was to make two trips to Walkerville during the day. The first was to pick up a staff member at the eleven o'clock train, then I was to take the ladies of the Auxiliary back to the four o'clock train for Chicago.

I couldn't think of who might be coming up. I'd learned that the Professor interrupted his trip and went back to Chicago with Mrs. G. as soon as she got word of Ken's illness. As for the ladies, I thought I would try to talk

Larry into taking them to the train. Max the coward didn't want to face Mrs. Silverman and listen to a sales pitch for her daughter.

There were some cute skits about farming done by the youngest girls' and boys' units just before breakfast. After the meal, the group broke up for activities and games. Each group got a chance to go to the Camp Craft building and see Marilyn Monroe, who was the biggest star of the program; and with a name like that, she couldn't miss.

Some "overnighters" were planned for later on that day. These were overnight camp-outs for the younger kids that took place at a forested area that belonged to a local farmer. The land, which had been rented for the summer, was just close enough for the kids to take a short hike in order to reach it. It was a nice place with trees and brush around the campsite, mostly rolling land that wasn't good for farming, but perfect for a sheltered sleep out in the woods. It engendered great excitement for kids who lived in a city ghetto.

It was getting close to eleven am. By now I had the timing down for trips to Walkerville. I kept trying to dodge Mrs. Silverman, and because I kept running into the Auxiliary Ladies everywhere, I decided to take off. I thought it was funny that Lee didn't put the name of the staff person down on my work order. I figured whoever it was would know the camp wagon.

I got to Walkerville, and saw that the small station parking lot was filled with cars and a few cabs. I had to park on the street. The train pulled in on time, and people piled off, including a group of sailors. Walkerville, I had learned from my chats with the locals, was a very patriotic town. The parks all had monuments to those who had fallen in defense of our country; some of them went back to the Civil War. I had learned that young men often joined up right out of high school to learn skills and get veteran benefits. Many had moved away from the town because of limited opportunity for employment.

People met up, and the station area started to clear. Cars moved out, and cabs picked up fares. Soon the area was empty except for a lone pale woman wearing a baggy raincoat, large sunglasses and a green "babushka" on her head. She stood next to a large metal trunk that apparently one of the conductors brought off the train, which gave a blast of its horn and started to chug out of the station.

I figured that whoever I was to pick up didn't make the trip or missed the train. I started the wagon. The woman noticed, waved at me and started to run toward me. Whoever she was, she looked very upset. She ran around the front of the car to the driver's open window.

"Oh, thank god you're here! Max? Is that you?"

I must have looked totally bewildered, so she cried, "Max, it's me, *MOIRA!*" She ran around to the passenger side, flung open the door and got in, slammed it, rolled up the window and punched the lock button. She sat frozen, with her arms wrapped around her as if it was winter.

I found my tongue. "Miss Wallace? I'm so sorry; I didn't recognize you. You're, uh, you look different."

And she did, too. No makeup, no jangling jewelry, hair hidden under an ugly scarf, and no 105-millimeter high-powered perfume; just the scent of fear. She didn't say anything. Instead she fumbled in her purse and brought out a pack of Pall Malls and a cigarette lighter. Her hands shook as she tried to light up. She took several short puffs, inhaled, blew smoke, took another, puffed, and another. She reminded me of Bette Davis, overacting in one of her films. She looked over at me and barked, *"Go get the trunk! It's heavy. Pull the wagon closer."*

Be careful with the trunk," she shrieked.
She didn't say 'please'.

I pulled the wagon into the station parking lot, got out and tested the trunk; It must have weighed a hundred pounds. I figured the leather handles would be the first victims if I tried to lift the thing with them. I opened the tailgate, and rocked the trunk on an angle so that I could grip the corners, and up she came. I slid the thing into the wagon, wondering what women put in suitcases that make them so heavy. I imagined that many of the fairer sex were secretly studying blacksmithing and had anvils, horseshoes, hammers and tongs along with their Bermuda shorts and bathing suits. Oh, yes, let's also include enough makeup to paint the Golden Gate Bridge, and thirty pairs of shoes for all occasions. I swung up the tailgate, and got back in the wagon.

"Okay, Moira, I got the trunk in the back."

"Let's get out of here."
She didn't say 'thank you'.

We headed for the camp. I drove and kept quiet just like the Professor said.

"I suppose you want to know why I'm dressed this way, why I'm, ah, a bit upset."

" Sure, if you want to talk, please feel free. I would be glad to listen."

"I - I, uh, I - was sitting alone. Some— um, sailors— were sitting a couple of seats behind me, laughing and telling dirty jokes. They were drunk. One of them came up and sat next to me. I was dressed for, um, business, you know, like when we met."

Boy, I remembered. I said nothing. I saw it coming.

"The sailor started, you know, flirting with me, and his friends were laughing and taunting him. He was really inappropriate. And then he...."

She choked and started to cry. Only squeaky, inarticulate noises came out of her as she tried to tell me what happened next, mangled words I couldn't understand. She stubbed out her cigarette, put her hands to her face, and wept like a little kid who'd had a bad scare.

I kept my eyes on the road, and eventually she got herself under control. She looked over at me and shrieked, *"He slid his hand up my skirt!"*

That did it. She totally fell apart. I thought, *So, it's all a show. She isn't the self-assured great sex bomb she pretends to be!*

 I said, "Miss Wallace, Moira, do you want me to pull over for a bit so you can get yourself together?

"Yes, please, Max, I can't go into camp looking like this." And with that, she yanked the driver's rear view mirror over so that she could inspect her face, which was now red and blotchy. Her eyes were red and watery, her hair a total mess. She pulled herself closer to the mirror, and moaned mournfully, like a cat whose litter box had dis-appeared. I couldn't tell if she was more upset by the sailor's hand going up her skirt, or her face being such a shambles.

 "Moira, there's a little coffee shop I know. Would it help if we stopped and got you some tea or coffee, maybe use their rest room?"

"Oh, yes, Max, thank you. I'm so upset. *But nothing happened,* you understand, don't you? Nothing at all. I slapped him, and yelled for the conductor, and then left the car. I went to the washroom and washed off my make up. I put on my raincoat and sunglasses, and went into another car, and sat with an old woman."

I wondered if it was Bessie Akers, since everything up here seemed to be connected.

I drove to the coffee shop. By now it was almost noon. No one was at the counter, so I called out, "Hello?"

Fritz came out from the back. He had an apron on and was largely covered in flour.

I said, "Hello, Fritz, I'm Max from the camp." Nothing registered. I tried again, "Professor Linzer's friend. I was here with him a couple of days ago." He brightened.

"Ach, sure, I remember now. And who is zis lady? Also for zeh camp?"

"Yes, this is Miss Wallace, the camp personnel director. Moira, this is Fritz, the owner of the shop, and a very good baker." He nodded, wiped flour off his hands on his apron and offered his hand to her.
She stepped back and said, "Very nice to meet you, Fritz. May I use your rest room?"

Fritz pointed to a hallway at the end of the front counter, and off Moira went into dry-dock for major repairs. She was clutching a large purse, that until now, I hadn't noticed.

I asked Fritz for two coffees, and some of his wonderful strudel. He beamed a big smile, and went into the back room. After a while he came out with two small place settings, and a plate of apple strudel. He poured coffee from a carafe, and informed me that he was in the middle of a recipe, and to call if I needed anything. Magda was in town, and he was running the whole show solo.

I sat and drank coffee. Minutes passed. I had some strudel. I looked at my watch. A quarter- hour. I poured a second cup from the carafe, and had another piece of strudel. A half-hour. I wondered if Moira had committed suicide in the restroom. I thought that maybe I should knock on the door and see if she had drowned herself in the toilet or what.

Finally, I heard a toilet flush. A door opened from down the hall, and I heard the jaunty click of high heels on the linoleum floor. Moira appeared with the raincoat folded over her arm. Her makeup and hair were flawless. She wore the tight skirt and a blouse opened a couple of buttons down. Jewelry hung from wrists, ears and neck. She wore a brooch on a silver chain one inch north of her cleavage. It said, "Go." It struck me that Moira accomplished much of what Diana Prince did when she became Wonder Woman, except that it took a half an hour and a restroom instead of a "whirl- around."

She smiled and said, "Oh, Max, I feel so much better!" I nodded and told her that I thought she looked so also. Just then Fritz walked out to see how we were doing and said, "Und, who is zis, Max? What happened to zeh other voman?" Moira laughed and said, "Fritz, it's just me, Miss Wallace. I've just freshened up a bit."

Fritz smiled and said, "Maybe you vill come back and show my wife how to do zis." We had a good chuckle.

Moira was now all business. She drank some of the coffee, ate a piece of strudel, and paid the tab, making sure to get a receipt. (She said she was on a traveling *per diem*, whatever that was).

"Let's go, Max. I'm anxious to get to camp."
We got back into the wagon and headed for the other side, where she said she would be staying.

"Ken asked me to come up and keep an eye on things. He said that Larry needed someone to advise him. He isn't used to running things all by himself. When we get to the cabins, I want you to bring in my trunk. There's some work in it I need to finish for a file audit. Some of the personnel files are incomplete."

"Is that why the trunk is so heavy? It must weigh a hundred pounds." She never answered, so I was left with my working theory of blacksmith tools. It occurred to me that she might notice the gaps in Mickey's file. No college transcripts! And there were probably other things missing as well.

I concentrated on driving. We got to the cabins on the other side, and I manhandled the trunk out of the wagon and into her room. It was pretty quiet there, as everyone was still at the All- Camp Program.

After I got the trunk in her room, Moira closed the door and said, "Max, I want to thank you for listening to me and taking time while I got myself sorted out."

"That's okay, Moira. I mean, I could see how upset you were."

"You have no idea. I'm still upset. Max, I need a hug."

I wasn't comfortable with this at all, but I stepped up. I put my arms around her and said, "You're okay, it was just a bad incident. You'll never see those guys again."

She got her arms around my neck and said, "It was so strange, Max, I was frightened and all stirred up at the same time. Max, I wanted to *do it! And I still want to do it."*
She kissed me, *"Max, let's do it! Now!"*

I started to say something and she glommed another kiss on my mouth. And I kissed her back. I flashed on images and heard voices in my head; my dad saying, "I ain't ready to be a grandfather, so use a condo-mum. Your mother will have a canary."

Bessie Akers saying, "Girls are loose up there!" Kitty saying, "Cat must have your tongue, 'cause Kitty isn't getting any!" My own promise, "Max Lewis is a man and next time…" And finally, the Professor shaking his finger, chewing his cigar and saying, "Be careful of the woman you want to save who wants to be saved; they're the most trouble!"

I didn't listen to any of it. We fumbled, trying to kiss and get loose from our clothes at the same time. She got my belt loose, I shoved my hands down the back of her skirt and grabbed her; we somehow shuffled our way like a four-legged spastic animal to the narrow twin sized bed and fell onto it. No love scene in a movie was ever shot like ours. It was a tangled mess of groping, manipulating buttons, zippers, grunting and panting. She breathed heavily in my ear that she had to be on top because she was the Director of Personnel!

I'll just say this much; it was very good. We were spent soon enough. I felt so intoxicated that I wanted to break open a bottle of champagne. She fell asleep. I looked at my watch and yelped, "The four o'clock train! I gotta get the Women's Auxiliary to the station! I gabbled, "Moira, I have to take the ladies of the Auxiliary to the train, it's on my clipboard."

She muttered, "Fuck your clipboard."

I tried to get up, but she was still sprawled on top of me. I edged my way out from underneath her, got out of the bed, and pulled myself together. I whispered quickly into her ear, "Moira, it was wonderful, thank you. I have to go."

"Don't go, Max, stay." And she dozed off again.

I sprang out of the door and instantly was hit with a stab of guilt and anxiety! I didn't use a condom! What if I knocked her up? Oh, Geez, what if...."
I felt a hand on my shoulder and I screamed, "Yaagh!" It was Victoria, the nurse who had just come out of the infirmary.

"Max, what's wrong, luv? Wait half a moment, will you? Max, I just want to... what's wrong with your face? Is that blood? Why is your shirt hanging out like that? Oh, it's lipstick!" I turned around, and she said, "Are those teeth bites on your ear?"

I recovered my composure, thought fast and said, "Yes, I bite my ears when I'm anxious. You shouldn't sneak up on me like that."

She said, "Oh, don't be silly. You've been horsing around with someone in that cabin, haven't you, luv?" Who's in that room?"

I said, "Our Director of Personnel."

Her eyes went wide. She said, "Max, go into the infirmary and look at yourself." She grabbed my arm, half pulled me into the infirmary, and pushed me in front of a mirror.

I almost didn't recognize my mirror image. My hair was messed up and there was lipstick smeared all over my face. I wore a goofy a smile that made me look like Alfred E. Neuman, the cartoon character on the cover of most MAD magazines!

Victoria said, "Better wash up, luv. You look a fright; even the campers will know you've been horsing around. Dear me. Moira was it? I don't think I'd have guessed that, luv. Anyone but her."

I said, "Victoria, it just sort of happened, I hope you'll be discreet. Can I count on you, please?"

I was washing my face in the sink below the mirror and she said, "Sure, luv, you can count on me."

I thought she sounded disappointed. I got cleaned up and hurried to get up to the main office and pick up the ladies. I don't ever remember feeling so loose and so— complete, like a man!

I remembered how my Jewish friends would talk about their Bar Mitzvahs saying, 'Today I am a man'. It felt as though this was my Bar Mitzvah in a crazy kind of way, a coming of age. And the whole service and party only took fifteen minutes. *Top that, boys,* I thought.

I hoped that this thing with Moira wouldn't cost me a lot of problems down the line. A saying of one of my Jewish friends came to me. It was Yiddish; he taught it to me when we were in German class. ***Venn der schmeckle steht, das sachel geht!*** Which means, if your Yiddish is rusty, "When you get an erection, all common sense is gone." Now I understood it completely.

I shook off that thought along with the echo of the Professor's warning to beware of women who need rescuing. I thanked Victoria for making sure I got straightened out, got in the wagon and took the back road to the camp side. I saw the ladies on the office porch along with their luggage.

Mrs. Silverman was standing with her arms folded, looking down the road while the others sat relaxing. I pulled up to them, got out and waved. "Hello, everyone, how did the All-Camp Program go? Everyone enjoy the day?"

Mrs. Van Lauder said, "It was very pleasant, Max, we had a really nice time, but we're anxious to go. We were worried about making the train. I'm so glad you're here."

I said, "I had a pick up at the station, and the train was late." Another lie, but it was necessary.
Mrs. Silverman picked a long hair off my shoulder and looked very closely at it, but said nothing.

That made me anxious. I got very busy, chattering about the planning that goes into the programs. I picked up their suitcases and packed them in the back of the wagon, worrying about any lipstick I might have missed. Mrs. Silverman slid into the front passenger seat, which I surmised would be reserved for Mrs. Van Lauder, as she was the president. I thought, *this is a fixed deal.'*

"Everyone ready?" I inquired with as much cheer in my voice as I could get. I was worried that they would ask whom I picked up. If I'd had to tell them it was Moira, they would want to know why she didn't come to greet them. My mind was racing. We got into the car and I said, "I'll have to step on it, but we'll make the train, don't worry."

I kept up the chattering up as best I could, but eventually I ran out of things to say. Mrs. Silverman said, "Who'd you pick up, Max? Was it Miss Wallace? She was supposed to come up to help Larry." I was hit by one of those waves you get in your stomach when you ride a roller coaster that suddenly drops at speed, or when you have a hand in the cookie jar and your mother walks in. *And, I'd just done a lot more than stick my hand in a cookie jar!*

"Yes, Mrs. Silverman. She had a bad ride up and wasn't feeling well. We had to make a stop and get her some antacids and aspirin in Walkerville. She had a migraine and was really feeling poorly. I got her to her room on the other side and she went right to bed." I thought, *Wow, I can spin the BS when I have to.*

"I'll bet. Lucky she had you to tuck her in."

I thought that Mrs. Silverman was a very sharp cookie. Thankfully we rode for a while in silence. Then Mrs. Van Lauder and Mrs. Dinwiddy started discussing a fund raising event, trying to decide whether it should be downtown or at Mrs. Van Lauder's home in Kenilworth. I thought Mrs. Silverman would get into that discussion and I'd be in the clear. But no such luck.

While the two in back were in deep discussion, Mrs. Silverman said, "Max, are you Jewish? I asked Ken to find out and he never got back to me."

"My mother is Catholic," I said, hoping that would do it.

"And your father?"

"Well, he's Jewish, but he never practices."

"Hm."
I could feel the wheels working in her head as she balanced and re-framed what she wanted on her personal Jewish mother's bucket list. Silence for a while, then, "So, what about you?"

"Me?"

"There's someone else here in front with us?"

"Ah, I'm not sure what you mean."

"I'm asking how you think of yourself, you know. Are you Catholic, Jewish, Buddhist or what?"

I could see that this dodging around could go on indefinitely until I either said I was an atheist, or a Nazi, so I just told her the truth.

"You know, Mrs. Silverman, I never was trained religiously in anything. I was never confirmed or had a Bar Mitzvah. (A flash image of Moira and me struggling onto get on the bed. I was wearing a Yarmelke!) "So, I guess I have no real religious identity."
Well, it was pretty close to the truth, and I figured I was now off the hook.

"Did Ken mention my daughter, Shoshana?"

Back on the hook. She didn't wait for an answer.

"Max, she's a real beauty, a great talent, and a wonderful girl. I'd like you to meet her when we come back next session. I talked with Ken a couple of months back. I shared my opinion that the campers should have some exposure to classical music. We agreed to have Shoshana travel up here and play for the kids. Have you met Richard Marrens? He's a counselor up here and a talented pianist. Anyway, he's accompanied Shoshana several times, and they will play during the second session. I'd really like you to meet Shoshana; such a gifted girl. *I know you would really like her.*"

My mind sometimes has an irrational mind of its own and I wondered if Susie Slater was the illegitimate daughter of Mrs. Silverman. *In spirit* for sure.

"That's wonderful, Mrs. Silverman. I look forward to meeting her."

Okay, we finally got it over with. She turned around to the ladies in the back seat and said, "Listen, a downtown venue makes more sense for a fund raiser. Do it at the Union League or the Yacht Club. I can get a room for *bupkis,* and we'll capture the lunch time executives who don't mind dropping a few bucks for me and the camp."

Venue settled, score it two-zip for Team Silverman. You couldn't help being impressed with her style of going for the jugular to get what she wanted. *A very smart lady,* I thought. I wondered if my future would be to marry Shoshana and run a real estate empire.

I shook off that horrible vision by stepping on the gas. We were close to Walkerville, the train station, and getting Mrs. Silverman out of my hair. I was really tired, and all I could think of was having dinner, getting back to the tent and sleeping. I didn't know the day was just beginning.

I pulled into the station; by now I thought I should have a reserved spot. I helped get the ladies' luggage onto the platform. We chatted about the program, I received thank-you's from the ladies and a warm handshake from Mrs. Silverman. I already thought of her as my mother-in-law. The train pulled in, and I helped get their bags aboard. I waved goodbye, and headed back to camp, breathing a sigh of relief. So much for my first encounter with wealthy important people. I thought it turned out all right. However, it was only the beginning of learning to deal with them.

Back to camp. By now I was totally comfortable traveling the roads of Wisconsin. It had been a long day. My mind was filled and buzzing with all that had happened. I only wanted to grab a nap and get up in time for dinner. Technically, I had no hours to fulfill. As camp driver I was on call, but could call it quits in the late afternoon or when I'd finished my errands. I parked the wagon behind the mess hall and walked down the road to the tents.

Chapter 10
A Little Stress Comes with the Turf

I was dead tired and in luck. No one was around, so I climbed into bed and dozed off. I was out almost instantly and dreamed that I was at a boxing match. I was at ringside about three rows back.

Mrs. Silverman was wearing a men's white dress shirt with a bow tie and black slacks. She was standing in the middle of the ring. She grabbed a microphone that hung down from the ceiling and announced:

" ATTENTION, ATTENTION!" A bell rang several times. "In this corner, weighing one hunnert and twenty pounds, from Waukesha, Wisconsin, 'Moira the Mauler!" The bell rang again and Moira, dressed in the tight skirt and open blouse, strutted around the ring with her arms held high, wearing gaudy bracelets and boxing gloves. "And in this corner, a featherweight *schlimiel* weighing one hunnnert and seventy pounds, from Brooklyn Noo

Yawk, "Larry, the Kid-Reznik!" Larry sat on a stool, and Frieda the cook was sponging his face. He looked out of breath.

"This is a 15-round heavy weight championship bout," Mrs. Silverman boomed. "Come out fighting at the bell!" Mrs. Silverman pointed to a slender woman with a long ponytail. She was wearing an off-the-shoulder evening gown and a diamond tiara. I couldn't see her face because she had her back to me. The woman rose and reached for the bell to start the fight, but it turned into a violin and she started playing the "Blue Danube Waltz." Larry and Moira were dancing and the crowd started booing.

Behind me, screaming and booing, were the Macho Male Counselors, Victoria the nurse, Kitty Katz, Tori the dancer, and Mickey, who threw her clipboard into the ring. All at once, Kitty threw her arm around my neck and was strangling me! I started screaming, and I was getting hit and pushed. Suddenly I awoke to find Bill Lightfoot shaking me.

"Max, Max, wake up! What's wrong? Are you all right? Max!"

"Yeah, I'm okay, I'm okay. What's wrong? What-r ya hitting me for?"

"What's wrong? I came into the tent to get my cigarettes and you were rolling around and screaming."

"What'd I say, Bill?"

"It was sort of hard to understand, something about warning Larry to watch out in the clinches. Made no sense. Listen, I'm glad you were here. Bruce Marshall asked me if I'd seen you. He said that if I did, to tell you that he's saving a chair for you at dinner. He said he wanted to talk with you."

"Okay, Bill, thanks. I'm up. It was just a bad dream, that's all. Hey, what time is it?" He told me that it was about quarter to six. I'd been sleeping for over an hour!

I was groggy and soaked with sweat, so I decided to jump into the shower. I showed up at the mess hall just as dinner was underway. As usual I looked for Mickey's table, but it was empty. Bruce was at a place in the corner with some of the other specialists. I took the empty seat next to him.

"Hi, Max, I haven't seen you since you dropped off Marilyn Monroe. Where you been?"

"I had to make a couple of trips to Walkerville; took the "ladies" back to the train and picked up Moira Wallace. She came up to give Larry some moral support while Ken is out."

"Anyone tell her what time dinner is?"

"I think she wanted to sleep; wasn't feeling well."

Max, I have a problem. I don't want to spell it out too clearly because it's about a certain girl we know from Chicago. Okay?"

"I got it. What's wrong?"

"So, this person wasn't the sharpest in my safety classes during orientation, especially when it came to the things you need to watch for in an overnight campout, okay?"

"Yeah, sure, go ahead."

"This certain person is out with her cabin tonight. They're over in the rented camp area. Their program calls for a cookout, a sleepover, and a hike back to camp tomorrow morning. Her kids are young, and she doesn't really watch out for them like I think she should. Also, during my session with her counselor group, she was scribbling on her clipboard the whole time. Then, when I asked her to pay attention, she got really huffy and said she was writing down everything I said."

"Well, that sounds okay to me."

"Yeah, if it was true. During a break everyone got up to go to the john or light one up, and I got a chance to glance at what she was writing. Looked like a love letter to Michael Vandon."
In a falsetto voice he said, "'Oh, Sweetie, how I miss you. I'm sending you XXXX's.' And that was only the start."

Death by a thousand cuts. I was running out of blood. "Yeah, okay, I get it. So what? She's been out with every guy in the camp except me and Fat Freddy. Michael will learn what she's like sooner or later."

"Well, I'm not worried about Michael. I'm worried about how she'll handle tonight. Sometimes I go out to check, to make sure everything is going well. She's so ornery that I'd like you to come out to the campsite with me, drive us out, maybe bring some extra water and snacks. You okay with that?"

"I'll go with you, but it won't help your relationship with her if I do. You know that, don't you?"

"I don't care about that. I care about the kids. Maybe if there are two of us she won't make a fuss. Let's wait 'til near sunset. Bring the wagon over to Camp Craft. I asked Fred to put a special nighttime snack together for the kids, and we'll take some water in a large thermos jug."

I needed to change the subject.
"Right. Say, Bruce, have you met anyone up here? Any girls?" He didn't answer right away, then he leaned over and said in a very confidential voice, "You know that little Phyllis, the Assistant Unit Leader in Mickey's unit? I think she's really cute and very nice. We're going on a date first day we can get off together. You have anyone?"

I didn't know how to answer that. I couldn't exactly say that I was banging Miss Wallace, that Kitty wasn't talking to me, and that Tori, the dancer must think I'm very strange due to the way I acted at the 'motivational meeting.' I could only imagine what Victoria thought of me, so I just said, "No luck so far."

Bruce nodded and said that he wanted to check out some equipment. He tapped his watch. "See you about seven thirty, okay?" I nodded.

Dinner was nearly over. I looked around for Marrens, the guy I'd seen playing banjo on the office porch. He was over with the older boys' group and headed up a tableful of campers.

I walked over, and introduced myself and said, "Are you Richard Marrens? Mrs. Silverman mentioned that I should look you up." He stood up and we shook hands.

"Yes, I'm Richie. Actually, I'm really a friend of her, daughter, Shoshana. Do you know her?"

This was a bit tricky, so I said, "Well, no, I'd just met her mother, who's on the Board of the camp. She told me you were friends with her daughter. I understand that she's is coming up next session and the two of you are going to play for the campers." I kept the chatting up just to see what he would say about this girl, and he kept it on a very political level. He was not a guy to make gossip. I was impressed with that, but didn't learn much about Shoshana.

I said I was looking forward to hearing them play and asked him about his banjo. He explained that he'd just started playing it a year ago. His "instrument", he said, was the piano. Piano wasn't the best thing to play in a camp setting, as he had trouble hanging it around his neck. The banjo was easier, and he found it was also a simple matter to break in with the guitar players because none of them played banjo. Then he asked if I played.

When I said that I didn't, he offered to show me a few chords if I wanted, and that it was a cinch to play folk music. I found him to be a friendly fellow. I said I'd try to find time for that.

I didn't learn anything about Shoshana, but figured if she hung out with this guy she would probably be okay. He excused himself, said he had to take the kids out to play some volleyball. I walked back to the kitchen, where the team was working to clean up the dinner mess. The cooks were gone for the night. Bob Wheeler was doing some paperwork in his office. He saw me and waved me over.

"Say, Max, did you bring Moira in from the train? I thought she was supposed to come up today."

Just then Larry came up behind me and said pretty much the same thing. And right behind Larry, Moira came striding into the kitchen and said, "Moira's here, boys, no thanks to any of you! I had to get Victoria to show me how to get here."

And there she was, all right, dressed in what I thought was her idea of roughing it in the woods. She was poured into a pair of Levi's with a tooled leather belt and buckle set that would have made any rodeo champion proud. The half-open blouse was replaced by a tight cashmere sweater covered modestly by a fringed leather vest. All she needed was a ten-gallon Stetson and a brace of nickel-plated Colt revolvers. She looked like a cross between Annie Oakley and Calamity Jane.

Bob said, "Moira, you've been to the camp a couple of times. You should know your way here from the other side by now."

"Well, Bobby-Boy, some of us just aren't used to the woods. One of you might have shown a little more concern."

I thought her enmity was pointed more at Larry than Bob or myself; she seemed to not acknowledge my presence. Bob said that they had a lot of things to discuss, looked at me, and said that I could stay if I wanted. I thought he was sending me a cue for departure.

I said, "Seems like this is a business meeting, so I'll let you get on with it. 'Night, all."

With that I was happy to get out of there. In the back of my mind I had been apprehensive about seeing Moira again. I wasn't sure how she would act. But her entrance sort of broke that ice a bit. I was relieved that there were others present. It seemed to me that we had used each other, and that our motivation was anything but a mutual love. I was pretty sure that there would be no more of the "horsing around," as Victoria had called it. I felt good and bad, guilty and elated, all at the same time. New feelings to accept and find a way of living with, I guessed.

I walked down the main road, thinking to go back to the tent and relax before I had to pick up Bruce for the trip to the campsite. I saw Martha coming up the road. I hadn't really had a chance to talk with her since the start of camp. Time seemed to go like the wind up here, and I had been really busy.

"Max, where've you been?" she said. "I haven't talked with you since the party, and the first session is nearly over."

"Hi, Martha, it's been crazy busy for me. I should've stopped by your Arts and Crafts shop to catch up. How's it going for you? Are you liking the camp? The work?"

"Oh, Max, I just love it up here. I'm so happy you called me. I have a great boss; Harvey and I have just hit it off. We're planning a really special sendoff for the kids at the end of the session. Larry said if it works we could do it at the end of every session. Oh, and before I forget…"
She fumbled in the pocket of her jeans and pulled out a purchase requisition. "Here, maybe you can take it up to the front office. Larry said he'd sign it."

I looked at it briefly. It was for fifty yards of chicken wire.

"Martha, whataya need with fifty yards of chicken wire?"

"Harvey has this great idea, and we're going to build something really neat. It's a secret but it'll will wow everyone!"

I stuck the order in my pocket, and we chatted for a while. I could tell she had something going with Harvey, so I wished her well. I decided that by now it was too late to go back to the tent. Instead, I headed back to the mess hall, got the wagon and pulled it around to the Camp Craft building.

Camp Craft was an interesting place. Along the side of
the building was a large rack on wheels that could be
attached to the wagon or a truck with a hitch. It held
eight canoes. The building itself was large and held
stacks of tents, miles of rope, tent pegs, water safety
equipment, hatchets, shovels and large containers that
could be filled with water and hung from low tree
branches. There were shelves and bins with all sorts of
camping foods, dried vegetables, fruits, cocoa, and re-
frigerators that held the fresh food. It was like a camping
department store.

 Fred and Bruce were piling up snacks and water containers, along with some other packages near the pile.

"What ho, Fred, lot of stuff here."

Fred wiped his brow and said, "Yeah, Mickey forgot a lot
of supplies for her campout. I told her that she was supposed to take what she could carry and said we'd deliver
the rest, but she never showed up. The kids are going to
want their dinner by now, I bet." He hefted a backpack
and held it up for me to see. "Dinner," he said. "It's too
late for her to start trying to cook, so I made up a batch
of sandwiches."

Bruce came around the side of the building and said,
"Good thing they're not on a canoe trip. We would never
catch up to them. Okay, Max, you ready for our en-
gagement with Miss Mickey?"

"Yeah, let's get it over with. Fred, you want to join us?"

"You gotta be kidding me, Max. There's something about that broad that just turns me off."

We loaded the stuff into the back of the wagon and Bruce and I scrambled in. I headed out the main road, took a left, and swung onto Route 54 for a short run. I made a left onto the road that led to the other side but took a right on a narrow dirt road before we got there. From that point it was only a few hundred yards to the campsite.

Once we got there it seemed like we were miles from anywhere. However, there was a short path through the woods that led back to the facilities on the other side. From there getting back to the camp was easy. It was a neat setup for the younger campers. A short hike from their cabins, and they thought they were in the wilderness. It reminded me of the "coal mine experience" at the Museum of Science and Industry back in Chicago. Visitors went down in an elevator that created the impression that they were descending forever; then *presto*, they walked into a "working coal mine." It seemed like they were hundreds of feet below the surface, but after the tour they went around a corner, and bingo, they were at the cafeteria in the museum basement.

Mickey's kids were sitting around a fire pit, and Mickey was trying to get a fire going when we arrived. They sat quiet, cross-legged, and looking like they weren't having much fun. Mickey had a smear of dirt on her forehead, her shirt was torn, and the tail hung out of her jeans. I could see at a glance that she was near to losing it. We got out of the wagon and walked over. I kept quiet and let Bruce handle this one.

"Hey, kids, how ya' doing? Hi, Mickey, need a little help with the fire?" Bruce was a master of jovial calm and understatement. I so admired that quality.

Mickey said, "Oh, Bruce, thanks so much for coming. I'm having just an awful time getting the fire lit. I can't find our backpack with dinner, and the kids are hungry and...."
She just trailed off. Bruce handed her the backpack, and while she handed out sandwiches, packets of fresh vegetables and apples to the kids, he made a circle of stones and said to the kids,

"Okay, listen up, kids. Who knows what kindling is?"

Little Ginny Jones raised a hand with a sandwich in it. With a mouth full of tuna she said, "Birch bark, dry grass or dry twigs, and if ya can't snap it, scrap it ! Right, Mister, Bruce?"

"That's great, Ginny! Now who sees some of those things?" The kids looked around. There was plenty of kindling close by, and they started bringing some of it over to him.

"Now, check it out, kids. This is really neat."

Bruce made a little teepee of twigs, put a few shavings of birch bark and some dry grass inside and said, "Presto, a one-match fire! Watch." He struck a wooden kitchen match and put it inside the teepee; it caught fire right away. He blew on it gently while adding some larg-

er sticks. In a couple of minutes he had a strong fire going.

"Now, eat your dinner and keep putting more sticks on
the fire so it won't go out."

Mickey came over and gave Bruce a hug and a warm
thanks. I could see she was relieved. Bruce asked her if
she would be okay for the rest of the night and she nodded, but I could see that she was nervous about being in
the woods. I stood like a mannequin, wishing that she
would at least acknowledge my presence.

Accepting that she just wasn't interested, I busied myself
unloading the rest of her supplies from the wagon. I was
invisible to Mickey. She never conceded my existence. I
felt like Claude Rains in the "Invisible Man." I felt an
emptiness I couldn't shake.

Bruce asked her if she and the kids had sufficient mos-
quito repellent. The kids would be spending the night in
sleeping bags and there were a couple of tents in case
of rain, but none had been set up. Bruce got that going,
and I helped while he gave me instructions.

When the site was all set up, he motioned to me that we
should go. Mickey thanked him again but said nothing to
me. I climbed into the wagon and waited while he gave
her some last minute pointers. She hugged him again.
Hugs for all; a cold shoulder for me.

Bruce stepped into the wagon and stated, "Well, I think
things should go okay. She was a mess, and it's a good

thing we came out for a check. The kids seem to know more than she does. It's scary."

I said nothing. I felt bad for her. I turned the wagon around and we went back to camp. I dropped Bruce at the Camp Craft building, and we went our separate ways. It had been one heck of a day, and I dropped into bed and slept like a bear in winter.

Chapter 11
A LITTLE TROUBLE GOES A LONG WAY

The next morning I woke up to a cool draft coming through the tent flaps. It was one of those cold fronts that come through Wisconsin, and this one was also damp. It was just the kind of weather that makes it hard to get going.

I dressed in jeans and a heavy sweatshirt and walked down to the ball field to watch the mist hovering over the grass. It was a natural phenomenon you didn't see or maybe wouldn't have time to notice in the city. The sun was just coming up and starting to burn the mist away. I thought the natural weather phenomena up here were beautiful.

I was about to turn toward the mess hall when a movement caught my eye. Across the ball field, where the path leading from the other side emerged, I saw Mickey and her little group of campers emerging out of the mist.

There was something wrong with the way they were walking.

Several had odd gaits. Mickey walked as if she'd been riding a horse for a week. I walked toward them, wondering if I should even approach her, given her demand that I not acknowledge her, and she, for a fact, never acknowledged me.

As I got closer, I saw that she looked very stressed. The kids looked tired and downcast; none looked up, only toward the ground. When I was about ten feet from Mickey she snapped angrily, "WHAT?"

I said, "Mickey, what's wrong? You look like you're at the end of your tether."

She dropped the armful of things she was carrying and let them fall to the ground. "Oh, Max, I feel so awful I could just cry."

The kids moved up and gathered around her, some hugging her legs and some putting their heads against her. None of the them said anything.

Little Ginny had a thumb in her mouth and with her other arm was hugging a Raggedy Ann Doll.

She said, "Mister, Max, I got a bad itch between my legs."

Others said they had an itch also, and that started everyone scratching their crotches.

Mickey said, "Max, I made some mistakes. Bad ones. I hope I don't get into trouble. Some of the kids got poison ivy. I was afraid of wild animals. I built up the fire too big and had some trouble with it. No one slept well, the kids were too young for a campout, and I didn't know how to help them with their fear of being out in the woods. I was afraid, too!"

"God, Mickey, are you telling me all these kids got poison ivy in their—um, private parts? How the hell did that happen?"

"Don't yell at me Max, I'm so sorry. Oh, god. I forgot to requisition toilet paper, and I guess the camp craft guys didn't catch it. So the kids had to, you know, go! And I told them we'd just do what the Indians did and use leaves."

"I can't believe this! Ok, listen. I want you to turn around and take the kids back to the infirmary, okay? Get Victoria and tell her what happened, and I'm sure she'll find a way to fix things up."

"Oh, Max, that's such a great idea! Why didn't I think of that?"

To my amazement she actually hugged me! I started to laugh. Laughter is contagious; and the kids started to giggle, and pretty soon even Mickey was smiling and tittering. I said, "All right, get going. I'll find Bruce, and we'll go straighten up the campsite and bring in the equipment. I'm sure this will be okay. You can't be the first counselor to make a mistake like this."

She turned the kids around and announced, "Come on, kids, we're going to fix up our itches. Okay?"

Still chuckling, I set out for the mess hall, and every now and then I turned to watch the little procession limping across the ball field. At least they were talking and seemed in better spirits.

Bruce Marshall was standing outside the mess hall when I got there, and he didn't look happy.

"Max, we have a problem. Lee up at the office got a call from the Wisconsin Conservation Department. They handle brush fires, and they were out at our campsite just now. One of their rangers spotted a fire where Mickey's cabin was camping."

"So? They put the fire out didn't they?"

"Well, yeah, they sent a crew and said it was out. They're going to file a report, and the camp could get a fine for our sloppy management. Also, I need to get out there right away to check on the fire. Can you take me out in the wagon? I want to take some equipment out there. And we need to bring in whatever Mickey's group used."

"Bruce, they put out the fire. What's the hurry?"

"Listen, Max, these guys aren't like a city fire department. A small deal like this is our responsibility and we need to make sure everything is running right."

"So, you want to go right now? I haven't even had coffee."

"Yes, now—sorry. Please, just bring the wagon to the Camp Craft building."

I nodded and jogged to the back of the mess hall where the wagon was parked. I pulled it around to the Camp Craft Building, where Bruce had a pile of equipment waiting in front.

"Geez, Bruce, what's all this stuff?"

"Well, I have a couple of bags of sand, two Indian pumps, shovels, and an axe. I think that's all we'll need."

"What's an Indian pump?" He looked at me with a look of disbelief and then said, "Look, I'll show you. It's just a simple tank that holds water. This hose has a pump on the end and when you pump the slide..." He demonstrated and a shot of water came out of the thing.

"Okay," I said, "Let's go."

We loaded the wagon. I was grumpy thinking that we were going to miss breakfast. Instead we would be dragging a lot of equipment to nowhere for nothing. Bruce was quiet and contemplative on the way out.

Finally, he said, "You know, Max, I don't have a very good opinion of Mickey. I never did in Chicago, and I think that out here I think she's a disaster. I can't figure out how she even got a job as a counselor. She has no college education, no camping experience or even any interest in it. On top of all that, I don't think she's even interested in kids. You make anything out of all this?"

I didn't want to break my promise to Mickey, and wasn't comfortable holding out on a friend I'd known since kindergarten.

While I was struggling to find an answer, he said, "I think Mickey either fooled someone or had a connection to get a job here. I've seen Larry hanging around her a lot. He's too old for her, but there's something going on."

I said, "Gee, Bruce, I bet you're right." I let it go at that.

We got to the campsite and it was a mess. The campfire had clearly been overbuilt; you didn't need to be a mountain man to see that. The fire had gone well beyond the stone circle built to contain it. Some of the bushes nearby were charred, and even a couple of trees overhead exhibited burned branches. The surrounding grass was blackened as well. I was wondering how Mickey and the kids got out of there without seeing a fire. The timing was all off. There wouldn't have been time for her to leave, come back to camp, and have the fire department come out. I didn't have time to think more about it, though.

Bruce looked around and muttered, "We were lucky. By the looks of that fire it, could have been a lot worse." He walked back to the wagon and came back with two Indian pumps and a shovel.

"Here, Max, take this and start spraying around those bushes. I'll start here and work my way right; you go left 'till we wet down the whole area. I started to protest. The fire looked out to me, but before I could get a word out I felt heat on my feet. Looking down, I saw that I was standing on a patch of grass that had suddenly flared up. I jumped and gave a yelp, and Bruce whipped around and shot a stream of water at my shoes. Just then more grass burst into flames. Smoke billowed up around the perimeter of the campsite.

Bruce came charging over, and we stood back to back. He yelled, "Max, strap that pump on and start using it!"

I got panicky, "Bruce," I howled, "We're surrounded!"

"Just get that pump going! We'll be okay!"

I don't know how long we were at it. It seemed like only a minute; time collapsed as we frantically sprayed. The smoke from the fire mixed with the water and steam hissed up at us. Ash flew all around as a small breeze whipped the flames higher. Bruce ran out of water, shouting that I should keep pumping. He grabbed the shovel and dug it into the sandy ground, using the dirt and sand to put out small flareups. In the end we got the fire doused. Bruce leaned wearily on his shovel and wheezed that I could stop pumping. I had been out of water for a while and didn't even realize it.

"Max, I'm glad you were here. I don't think I could have handled this on my own."

He was calm as usual. I was shaking. I had never been involved in anything like a fire before, and for a while I wasn't sure we would get out of this one alive. It wasn't that the fire seemed so massive; it was that for a time we were completely surrounded, and the heat, smoke and steam were really terrifying.

"Bruce, what if Mickey's kids had been caught here?"

"That's what I've been trying to tell you, Max. She doesn't belong here. She could get these kids hurt or worse. It doesn't take much to get in trouble in the woods, and her judgment is very poor."

"Are you going to report her for this?"

"I have to. Let's go, I think we've got this thing managed. Take me to the office."

We packed up the camping gear that was now either scorched or soggy, dragged ourselves into the wagon, and were back at the front office in a short time. I parked in front and we went in. Lee took a look at us and started to laugh.

"Well, what have you guys been up to? You look like you've been tunneling to China."

I said, "Lee, what are you talking about?"

"You guys go in the washroom back there and look at yourselves!"

We did. We were covered with soot. It was in our hair, on our clothes, and certainly on our faces. I looked down and saw that the soles of my gym shoes had melted. It looked like I was wearing pancakes with shoelaces.

Bruce smiled at our images in the mirror. I started to giggle, more from anxiety than humor. Lee kept cackling, and then it caught Bruce. Soon Larry came out of Ken's office. He'd taken it over since Ken was out, and he wanted to know what was so funny. Well, he saw us and joined in. Then Moira came out of Larry's office, where she was working. You get the idea. But it wasn't so hilarious when Bruce asked if the three of them could go into an office. They closed the door, and I left wondering if it would be curtains for Mickey.

I left the wagon where I had parked it. I walked back to the tent area, threw cold water on my face, got a change of clothes, dug in my duffel bag for my only other pair of shoes, and went to get cleaned up.
 After that I decided that I owed myself a good hearty breakfast and went to the mess hall for whatever was left. Cold eggs were all I could find. My luck was running low this morning. I was about to leave when Frieda asked why I looked so down. I gave her a brief summary, and darned if she didn't fix me an omelet. With real eggs no less, not that powdered stuff from a chemical company!

I had been gone an hour by then, and went back to the office to get my clipboard and get the day started. It seemed like I'd already put in an entire day. Lee looked up and said, "Boy, you missed some fireworks after you left."

I said, "Thant's just fine with me, Lee, I already had enough fireworks for the summer, thank you. What happened?"

"Well, Bruce, Larry and Moira went into Ken's office, and just then I got a call from Victoria over at the infirmary. She wanted to talk to Larry, and I told her he was in a meeting. She insisted and said it was important, so I knocked on the door and Larry took the call. I don't know what she said to him, but soon after that there was a lot of screaming back and forth between Larry and Moira. Bruce left disgusted and finally they stopped fighting. It sounded awful for a while."

"So, you don't know exactly what happened?"

"No. But I've worked here at camp for six years, and I never heard anything like it between camp leadership."

"Well," I said, "I think there's a lot of stress since Ken's been gone. I'm hoping things will work out. Where is everyone now?"

"Larry's in Ken's office, Moira's in Larry's office, and both of 'em said they didn't want to be disturbed. My switch-board here shows that they're both on phone calls now."

I got my clipboard out of my mail cubby where I kept it. Lee would put in work orders or signed requisitions for things to be purchased, or people to be picked up in town. I sat at the spare desk in the office area to get my day organized.

"Hey, Lee, who am I picking up at the 11:00 o'clock train? It says here I have to meet it."

"Oh, right," she whispered, "It's Professor Linzer. He's coming back up to spend some time here. Ken asked him. He's concerned that Larry and Moira need some extra guidance."

"Does that mean that Ken won't be back? Have you had any more news?"

"Max, keep this under your hat, okay? Mrs. G. called yesterday and Ken is still having problems. His gall bladder apparently kicked off something with his heart, so they want to do more tests. The doctors told him to take it easy till they figure out if there's a bigger problem. And, between us chickens, if Ken can't be here, it will be good to have the professor. I've known him since I came to work for the camp, and he's a cagey old guy who will get things on a better track."

"All right, hey, it's near ten A.M., so I'd better get on the move. I need to get the wagon unloaded before I can go to town. I see you have a pickup order on my clipboard for... What's this? Fifty pounds of beef balls?"

I started to snicker, and Lee said, "Oh, that's Frieda again. She wants *meat balls!*"

Lee blushed and giggled. I snorted, "I gotta get out of here, this place is nuts!"

"*Nuts!*" she cried, turning red as a beet, and started laughing all over again.

I left the office and drove over to Camp Craft to drop off the equipment. I was hoping to catch Bruce, who came out as I arrived. He ambled over to the wagon.

"Max, I want to go get cleaned up, but you should know that Mickey left the campground last night not long after we were there. She took the kids to the infirmary and got them into one of the empty cabins. They stayed there the whole night. She was trying to sneak them back into the camp when you saw them on the ball field this morning! I can't believe what she did!"

"Wait, Bruce, how do you know this?"

"Victoria called Larry while I was in the office talking to him and Moira. She said that the kids had caught poison ivy and were dirty, tired and pretty hungry, so she helped get them straightened out. Mickey gave her a cock-and-bull story about the campout going haywire. Victoria smelled a rat, checked out the empty cabin, and found some of the kid's stuff there. Her call started an argument between Larry and Moira.
Moira wanted to fire Mickey right then. Larry said they needed to talk with Ken, that Mickey hadn't enough training and would be okay with some support. It was pretty ugly. I hope I never get onto the wrong side of Moira."

"So, is that where it stands?"

"I don't know; it wasn't any of my business. I made my report and left. I gotta get cleaned up. I stink like a campfire."

He stalked off, and I don't recall ever having seen him so upset. I think that's when I finally let go of my fantasy that Mickey and I would ever be together. After that I felt bad for her, but whatever love I had withered like a plant that somebody forgot to water.

I had work to do. I always felt better when I worked. I forgot my troubles whenever I had a purpose. I unloaded the Indian pumps, shovels, sand bags (that we forgot to use,) and the axe. I brushed sand out of the back of the wagon and headed for the Walkerville Locker, fifty pounds of 'beef balls," and about a hundred and fifty pounds of goof ball: the Professor. I laughed at my own humor and felt a twinge of guilt. I actually liked the professor. I thought the place needed Mr. G. more than anyone, but the professor was a good backup. I kicked over the engine, put the wagon in gear and headed for Walkerville.

By now I had a nice friendly relationship with Charlie Wilson, the clerk at the Locker.
"Hey, Charlie, how's it going?"

"Hello, Max. Say, you aren't going into the camp's locker, are ya?"

I mean, what else would I do there?
"Yeah, I need a box of meatballs. why? Is there a problem?"

"Max, we just had a delivery for the camp of forty boxes of government farm surplus butter. We stacked it in your locker back there. Might take you a while to get at that box of meatballs."

He was never more right. I had to hustle to unload the butter to get the meatballs, and then load all the butter back in the locker. Meanwhile, I had to stack the boxes in the narrow aisle, and of course, the guy who rented the locker next to the camp's came in to get his dead bear head and pelt because the taxidermist was ready to stuff it. It took forty-five minutes of horsing around with boxes to get the meatballs, and I was half frozen by the time I got to the train station. The Professor was sitting on the bench at the station, waiting and smoking a pipe.

"Hi, Max! Boy, you look like you've been out skiing! Where'd you get that healthy glow?"

" Hello, Professor. You can get one too if you want to spend an hour at the Walkerville Food Locker loading boxes. About zero Fahrenheit there, gets your blood moving."
The Professor laughed and said, "C'mon, you can warm up loading my baggage. I'm anxious to get out to the camp."

I got his luggage on board and headed out of Walk-erville.
I said, "Professor, nice to have you back up here. I enjoyed our chat last time. By the way, you never told me how you knew Fritz and Magda, remember?"

"Max, it's an interesting story and I'll share it, but please keep it to yourself. Fritz was formerly a tank commander with the Wehrmacht during World War II. He was captured early when the Allies landed at Tunisia. That was the eventual Italian campaign; first Sicily, then up the Italian Peninsula.

Anyway, he never wanted to be in a war, and was not a member of the Nazi Party. When he surrendered, he became a prisoner here in the US. Not many people know that we had a lot of German prisoners here during the war. At the time I was in Army Intelligence here in the US, and we were responsible for sorting out prisoners and getting them jobs on farms around the country; only those who we thought would be safe, mind you. The farmers were short of manpower. So I got to know Fritz well. I placed him with a farm up here in Wisconsin."

"It wasn't with Titus Akers, was it?"

"No, but I heard about your adventure with Marilyn Monroe. Mrs. Van Lauder told us the story at the last Board meeting, and it went over really big!"

He chuckled at the memory.

"We placed him at another farm near here, a family that spoke German. Fritz was a model prisoner. He met Magda up here, and after the war stayed on until he could earn enough to buy that little coffee shop. I only wish his location would have been closer to Walkerville. But he tells me that he does okay. Max, let's talk about some current issues, all right?"

"Okay, Professor, What's on your mind?"
He got out his pipe and stoked it with some tobacco. He took his time packing it down, lighting it, tamping the hot coal down, re-lighting the pipe. I wondered if he was re-

ally all that concerned about the pipe or what he wanted to talk about. We were about twenty minutes from camp by now.

"Max, you have any idea why I've come back to camp? Just give it to me straight, you don't have to diddle around, okay?"

"Well, Professor, I'm guessing now, but here's what I think. Ken might be a lot sicker than anyone is letting on. The Executive Director, Margie's boss, might be worried about how Larry and Moira will run the camp. There's been some weird things going wrong up here since I came up— like Jack Ryan falling off the mess hall roof, a forest fire that was our fault, maybe other stuff I don't know about. Am I close?"

The professor didn't answer right away. He sucked on his pipe and let smoke out of his nose. Finally, he said, "What else, Max?"

"Isn't that enough? I think Ken wanted someone up here who had some authority and judgment."

"Yeah, that's good. Look, Max, I value the perspective of the camp driver. In the past I've learned a lot about what goes on from the camp drivers here, even that adolescent ape, Crash Kelly. Took a while to sift out his anger, but he knew what was going on. I'm betting you do too, even with the short time you've been up here. I'd be interested to know whatever perceptions you have of how things are going. Just let it fly; just between you and me."

I thought about that for a bit. I liked the Professor; he was a straight shooter, right or wrong. He said what he believed, and unlike a lot of adults, he seemed to be truly interested in what younger people thought. So, as he asked, I just let it fly.

"Professor, I don't think all of the staff have been trained well enough. I thought Jack Ryan's attempt to rappel down the mess hall was a grandstand play to look like a hero to the girls. I didn't think that Larry should have let him do it. And one more thing; I have some thoughts about the kids, the campers. I got to know a couple of them."

"What about them?"

Well, Professor, you have kids from some affluent families, and you have some colored kids and other poverty-level kids. Right?"

"Yeah, sure. Please, go on."

"So, how come all the camp staff are white upper-middle class kids from good colleges? How come you don't have any colored staff? How come the one Indian guy I met up here who's going to college doesn't fit in with the rest of the staff, feels like he can't belong and ends up washing dishes every year? And I got one more thing bothering me. The camp philosophy is all about friendship and learning to get along, but you have a couple of administrators who get along like cats and dogs, and I bet I don't have to name anyone, okay?"

The Professor was quiet for a few moments, tinkering with his pipe. Then he muttered to himself, "Well, I asked for it, and I got it!"

"Hey, Professor, I'm not going to get canned for what I said, am I?"

"Max, if it was in the budget, I'd give you a raise for what you just said."

I still didn't know what a budget was, but I knew by now it had cost me a couple of raises, the last one from Mrs. Silverman. I was worried. I hoped I'd get paid for all my friends that I helped to find jobs.

"Thanks, Max, that gives me some thoughts for what I need to do. Oh, and about Ken, yes, they're still not sure what's going on with him, but I think he'll recover. We're almost at camp. How about dropping me at the office, and would you take my luggage over to Ken's place? I'll be staying there."

The Professor was quiet after that, and gazed pensively out the car window and puffed on his pipe. I could tell the wheels in his head were moving, though. You could almost hear them grind.

I dropped the Professor off at the office porch and dealt with his luggage. It was now lunchtime, and I needed to deliver those damned meatballs before they thawed, so I went to the mess hall and got them in the freezer. Lunch was underway, and I went in and found a seat with the kitchen boys. Mickey and her cabin were there. The kids looked better than they did earlier in the morning. She managed to swivel her back to me when I walked into the dining room.

"Hey, stranger," Leon queried, "Where you been hiding?"

I told the guys that I'd been on the road doing this or that and missing meals on a regular basis. Then I dug into the food. Martha came over and asked about her chicken wire, which I'd totally forgotten about. The requisition was still in my pocket so, I promised her I'd get it signed and pick the stuff up later in the day. Yet another trip to Walkerville. Things settled down for the rest of the day.

Chapter 12
Transitions and Changes Unexpected

The first session was nearly over. In a few days, we would be seeing to it that the kids got packed up, their luggage moved to the area in front of the mess hall and a reverse of their arrival only three weeks earlier. Before that would happen, there would be a ceremony marking the end of the camp experience for the kids. Whatever that would be was something of a mystery.

I'd received purchase orders for chicken wire, lumber, and a lot of other art supplies, and had delivered it to Martha and Harvey. They were super-secretive about their project and said only that it was to be part of the end-of-session ceremony. I guessed that the waterfront staff was also going to play a role in it because I saw Ted Wilson, the Assistant Waterfront Director, in the Arts and Crafts building a number of times, and once in a while I saw Harvey down at the waterfront talking to Al Swanson, their top honcho.

Meanwhile, every time I was up at the front office, Lee told me that Larry, Moira, and the Professor were spending a lot of time in meetings. She said, "Honestly, Max, I'm the one who types up minutes of meetings around here, and no one will even tell me what they're talking about. Sometimes they're on the phone long distance with Ken, and once they even had a conversation with the Board Executive Committee. Something is going on, but it beats me what."

"So, what's in the minutes then? You type them."

"Ah," she said, That's the big question. They're not giving me anything to type. After they break up, Moira goes into her office and is in there typing the minutes herself. We never had any of that secrecy when Ken ran the place. Oh, that reminds me. You have yet another pickup at the train this morning."

"Oh? Who's coming? Ken, maybe?"

"No, it's a new staff member. Her name is— let's see...."

"Hm, sounds Chinese."

"No, silly, it's... her name is... I have it here in my papers... Okay, Anita Jackson."

"Right, I'll get her. Where do I deliver her?" It was a hard question to ask; however, I had to know.

"Um…" she shuffled more papers, and the suspense was hard to handle. " Moira said… Unit 2, cabin 1."

"Lee, are you sure of that? Unit 2, cabin 1 is Mickey Kamen's cabin."

"Yep. Moira was emphatic when she told me, and the way she talked I didn't want to question her. I knew it was Mickey's cabin."

"I got a bad feeling about this. Any, uh… anyone going back to Chicago on the four o'clock train, by chance?"

"Not that I know of— so far, anyway. Here's another requisition of supplies for Arts and Crafts. Boy, whatever they're cooking up is busting their budget line."

I looked at the list; some hardware items, a few quarts of water-base paint, and a dozen goose feathers. Goose feathers?

"Lee, where the hell do I find a dozen goose feathers?"

"Oh, there's a butcher shop in town on Second Street, right off the main square. I called all over to find goose feathers. The butcher told me that most people don't order them at his place, but he knew where to get some. Geez, he wanted two bucks apiece for them. Larry told me to order them anyway. The shop is called 'Lutz Premium Meats.' Ask for Rudy. Better get going. It's past ten already. Oh, Max, one more thing. There's a staff meeting for everyone tonight after bedtime. You and the other specialists are asked to come; everyone except the kitchen boys. Okay, move it!"

I rushed out of the office door, looking at my list that now included a goose chase for goose feathers. Unbeliev- able. On the way out, I bumped into Tori the dancer. She said, "Hi, Max, where's the fire? You almost knocked me off the porch!"

"Oh, so sorry! I'm heading for town. Didn't mean to bump you, Tori."

I have to admit that tall good-looking women intimidated me, and Tori fit that category like rubber gloves on a surgeon.

She said, "It's my day off, and I was hoping to catch you and get a lift into town. They have a small dance school, of all things, up here. I want to spend some time there. Would you take me in?"

"Sure, I'd be happy to. I'm heading out to town right now. You ready to leave?"

"I'm all yours!"

"I wish."

She laughed, took my arm and said, "Just like Fred As- taire and Ginger Rogers!"

I repeated, "I wish", and she voiced that sparkling laugh again. I thought, *could it be she likes me?* but the little matter-of-fact voice we all have in our heads declared, *"Run the errand, dummy. She just needs a ride."* We got in the wagon and headed for Walkerville. I had a hard time keeping my eyes on the road and off her legs. I wondered how many accidents could be attributed to shorts. *"Not shorts,"* said the little voice, *"Legs!"* To which I said out loud, " Oh, shut up."

And Tori exclaimed, "Huh? I didn't say anything."

"Oh, I'm sorry, I was thinking about something. I just got carried away. Where did you find out about a dance studio up here?" I queried, to change the subject.

"I go to dance and singing lessons in Baltimore. Where I'm from. I met a girl there who's from Wisconsin, and her parents run a small studio here that's pretty well known in this area. I told her I would pay them a visit if I got the camp job."

"I thought that dancers and singers and show people worked in summer theater this time of year. How come you're not doing that?"

"Yeah, I wish."

My inner voice said, *she wishes too,* and the matter-of-fact voice replied, *yeah, sure.*

"My parents are against my doing that, and told me I would have to be either twenty-one or on my own financially to do summer stock. I'm too young and too broke this year. Maybe next year; I'll be twenty one by then.

So, it's kids and camp for me now. I do love the kids, though. How did you wind up here, Max?"

"Long story, but the short version is that my sister works for the social service organization that runs the camp, among other things. She got me an interview to be a dishwasher. It's another story how I wound up with this job."

"You know, there's talk among the staff that you got into a fight with that guy Crash, and they fired him? Is that true?"

"Oh, that's just a rumor."

"You know what I think? I think you're the kind of guy who wouldn't say."

Time, I thought, *to change the subject*, "We're almost at Walkerville. Where did you say the studio was?"

"My friend said it's on Second Street, right off a town square, number 130. She said you can't miss it; there are a bunch of store fronts, and the studio is in one of them."

"I have a pickup on Second Street so we'll just park there and look around."
We reached the center of town. I hadn't spent much time there since I started driving for the camp. The train station and the Locker were my main destinations; they were out a bit further from the main drag.

The square was bigger than I imagined it. There were
trees, a playground, and a large monument to those who
died in the Civil War. On each corner of the monument
stood canons. I recognized one as a Napoleon and another as a Parrot rifled canon.
Old men sat on benches and some fed pigeons. On the
far side I saw kids playing with small toy sailboats in a
pond. Mothers sat nearby watching. The scene reminded me of a French painting I saw once in an art book. I
spotted the butcher shop off the square, and further
down was a sign that said, "Metropolitan Studio. Learn,
Dance and Live!"

"This way, Tori." I pointed to the street and we strolled
over. "I have an errand and someone to pick up at the
train at eleven o'clock. How are you getting back to the
camp?"

"Oh, my friend's parents said they'd drive me. We're
having lunch together so that they can find out about the
kind of lessons I take in Baltimore. I'll be fine. Max,
thanks so much for taking me. You're a doll. I'll see you
at camp."

She squeezed my arm, and I mumbled a "you're welcome.'

She walked off with feline-like magical moves, and I
watched her go. I wasn't used to being with girls like her,
and it bothered me that I felt intimidated. I didn't understand how I could be comfortable in a fight with a guy
like Crash, who came at me with a knife, and so shaky
with someone like Tori, who was so pleasant to be with. I
had learned how to fight; I figured I'd probably have to

learn to be around women who rattle me, like Tori and Kitty Katz, for example. Enough philosophy; I had a mission to accomplish.

I had important things to do, like getting to Lutz's for goose feathers. It wasn't exactly like looking for the Northwest Passage, but it was my job.

A bell jangled when I opened the door and a man came out from the back of the shop. People have a notion how someone will look in a butcher shop, a stereotype. I expected a big guy with a meaty red face wearing a straw boater and a white apron with blood all over it. But this guy was about five feet six, weighed maybe one thirty tops, and his face was pale. I was even off about his apron. It was clean.
"Hi," I said, "are you Rudy?"

"Yep, you the guy from the camp for the feathers?"

"Yep."

"Hang on a minute." He went into the back, came out with a small package of beige butcher paper, and put it on the counter.
"Camp lady said to send her the bill, so just sign this for me." I signed.

"Say, where'd you get goose feathers? Just curious."

"Oh, a guy named Charlie Wilson up at the Walkerville Locker got 'em. He's a hunter, lot of guys up here hunt. It wasn't too hard for him to get the stuff."

"Right. Well, thanks."

I took the feathers; the package was light as, well—feathers. I thought I could have gotten them for a lot less than twenty-four bucks. I heard my dad saying, "Geez, Max, why didn't you think to ask the locker guy about the feathers? Could'a made a few bucks there."

Off to the train station. I was late; the train got there before I did by a good quarter-hour. I looked around. Only one person was there with a bunch of suitcases. She was colored. I figured she was waiting for someone else. After a minute or so she walked over to the wagon.

"Must be from the camp, right? Can't be more than one pale green ugly Chevy wagon around here. Am I right, or am I right?"

I hadn't expected a colored woman. I said, "Yes, I'm Max. Are you Anita?"

"Mm-hmm."

I slid out of the wagon, offered her my hand and said, "I'll get your luggage. Please, hop in and make yourself comfy."

I started collecting her bags. By now I was used to heavy suitcases, but hers were over the top. I thought that she should be traveling with a dozen Sherpa guides. I got into the car, and she was staring at me wide-eyed.

I said, "Is there something wrong? I'm sorry I was late."

She said, "Just not used to such nice service from a white-bread honky!"

I felt hurt and must have looked it, because she picked it up immediately.

"Hey, look, "Max, is it? Let's start over. I'm just kidding you, okay, honey?"

"Okay, Anita. You sort of caught me off guard. I meant no offense."

She said, "You know, I'm a bit nervous about coming up here and doing a job I never did before."

Instead of starting the wagon, I leaned back and took a fresh look at her. She had enormous eyes, long thick hair pulled straight back in a ponytail, high cheekbones, and a very sexy mouth with a wall-to-wall smile and beautiful teeth. I didn't get intimidated, at least not right away, as I guessed she wasn't a woman with whom I would ever have a relationship. But I thought she was one of the sexiest women I'd ever met!
"So," I said, " Are you replacing one of the camp coun-selors?"

"That's the plan. I got a call from Dr. Linzer a couple of days ago. He asked if I could come up and help out. I never worked at a camp before. I did teach pre-school, though, and he said the job was with younger kids."

"So, you could just drop what you were doing and come up?"

"Well, yes. It was easier than you might figure. I'm in school, not working. I was actually looking for a summer job, so getting Dr. Linzer's call worked out really well."

"How do you know the Professor?"

"Oh, he helped me get a scholarship for my graduate work. I'm at the University of Chicago; SSA, the social work program. They call it 'Social Service Administration.' Dr. Linzer and my uncle are friends. He wrote a letter of recommendation for me, helped get my scholarship. I'm done with my first year; one more to go for a MSW. You know what that is?"

"Master of Social Work, I think."

"Yes, that's right, it's a Master's of Social Work. I want to work with disturbed children."

"So, you're a group social worker like a lot of the camp staff?"

"No, I want to do therapy when I get my degree, work on an individual basis with children who have emotional difficulties."

"That makes sense to me. I haven't figured out much about the group workers and what they do."

I didn't say it, but I thought it was a shame that she didn't want to work with disturbed camp staff; there was plenty to learn up here. I liked this woman. She was open, sexy, sensitive, and, I thought, tough. I didn't know any colored women; I didn't know any Indians until I came to this place. My world was small and simple. My parents' values were straightforward and simple. I felt there was so much I didn't know about people, about how complicated relationships were. I felt that my world was growing in ways that were new and different, and camp had opened that world up for me.

"Well," I said, "There are plenty of social workers up at the camp, so you'll have plenty of meetings to get to know them. They have meetings about everything, it seems. Last night I heard them talking about whether to have dinner or not."

"Oh, no, you didn't! You're just kidding me."

"They did! It was a very complex discussion. Pros, cons, impact on the environment, nutritional philosophy and concerns, starving kids in Alabama...." I went on and she began to laugh. It was a good hearty laugh, and I liked to hear it.

So, do you know what you'll be doing?"

"Um-hmm," Dr. Linzer had a woman call me to explain the job. It's with a group of younger kids who need a little TLC."

"TLC?"

"Tender Love and Care. What I was told was they're experience was less than what the camp thought they should get, and the lady told me I'd take over for their counselor."

"Was the 'lady' by chance named Miss Wallace?"

"Mmm, how'd you know that?"

"She's the Personnel Director."

My heart sank at the conversation. It meant that my fears about Mickey getting the sack were justified. I was puzzled, though. How could I feel bad if I no longer cared about her? I kicked the engine over and said, "Well, we'd best get you there."

We drove in silence for a while. Anita asked if we were close to the camp, and I sensed that the closer we got, the more tense she seemed. When we started off she had been cheerful and chatty, but it trailed off, and I wondered if she was as tough as she initially seemed. Finally, she broke the silence.

"Max, I'm not sure how to say this, but, ah, will I be the only person of color up at the camp?"

"Well, pretty much, except for some of the campers. But, hey, I'm Jewish (I said it!) and my friend Bill Lightfoot is Indian and everyone is pretty friendly, but, yeah, you'll be the only staff 'person of color.' I don't think it will be a problem; there're nice folks there."

She became quiet again. I realized that this time Mickey's lies, evasions of the truth, and all- around second rate performance had finally caught up with her. I saw Moira's hand in this. She'd finally gotten her way, and it was curtains for Mickey.

We arrived at the camp, and I told Anita we should check in at the front office. Afterward, I'd take her to her cabin and help her to get moved in. I took her into the office and introduced her to Lee, who started in with the orientation routine. I said I'd wait on the porch. Lee prompted, "Max, don't forget, there's a staff meeting tonight on the other side. I was told to tell you especially to show up."

"Okay, Lee, I remember. I'll be out on the porch."

I sat on one of the lounge chairs figuring I should help Anita with her luggage and maybe show her around a bit. Down deep that I wanted to see if she was really assigned to Mickey's cabin. I wanted to know if Mickey's stuff was gone, and to know if Mickey was gone as well. It was also past lunch time, and I thought I should do what I could to get Anita some food if she was hungry.

Just then I saw the Professor, Larry and Moira coming up the road from the mess hall. Larry and the Professor were walking side-by-side, and Moira lagged a little behind them. It seemed like the three of them were engaged in a tense exchange. They were too far away for me to hear anything. As they got closer, the Professor put his hand up and they stopped talking. Moira wore a sour expression on her face.

"Hi, everyone," I said, with overstated cheer I didn't feel. "Have a good lunch?"

The Professor said, "Hello, Max. Getting a bit tired of macaroni and cheese, but yes, lunch was good. Say, did you pick up a young woman at the train this morning? Name's Anita."

"Yessir, Professor, she's right in the office getting set up with Lee."

The three of them marched right into the office. Neither Larry nor Moira bothered to say hello. Moira in particular seemed evasive in any acknowledgement. Larry simply seemed otherwise preoccupied. They still hadn't come out after twenty minutes or so. I thought I should go inside to find out what was holding up the works. After all, it was getting late and I'd missed another meal. Seemed like I was always hungry. Then I remembered the goose feathers and thought I should deliver them to Arts and Crafts. First things first. I strode into the office. Lee was alone.

"Hey, where'd everyone disappear to, Lee?"

"Oh, they're in Ken's office, all of them, and they've been in there since the 'Three Musketeers' showed up from lunch.

I said 'nuts' and Lee tittered and blushed. I guessed she was still thinking about the 'beef balls.'

"Lee, I'll be back. Tell Anita I'll get her to her cabin. It shouldn't take me more than fifteen minutes to get back here. Okay?"

"Okay, Max."

I left and went to Arts and Crafts. Only Harvey was free; Martha was with a bunch of kids doing instruction on a potter's wheel. The floor and walls were splattered with clay. The kids looked like the 'Clay People' from an old Flash Gordon film, but they were having fun.

"Harvey, I got you the goose feathers," I said, handing them over. He opened the package and blurted, "Ooo-whee, babe, these are just what we need!"

"What're they for, Harv?"

"Big secret, man. You'll see at the end of session. Whoa, gonna be cool, daddy-o!"

I left thinking, *what a schmuck*, and doubled back to the mess hall. I got a couple of sandwiches together, bagged up some potato chips, and reached in the cooler for some cokes. Then I hightailed it back to the office. Anita was waiting on the porch.

"Anita, how about a picnic? I got some sandwiches for us. Are you hungry?"

"Max, I'm famished!"

So we ate a quick lunch. Anita wolfed down the sand-wich. She skipped the chips.

"Gotta watch the figure, honey."

After we finished, we drove over to the girls' units. I gave a running commentary on the physical layout of the camp, echoing the presentation given to me only a few weeks back by Crash.

I parked the wagon near Mickey's cabin and got a couple of Anita's bags out of the back. I felt an emptiness in my stomach despite the hefty sandwich. I walked up the three wooden steps and into the counselor's cabin. My hand clenched the doorknob to Mickey's cabin, and I froze with anxiety. This was it; I was going to learn if she was really gone. Even though I knew it had to be, it bothered me that I had lost her for good this time.

Her room was empty; no clipboard, no clothes hanging or on the floor, no pictures on the wall, wet bathing suits on a hook, socks on the bed, or schedules for activities. There was nothing that an occupied counselor cabin would contain. Without realizing it, I let the suitcases I was holding slip to the floor. They went down with a thump. I stood, stone-like, staring at her empty bed. A chill went through my body, though the afternoon was warm. My nose began to sting, and I felt tears coming. Mickey was really gone.

I heard Anita coming up the stairs to the cabin. She chirped, "Max, I got the last bag. I can't thank you enough for.... Hey, are you all right? Is something wrong?"

I felt her hand on my shoulder. I didn't move. I was near tears and didn't want to be embarrassed. She came around and gazed into my face with concern.
"Max," she said, "Are you sick? You don't look so good. You're really pale."

"I got a pain in my stomach just now." I faked it by leaning over and groaning, "Cramps! I'd better find a bathroom." I pulled away from her and tore out of the door, down the stairs, and into the wagon. I heard her call, "Jeez! I hope you feel better! Don't forget the meeting tonight."

I pulled away from the cabin at full tilt and nearly hit some campers coming up from the lake. I jammed my foot on the brake, and tried to get hold of my reeling emotions. I parked behind the mess hall, and walked down a seldom-used path toward the lakeshore, a couple of hundred yards from the beach and its turmoil. I sank down on a fallen log, put my face in my hands, and cried like a seven-year-old kid who had lost his favorite toy.

It took a while, but I got it all out at last, and started feeling better. I was done with Mickey for good. I began noticing little frogs jumping at the water's edge. I heard birds in the trees, and saw small fish swimming in the lake near the shore. My world was starting to open; I felt lighter than I had in weeks. I splashed some water on my face, straightened my back and walked back to the wagon.

I still had some things remaining on my work orders for the day, and wanted to keep busy. Even though I felt better, I kept thinking about Mickey. She was gone as suddenly as she had appeared, like a magician's model in an act. The camp seemed empty for me. Mickey had caused me only heartache, and I had at last cried her out of my system. I still wished things had gone differently. She was like a wound that had healed but still left pain.

Chapter 13
No End to the Surprises Up Here

I finished up my day and went back to the tents to clean up for dinner and the meeting that was to follow. As I entered the mess hall, I looked for Mickey's table but Phyllis and now Anita were with the kids. I didn't see Mickey anywhere. Kitty was also missing; maybe she was off today. I sat at a table with the other specialist staff. Everyone was especially quiet, and dinnertime rolled by quickly. We had meatloaf, my favorite, although there were the usual complaints from others.

I was sitting next to Bruce, who leaned over and said, "You know anything about this meeting tonight?"

"Nope. Is that why everyone is so quiet? Something going on?"

"There's a rumor going around about a staff shakeup, and some other announcements. Thought you might have picked something up at the office."

"I think something's going on, all right, but I don't know what. Lee tells me that Moira, Larry and the Professor have been in lots of meetings, and sometimes there's a lot of arguing. She let on that Moira has been typing the minutes of the meetings instead of her. You can make of it whatever you think. I don't know anything for sure."

Bruce turned toward Freddy and told him what we were talking about. Fred replied that the brown gravy for the meatloaf had too much salt, not enough pepper and that the flour hadn't been fully folded in and mixed.

 Bruce goggled at Fred like he was out of his mind. "For Pete's sake, aren't you interested in what's going on in this place?"

Fred looked hurt and said, "What could be more important than their recipe for brown gravy, I'd like to know! If they weren't having shortcake and strawberries for desert, I'd walk out of here right now. You don't have to get so rough."

Bruce flashed him a disgusted look and went back to eating. I finished up and said, "I'm going back to the office to check if anything's going on there. I'll let you know if I learn anything."

I'd just gotten to the office porch when the door opened. Out came the "Three Musketeers" as Lee had tagged Larry, Moira and the Professor.

The Professor exclaimed, "Oh, good, Max. We have some things to take to the other side. Could you drive them over?"

"Sure, Professor, where are they?"
He pointed to the counter inside the office. There was a pile of manila folders, a projector and a screen. Next to those items was a large box from "The Walkerville Bakery."

"So, what are we having at the meeting, movies and chocolate eclairs, I hope?"

Moira said, "It's an overhead document projector, Max. And the box is donuts for the meeting, not eclairs."

I nodded, and without further conversation, I loaded up the wagon. Larry was unusually quiet. I wondered if he was trying to memorize another motivational quote from Zechariah for the meeting. The last one from the pastor was such a hit with the staff.

"Okay, I'm loaded up. Anyone want to go over with me?"

Larry said he still had some work to do and the Professor said he needed to clean up a bit. But Moira said she would go, as she was lodging there. I figured she also wanted to make sure I didn't snoop inside the folders. This was the first time we would be alone since our "horsing around" episode the day she arrived. I was a bit apprehensive about that.

We got in the wagon and I stifled my usual chattiness that served as a cover for anxiety. Moira was quiet for a couple of minutes. Then she said, "Max, you know, the day you brought me to camp?"

"Mm-hmm."

"You haven't told anyone about that, I hope."

"No, Moira, I would never do that. But there's something you should know from me."

"WHAT??" she blurted with a sudden intensity that startled me.

"When I left your room I bumped into Victoria and...well, my face...."

"WHAT, the LIPSTICK? OH, GOD!" She was quiet for a while, and then she muttered, "It's all right, Max, I can fix it."

"Moira, there's nothing to fix. I asked Victoria to keep the incident to herself. I mean, as far as she knew we were just necking, you know. I didn't say anything about what we did."

"It's all right, Max. Just for your information, I have been reviewing everyone's personnel files, and Victoria is in the US illegally. She came here on a visitor's visa that expired more than three years ago. I'll have a little talk with her and let her know that one word from me and she'll be lucky to get a job in the back ward at Timbuktu General .

"Gee, Moira, I don't think you need to...."

"Max, shut up and let me do the thinking, okay?"

"Okay."
So, that tied up any loose ends (so to speak) between Moira and me. I figured that we both got something we wanted (or needed) and as long as she felt safe about what happened, it was all good.

"So, what about it, Max?"

"What about what?" She reached over and slid her hand along the inside of my leg. I nearly ran the wagon into a tree. Suddenly she was right next to me and I could hear her breathing getting faster.

"I want to do it again, don't you? But this time we need to be a little more careful."

I'm not comfortable talking about what happened next. I'm actually a little ashamed about it.

But it was even better than good. The trouble was, I feared that I was being taken advantage of. Yeah, I know, you're thinking, "It should only happen to me!" But being used and controlled in a situation that has no love involved can leave you with worse marks than lipstick.

Still, I now had half the package. What I needed was a girl I could love who would love me back. I saw that as a way to break out of the crazy relationship that was developing with Moira, a relationship that filled only part of my needs. And, damn, the Professor was a very smart guy!

I'm also ashamed to say that I crept out of her cabin fearing another sneak attack by Victoria. I got back in the wagon and high-tailed it back to the camp.
I took the wagon back to the mess hall and for the next hour I washed it, cleaned out the inside, washed the floor mats, and would have simonized the damn thing if I'd had some car wax.

I knew that I was washing away my own guilt. The thing with Moira was just sex, and it felt wrong. The relationship was so incomprehensible to me. Her behavior was bizarre; the aggressive way she treated women, came on to men, pushed them away and practically attacked me. There was a lot I didn't understand about her, and it made me nervous.

I washed the wagon again, but didn't feel any better. Then I went back to the tents and had a hot shower. I still felt dirty and prayed I wasn't going to be addicted to having sex with Moira. I mean, it *was pretty good!* Okay, I admit it; but I was a mess, too.

I got to the meeting on the other side, and just like the last time, the room had been set up "auditorium style.' And, just like the last time, the room was already filled with staff and way too hot and muggy. I found an empty chair in the back and settled in. I was next to Richard Marrens, and then Lee came and took the chair on the other side of me. A door opened, and in came the "Three Musketeers," followed by Kitty. They sat at a front table facing the audience. Larry got up and asked for everyone's attention, again getting little useful response. The professor finally got up, and put a finger over his lips and said, "Shhh!" That worked like magic.

He called the meeting to order.

"Thank you all for coming tonight. It's a pleasure for me to be here. For those of you who don't know me, let me introduce myself. I'm Doctor Alfred Linzer. Most folks up here call me the Professor. I teach at the University of

Chicago, have a private practice in psychiatry, and am a member of the Board of Directors of the camp.

Okay, with that out of the way, I want to get into tonight's meeting. I'm sensitive to your time, that you've been active all day and want to get active tonight, if I remember my early years right."

There was a lot of laughter at that; the Professor knew how to work a crowd.

"Right. I'm aware that there have been rumors about a number of things going on at the camp. I'm going to address those items and spell out some changes. Moira, would you please ready the projector?"

Moira stood, took a package of clear plastic sheets out of a folder, and turned on the projector. Up on the screen behind her was a list of items that the Professor reviewed.

He continued, "First, our director, Mr. G. as you call him and Ken to me, will continue to be out for a while longer. The problem he experienced with his gallbladder has upset his heart rhythm, and he will require some further evaluation before he can be cleared to return.

Second, there are some staffing changes to announce. Linda Baron, the Assistant Unit Leader of Unit Five, has had to return to her home in Pittsburgh. Her father has recently become seriously ill and her mother needs her assistance. We hope that she will be back, but frankly, the chances don't seem good."

He nodded to Moira, who changed the sheet under the projector. The heading said, "Staff Changes."

"So, here are some alterations you need to know about. First, we are promoting "Kitty Katz." (A chuckle was heard at the mention of her name) "to Assistant Unit Leader to replace Linda." (A smattering of applause and positive murmuring sounded. Kitty was well liked).

"Kitty's cabin will be taken over by Mickey Kamen. Mickey, would you stand up?"

And there she was, standing up in the first row! She turned around and waved to the group, one hand on her hip. I hadn't spotted her over the crowd sitting behind her, and because she is fairly short. Or maybe because I had stopped looking for her! I reacted by jumping up. I knocked my chair over with a crash. She caught my eye, and looked at me as I stood with my mouth open. She *smiled at me!* Or maybe it was a sneer. Her lip curled, and, for a brief moment, she wore a devilish expression.

There was more applause, mainly from the macho guy counselors. Lee grabbed my arm and said, "Max, sit down, what's wrong?" I turned, picked up my chair, and sat. I was stunned. I had her fired and gone, and there she was, up from the ashes like a phoenix bird. The Professor went on.

"To replace Miss Kamen in Unit Two we have brought in a new counselor, Miss Anita Jackson. Anita, please stand and take a bow."

Anita was in the front next to Mickey. She turned around, gave a big gorgeous smile and waved. The group seemed momentarily surprised, then gave Anita the warmest applause yet, even a couple of "wolf whistles." They really wanted to make her feel accepted. I was still too shocked by seeing Mickey and just kept quiet. The Professor nodded to Moira, and she put another sheet on the projector.

"Right," the Professor said. "So, now we have some other announcements. You all know that camp has three sessions comprised of three weeks each. Well, we've received word from the office in Chicago that the third session has not had a good response, applications are…"

I stopped listening to the Professor. It was all up there on the screen. They were canceling the third session, stretching the first session by a week-and-a-half, and having an extended second session. The Professor was reassuring the staff that their summer jobs were safe.

Some of the campers would be leaving, but others could stay if their parents gave their approval. Scholarships would underwrite those whose families couldn't afford the extended time. Finally, the Professor discussed the increased fund raising that the Board would take on to cover the decrease in funding from the low camp registration.

He asked if anyone had questions. I had plenty, but kept my mouth shut for a change. Finally, he invited everyone to stay for coffee and donuts. The group stood with great relief. Everyone had his job intact for the summer. I was happy for Kitty, but didn't understand how Mickey kept sidestepping disaster.

The male staff started stacking chairs while some of the girls went into the kitchen to start the coffee and get soft drinks out of the refrigerator. Moira and Victoria left together, and I thought *Watch out, Victoria, the bombs are going to drop.*

The Professor was working the crowd as though he was running for office. Some of the Unit Heads were talking with Larry. I got through the crowd and informed Anita that she'd got the "Royal Welcome." She flashed me a floodlight smile, and we chatted. Others came to meet her, and I took the opportunity to look around for Mickey. Of course, she was busy with several of the macho males. I went up to Kitty and said, "Well, congratulations on the promotion. I think it's well deserved."

She said, "Oh, thanks, Max. Listen, can we get a Coke and get out of here? It's stifling."

We pushed our way back to the kitchen area, went inside. We got a couple of Cokes and swung out the back door. It was a quiet night, and a lot cooler outside than the meeting room. Kitty didn't hesitate, but walked straight for the bridge. I followed figuring, *Okay, what now? Another bridge and the coup de grace on any further relationship with her, I bet.*

"Max, if I tell you something will you keep it a secret?"

"Sure you can, Kitty. What's bothering you?"

She leaned with her elbows on the bridge rail, and sipped her Coke. She was looking out over the lake, and I thought she was trying to find words that worked with her thoughts. I waited. I took a gulp of Coke. She took a sip of Coke. I leaned on the bridge railing, and she straightened up and planted a hip against it. Some kind of night bird flew in circles, screeching. I thought, she was going to tell me she liked me. The shifting, screeching and sipping were beginning to wear on my nerves, and I said, "Kitty...."

"Max," she cut me off, "I want to talk about Mickey."

I thought, *Ouch*. "What about her?"

"This promotion of mine? The transfer of Mickey to the older girls' unit? Max, she's a total disaster and they want me to mentor her, teach her how to be a better counselor. I got called into the front office, Larry promised me a raise and a promotion if I'd get her through the summer without any more of her screw-ups. He wanted me to train her and keep an eye on her. What do you think?"

"Gee, Kitty, I don't know anything about her."

"You don't need to bullshit me, Max. I had a heart-to-heart talk with Mickey when I accepted the job. I know the whole deal between you and her. I know how much you like her, and I know how she ended your relationship."

"Oh. Ah, well...um, in that case why do you want to talk to me about her?"

"I want to confirm what I think about her. I think she's manipulative, a liar, and a phony. She was feeding me a line of crap to make me feel sorry for her. She told me that you and Bruce sabotaged her campout by building a fire that was too big and impossible to manage. She said that Bruce made sure there would be no toilet paper, which led to her using poison ivy. She blamed both of you for her failures as a counselor. She told me that with my help she was sure she could do a really good job. That she just needed someone to help her. She said that she told all this to Larry and that he overrode Miss Wallace, who wanted to fire her. I want your take, and I want it straight."

She took a long pull on the Coke. I did too, but wished it had been bourbon. Well, all of it was painful to hear, as you might have guessed. First, because everyone in the universe knew Mickey for what she was except for Larry and me. And second, that put me in a depressing loser's category that included just Larry and me. I tried to spin my answer straight without sounding like a bitter, dumped ex-boyfriend. I figured if I could accomplish that, I might consider a career in advertising.

I took a deep breath and said, "I think that Mickey wants to do what's best, but somehow she messes herself up and then tries to dig out of it without taking the blame. Maybe she does need someone to help her learn to do things right, someone she can trust or at least someone she'll listen to. Bruce tried to be that person, he tried to reach her, and he was worried about her. We went out to her campsite to help her. The things she had to do were over her head. She has no experience with kids or camping. She needed a summer job and slipped by Larry using her looks. Miss Wallace made mistakes in reviewing her application form because she was overloaded with work." (I didn't want to tell Kitty that Moira was overloaded with male applicants.)

"I think you should give her a chance, Kitty. It's the best summing-up about her I can give you."

And it was. I could almost believe most of what I said, but my heart wasn't in it a hundred percent. Kitty didn't say anything for a while, just stood sipping her Coke and thinking.

Finally, she said, "Max, you still like her, don't you?"

"Maybe some part of me does, but I'm pretty much done. She dumped me, and it's taken a while to get used to it. When I came up here to work I figured I would have the summer to get over her. I had no idea she would be here too."

I went on telling Kitty how I had called Martha, Bruce and others to help them get jobs, but not Mickey. I asked if Mickey had said anything about how she fudged her application and played up to Larry at the interview. She'd wanted to get that job and did whatever it took. Kitty looked sour about all of Mickey's scheming, and I realized I had spilled too many beans. I said, "Kitty, give her a chance, maybe you can turn her around. It would be a wonderful thing for her."

"Max, you're quite a guy, too nice and too honest. I like the way you didn't pull punches. Okay, I'll give her a shot. I have one more thing to say."

I thought, *Geez, what next?*

"I owe you an apology. You remember the first time we met?"

"Hard to forget it."

"Yeah, well, I turned around and liked you right from the start. I sort of overplayed things. I meant it to be funny, and it didn't work out so well. Then you gave me that routine about watching out for fast guys, right here on this bridge, and I overreacted. I thought you should've seen that I liked you, and instead, you came on like my father. It was so, so silly. I'm-- I'm-- I just want to say..." I stepped up and slipped my arms around her and gave her a good solid hug. She put her head on my shoulder and her hands on my chest. All at once, she leaned back and goggled at me like she'd glimpsed a ghoul from a horror movie and grated, "Jesus, you smell like Miss Wallace! What gives with *that?*"

Oh, god! I thought back quickly, I had showered for ten minutes with lava soap. And then it hit me; I hadn't changed my shirt from the last "encounter" I'd had with Moira!

"Are you kidding me? That's my aftershave!"

"Oh, sorry, for a minute I..., oh, but that's silly isn't it?"

"It certainly is," I said as indignantly as I could. I was starting to think that maybe some lies weren't so bad now and then. I mean, what did the truth get me so far?

Time to cash in. "How 'bout a little kiss?"

I got one, and it came with a lot of tingles. Maybe my little mess was getting cleaned up bit by bit. I walked her over the bridge, across the ball field and to her cabin. And got another good night kiss. She murmured that she was getting a day off and wanted to know if I'd like to go camping with her, Phyllis and Bruce. I said sure, that would be fun, and to let me know what day she was off so that I could clear it with the office. Today had been quite a day, and all I wanted right now was a good night's sleep.

I walked back to the tents and found Bill and Leon playing gin rummy on an empty nail keg. They were sitting on low stools. Several beer cans that were "off limits" at camp were lined up on the ground.

"Hi, guys," I said, "You missed an interesting meeting."

Bill said, "Nah, we got the word earlier at the kitchen. Bob called the staff together and told us about the changes in the sessions, that we'd all keep our jobs, stuff like that. He said we were getting the early word early since the cooks leave for home after dinner and the kitchen boys never show up at the meetings. We're fine with all of it; makes no difference to us about the sessions and who's doing what. Long as we get paid."

"Okay. Say, where's Michael?"

"He went into his tent. The last I saw of him he was eating potato chips and reading a book."

Just then we heard a blood-curdling scream from Michael's tent, then another, and "Yaaah, get offa me! Jesus, get offa me—Yaaaah!"

We raced to the tent to find a huge raccoon sitting on Michael's chest munching on potato chips. Michael was lying flat with his arms spread wide and a terrified grimace on his face. The raccoon looked around at us. He continued to munch on the chips and had crumbs on his mustache or whiskers, or whatever they're called. He didn't look like he was in a hurry to leave. We froze, not having any idea what to do.

Leon ran back to his tent and came trotting up behind us shouting, "Looks like I'm gonna get me a 'coon!' I turned around and saw that he was hefting a gun.

"Leon, what the hell you got there?" He said, "Just a twelve gauge shotgun, don't worry, I'm a really good shot."

I babbled, "Leon, you can't shoot that thing! He's sitting on Michael's chest! You'll kill him!"

Leon mused, "Yeah, that's a point." Then he stepped up to the tent opening and started screaming at the raccoon, poking the barrel of the gun at him. Michael screamed, "Jesus, do something!" The raccoon had had enough of the screaming, I guess, and jumped off of Michael who said, "OOF" as the raccoon used his stomach as a diving board. The critter scampered off the tent floor, through the side flap, and ducked under the wooden platform. I was thinking, *What do I have to do to get some rest here?*

We dropped to our hands and knees and could see the raccoon hiding under the tent platform, his eyes glowing. Leon said, "Watch out, boys," and shoved the barrel of the shotgun under the tent. I hissed in a fierce whisper, "Leon, you can't shoot that thing here! There are three hundred campers sleeping...."

KA-BOOM!

I don't know if you've ever had a twelve-gauge shotgun go off in your ear. Let me tell you, it's pretty noisy. The shot charge comprised a couple hundred #6 lead pellets. It hit two targets under the tent. The first was the raccoon, and the second was a large rock.

 The raccoon scampered off into the forest, at least most of him did. He was working on three legs and no tail when I saw him leave. The rest of the shot charge ricocheted off of the rock and came back to hit me in the upper leg as I'd bent down on one knee. Bill was hit in the ankle. Leon said, "Damn, I missed!" But I didn't hear him very clearly, since I was listening to the Bells of St. Mary's clanging away, all out of tune. Of course, just at that moment Larry came running up panting, "Is there something wrong? I heard a loud...."

Startled, Leon whipped around with the shotgun level at his hips. Larry's eyes looked like a couple of big white doilies with a black olive on each one.

He backed away slowly, nervously chattering, "Boys, you have to get rid of the guns. We can't have them at camp; same rule as alcohol." And he turned around and scurried off. I figured that we'd get into a heap of trouble over this. Michael came out of the tent with the bag of potato chips and said, "Bill, you were right. I shouldn't have kept snacks in the tent."

"Live and learn, Mike," said Bill.

I pulled my pants down and saw several small lead pellets imbedded in my thigh. There was a little bleeding, not too bad. Bill had some pellets in his ankle as well. Most of the shot's energy had been expended on the rock.

I said, "I think we should head to the infirmary and get some kind of antiseptic." Bill and I limped over the bridge and found that the infirmary lights were still on. I knocked at the door just as Moira was opening it. She looked surprised and said, "Max, Bill, what are you guys doing here?" I sort of wondered the same about Moira, but it wasn't my business.

I thought fast, acted excited and blurted, "One of the guys was showing us how to handle a shotgun safely, and it went off! I guess the safety catch was broken. Larry already chewed us out for it, and we know the gun will have to go. In the meantime, Bill and I need a little first aid. Could have been real bad, real bad— you know, someone could've been hurt bad, *real bad!*

I couldn't tell if Moira bought this line of crap, but it was the best I could do on the spur of the moment. I was becoming a regular little Pinocchio. But what should I have said? That a raccoon was sitting on Michael Jenner and the only thing we could think of was to shoot him (the raccoon) with a twelve-gauge shotgun? I mean, who would believe that?

Moira walked off. I heard her mutter, "Dummies." under her breath. Victoria beckoned us into her shop. She said, "Boys will be boys, boys. How silly. Okay, where'd you get hit?"

I dropped my pants. She looked at my leg very professionally.

"Ah, not so bad, luv. Give me half a second. Everyone have a tetanus shot lately?"

She picked up a little probing tool and a tweezers out, dunked them in something and dug into me a bit. Wasn't so bad. Some antiseptic went on - that stung- and she finished with a bandage or two. She said, "You want these as a souvenir of your stupidity, luv?" She dropped a half dozen-pellets into my hand. And then she turned to Bill.

"Well, luv, want to drop your pants?"

Bill said, "Got hit in the ankle." She took care of his wounds and declared, "If you boys have any brains, you'll get rid of the gun. Next time I might not be able to patch you up so easily."

Bill and I ambled back to the tents. I thought that we got off pretty easily. When we arrived, I said, "Well, boys, time to turn in. It's been a hell of a day." I didn't sleep well, though. I kept hearing bells and whistles, and I waited for an angry, bloody giant raccoon to slip into my bed.

I was sore the next morning. I'd suffered my first gunshot wound. The area where I got hit in was tender and a bit puffy. I got down to the mess hall and grabbed some breakfast, sort of waiting for Larry to come over and give me hell for last night. Nothing happened. I learned later that Bob Wheeler told Leon to take the gun home or he'd be fired. That ended the episode. To this day I wonder how the raccoon made out with three legs and no tail.

Bruce showed up at breakfast and asked if I'd heard a loud noise last night like a car backfiring last night. I told him that I'd fill him in later. He sat down and said, "I need you and the wagon to check something out."

I said, "I hope it's not another errant campfire."

"No," he said, "This one is a safety check on the canoe rack."

I asked, "How do we do that?" And he answered, "Easier to show you than discuss it."

"No problem. I have to stop at the office first, see if there's anything on my schedule that might override your request."

After breakfast I walked down to the front office. Lee was already open for business with files scattered around, a cup of coffee and a bowl of cereal on her desk.

"Mornin' Lee, how's business?"

"Oh, hi, Max. Just getting started. Just the usual chores and errands. Only thing unusual for you is a call from Mrs. Silverman. Her daughter will be coming up in a few days to do a concert for the camp at the beginning of the next session. You'll have to pick her up at the train."

"Lee, is Mrs. Silverman coming up as well?"

"Oh, she sure is. From what I hear, she never misses her daughter's concerts."

"Anything new here with the 'Three Musketeers?'"

"They're not in yet. As far as last night's meeting went, I haven't heard anything one way or the other. In any case they're not letting me in on much these days. Pretty secretive around here all of a sudden."

I walked back to the Camp Craft Building, but couldn't find Bruce. I did find Fred, who was packing food for an overland hiking trip that was to be the last major outing for the older boys' unit. He said that Bruce had left a message and would catch up with me as soon as the last of the camp outs and hikes were finished.

The last week-and-a-half of the first session was pretty much one of routine. No more disasters; campouts were accomplished without forest fires, no one drown in the lake. The worst problems from the overland hikes featured only hornet bites, trench foot and the occasional sprained ankle.

The staff seemed to be operating with better efficiency. By now a few counselors had been let go (but not Mickey.) The rest had learned how to manage working hard all day, fooling around at night, finding sleep when they could, and involving themselves in reasonable relationships. There were hot romances and some broken hearts as the male and female staff met, mated and went different ways. Bessie Akers was right about how the girls were "loose" here at the camp. I found that the college level staff members were a lot more casual about sex than I was used to.

 I stayed away from Miss Wallace, and she, thank the stars, kept aloof and away from me. I didn't know why, but I was curious about her. I didn't understand why she had come on to me so strongly and then just as quickly cooled it. But it was all fine with me.

The Professor was catching on as to how the camp needed to be managed. He and Larry continued to spend time together. My guess was that the Professor was mentoring him and maybe even doing a bit of therapy. Larry seemed more relaxed than he was after Mr. G got sick.

I had some dates with Kitty on my days off. She said that she'd been working hard with Mickey who she still thought was a total disaster. Our best times together were with Bruce and Phyllis, who now seemed to be now steady pair. We did some overnight camping and canoeing as a foursome. That was a lot of fun for me. I'd never been in a canoe, only a rowboat. Kitty was an expert, and Bruce, being an Eagle Scout and all, was really the best person to have along on any camping or canoeing trip. He amazed me with his knowledge of camping, starting fires as easily as my mom did on her gas stove, and troubleshooting problems before any of us even knew they were there.

One memorable day-off camping trip I took with Kitty, Bruce and Phyllis stuck in my mind. We took the wagon and the canoe rack with two canoes. We drove east on 13 to Port Edwards, then south on Highway G to Lake Bennett. We found a quiet, secluded place to camp and did some canoeing there. Everyone hooted at me because I was clumsy with the paddle and couldn't get the rhythm of the "J-Stroke" down. We spent a lot of time going in circles before I got the hang of it.

We had a light lunch and later cooked out dinner. Bruce surprised us with a kettle of Freddy's very own "Strongman Stew." He brought it out in an iron kettle and set it up over the campfire on some sort of tripod. As it warmed, it filled the air with a rich meaty aroma. We thought it was delicious, maybe because we had been out on the water and in fresh air all day. We spoke and laughed together 'til the sun went down. It was late in the summer by then, and the light faded more quickly. I had brought along a sleeping bag for the trip. Kitty called me a tenderfoot. She wanted to sleep on a blanket under the stars and get all that wonderful night air flowing through her clothes. She also wanted to move away from the fire, explaining that firelight made looking at the stars difficult. We took our belongings and moved a bit farther from the water, behind some trees and away from the campsite. We talked for a while, and then turned in. I gave her a kiss, she told me what a wonderful day it had been, and asked if I would join her on the blanket. I just wanted the sleeping bag. I was done for the day. I went under as soon as I had the bag zipped.

Sometime during the night there was an unexpected shift in the weather. The wind picked up and the temperature dropped like a rock. I slept right through, oblivious and warm as toast. It must have been around one A.M. I felt a tapping on the sleeping bag. I roused and saw Kitty, her nose almost touching mine in the dark.

"Max, I'm freezing! It's got to be in the thirties! Let me in, pleeeze!"
I was half out of it, but I zipped the bag open and she crawled inside. It was a pretty tight squeeze. She was freezing, and that woke me up fast. Her teeth were chattering together and she was shaking all over. Her nose was squished against my neck, and it felt like an ice cube. I got my arms around her and pulled her close.

"Hey, you'll be okay in a couple of minutes."

"I'm so c-cold! I fell asleep and woke up when the wind blew the blanket into my face. I tried to wrap myself up in it, but the temperature kept dropping. I didn't want to bother you.

I could feel how cold she was, and I started rubbing her back. "Mmm, that's good, a little slower, if you please. Mmm. HEY, I said slower, not LOWER!"

"Sorry," I said, "Couldn't hear you, so noisy in the sleeping bag." She didn't argue, andI sort of couldn't help myself. It got warm pretty quickly in that sleeping bag. I think we both knew what was going to happen. We started kissing, and after a bit she said, "Max, you need to use a rubber."

"A rubber."

"Yes, of course."

 My mind flashed a picture of my dad handing me the little paper bag from the drugstore, and then I saw my hand dropping it into the duffel bag. I saw the duffel bag in the corner of the tent back at camp....

"Ah, Kitty, I don't..."

"My god, you come all this way on a camping overnight trip and you don't have one?"

"Kitty, I didn't know we'd...I mean, I'm sorry I didn't think that... you know we haven't even..."

"Max, be quiet a minute. I need to count."

"You're counting? What could you be counting? I'm trying to apologize and you're..."

"SHH, be quiet! Okay?"

We were quiet for a moment or so, and then she whispered, "Okay, let's go."

I unzipped the sleeping bag. She hissed, "What the hell are you doing? It's freezing out there!"

"You said, 'let's go', so I thought we…"

"Max, you sweet jerk, I was counting the days of my menstrual cycle. We're okay, let's *go*."

We went. I don't remember anything more about the camping trip, honestly, and wouldn't tell you anyway if I did.

The next morning, Kitty said, "Boy, it's a good thing I'm a science major. When we get back to camp, I want you to talk to Bruce and sign up with the Boy Scouts. They come prepared."

Finally, the session was nearing its end. The night before the campers were to leave there was a gathering at the lakefront just as the sun was setting. The beach was filled with kids, staffers, and specialists for a special presentation. This was what all the mystery was about; the stuff I had been buying for Arts and Crafts, the goose feathers, a ton of chicken wire, paint and a bunch of other stuff. I walked down to the lake with Bruce and Freddy and we found an empty part of the beach with some grass growing sparsely on it. I never liked to sit in sand.

As the sun went down, Larry rose and stood behind a podium. He began a somber speech, but some sort of feedback in the microphone system started screeching at a couple of hundred decibels. This startled a lot of birds that had settled down for the night in the trees all around the beach. Suddenly, speakers were squalling, birds were squawking, flapping and flying around the the kids. Some birds, thinking they were under attack, dive-bombed the spectators.

Finally, after several campers had been blasted by bird droppings, Larry turned off the mike and asked if every-one could hear him. Everyone said yes whether they could or not. He started his speech again, and it was all about friendship, learning about each other, fidelity, brotherhood, you get the idea. The kids were getting restless, as you could imagine, and I figured that the staff, was waiting for more quotes from Zechariah. Larry didn't disappoint and closed his speech with,

"O sword! Rouse yourself against my shepherd, the man in charge of my flock. Strike down the shepherd and let the flock scatter; and I will also turn my hand against all the shepherd boys."

I tried to understand why Larry kept up with this theme; maybe he had a secret anger against the counselors. Or maybe I was missing something deeper.

Then he gave a signal to my friend, Ted Wilson, the Assistant Waterfront Director, who flashed a light at the far left and right sides of the beach. Hidden behind a copse the trees near the water's edge were two canoes, one on each periphery of the beach. They began paddling out to the middle of the lake. Anchored out there was a raft that was difficult to see, since the light was dim and a background of dark forest lay behind it.

Standing tall in the bow of each canoe was a male staff member dressed like an Indian. Each was brandishing a torch and heading out for the raft. The light was now so low you could only just make out their silhouette.

Larry was narrating the scene and talking again about friendship, loyalty, brotherhood. Suddenly one of the torches winked out, and from across the water we heard,

Ker-plunk!

Someone in the left-side canoe hissed, "Hey, what happened?" The voice carried clearly over the water. "Jerry fell in the water! Jesus, throw him a preserver!"

A smart-ass camper on the beach wryly remarked, "Another Injun bites the dust!" And another wisenheimer answered him, observing, "No, dummy, another Injun gulped the water!"

Well, by now the dramatic effect had lost something. Then someone farted, and three hundred campers dissolved into laughter. Finally, the lone remaining torchbearer in the other canoe, managed to set fire to the raft.
There was a huge blaze as the word 'FIENDSHIP' took fire in letters about eight feet high. I was pretty sure they meant "Friendship," but someone misspelled it and overlooked the "R". This initiated some chuckling among the more literate staff members, especially Lee, who was an adept proofreader.

The rest of the raft's secrets came to life. A ten-foot tall Indian Chief, complete with war bonnet, poised stoically on the raft as it was engulfed by flames. I finally learned what the chicken wire, goose feathers and all the other weird materials I'd been buying in town were for! Despite the spelling slip-up, I thought it was really an impressive production. The campers, however, saw only the humor, and I think some of them were still snickering when they clambered onto the buses the next morning. Bill, however, didn't think it was so great. .

"Hey, Max, how would you feel if they were burning George Washington? I'm out of here."

And so ended the initial session of my first time away from home. Its high points: my fight with a knife-wielding jerk to save a girl who dumped me; cowboy wrangling with Marilyn Monroe; learning first-hand about forest fires; mixing it up with the Ladies of the Board; my sexual entanglement with a very mystifying woman; a growing interest in a many-faceted girl; and getting shot in an argument with a raccoon over a bag of potato chips. That adventure was an experience I never forgot, and one I would still call a genuine blast.

I had learned a lot in the last month. I was still employed, and mostly in one piece. I thought back to how my family was of the opinion that camp would be a great place to spend the summer. Now I wondered if they really wanted to get me killed. I also wondered what new and interesting things would happen during the second session. Sometimes it's good you never know what the future holds.

Chapter 14
The Beat Goes On

The new batch of kids were in camp, having come up in buses from Chicago. There weren't many fresh ones, and those who left went back on the same bus. Little Ginny Jones stayed on and was still in Mickey's former cabin. She looked overjoyed to have Anita Jackson as her counselor. In fact, all the kids who stayed in that cabin looked contented; a turnaround from the experience they'd had with Mickey. Kitty was working hard with her. I'd heard that there had been an incremental improvement.

We were about a week into the new session when I walked into the office to get my daily work orders.

Lee said, "Max, there's a problem in Unit two. Larry asked that you take the wagon down there right away and see Victoria. Oh, and here, take this."

With an effort she hoisted a canvas bag up on the front counter.

"What's this, Lee?"

"A bag of coins. You're going to need it."

"For what? What's the mystery?"

"Larry said that you should talk to Victoria and not to say anything to anyone else about it."

"About what?"

"I don't know! Just go!"

"Where's Larry?"

"He's not to be disturbed."

"He's already disturbed enough, I guess. Okay, I'm going."

I hefted the bag. It must have weighed about ten or twelve pounds. I got into the wagon and drove down to Unit Two, the youngest girls' cabins. When I got there I saw a line of girls filing into the bathhouse in their pajamas. As they entered, someone inside was taking their pajamas and throwing them into a large canvas laundry bin that was nearly filled with other clothes and underwear. Victoria was standing outside the bathhouse with a clipboard, and she seemed to be checking each girl's name off as the kids filed in. I couldn't imagine what was going on.

"Hi, Victoria, what's cooking? Why the mystery up at the office? Why are the girls all going into the bathhouse? What's with the bin of clothes? What gives?"

Victoria handed the clipboard to Bruce's girlfriend Phyllis, the Assistant Unit Head, and grabbed my arm. She yanked me around the corner of the building.

"Max, you have to keep this confidential. The girls have impetigo."

"What?"

"Impetigo".

" What's...."

"It's a skin infection from streptococcal bacteria. Forms honey colored pustules that ooze, along with red sores. It often comes from a lack of good hygiene. Listen, I don't have time to give you a medical education. I need you to take all these infected clothes to the Laundromat in Walkerville. Bob Wheeler said it's on third Street off the Square. Wash and dry all this," (She pointed to the canvas laundry basket,) "and bring it back as soon as possible. And for god's sake, don't say anything to anyone in town about what you're doing! Did you get the coins from the office?"

"Yeah. What's the secret? Why can't I say anything?"

"Bob says the town is a rumor mill, and if anyone finds out there's impetigo at camp you can bet we'll have the health authorities on our necks. Get it?"

 "Got it; makes sense. Can I catch anything from this batch of clothes?"

"Hm, good question. Well, if you do, come to the infirmary. You can shower there and I'll give you some ointment. Just don't scratch your crotch 'til everything is clean, okay, luv? Oh, and one more thing: pick up Leon, that big kitchen boy, and take him with you. Bob thought that two of you would make things go faster, so he's assigned him to work with you. He's up at the mess hall waiting."

I was repulsed, but I get my work done. I'd never heard of impetigo, and I hoped I never would again. I loaded the canvas basket into the wagon and headed for the mess hall. Big Leon was waiting outside when I pulled up.

"Hi, Max," he said, as he levered his bulk into the front seat. "Bob told me we had a special job to do in town, but he didn't say what. You know what's going on?"

"Yeah, wait'll you hear this one." I filled him in, and surprisingly he got very anxious. You don't expect someone who's six-five and a couple of hundred pounds of muscle to be afraid of a bacterium, but everyone has their "little deals," I was learning. He was a good man at hunting raccoons with a shotgun, but it's hard to hit bacteria even with a shotgun.

We pulled out of the camp and I said, "Okay, Leon, here's the plan. When we get to the Laundromat, we'll load up as many of the machines as we can get. I have a bag of coins. We'll just work the machines, get the stuff in dryers and don't say anything to anybody about what we're doing, okay? Bob said that the town's a rumor mill, and we don't want the Health Department getting wind of this."

"Max, what if someone asks why we're washing all these kids' clothes? What do we tell them?"

I had to think about that. We drove in silence for a while and then it hit me.

"Okay, we tell them that we're from Proctor and Gamble and we're testing a new soap on kids' clothing. We'll say that it's top secret, so we can't mention anything else, but they should look for the new product in six months." I felt pretty smug about that line 'til Leon said, "Yeah, but we'll be using the soap they have there, won't we?"

He had me for a moment. Then I said, "We'll use the soap boxes they have there, but just wink and say that we've switched the soap for the experiment so nobody gets wise."

"Gee, Max, you think anyone will fall for this bullshit?"

"Ask me on the way back. It's the best I can do."

We tracked down to the " Wisconsin Wash-World Laundromat" on Third Street, and fortunately it was modern, well equipped, and not too busy. Leon and I dragged the canvas laundry basket through the door. The woman manager who sat behind a desk at one end of the place took one look at us and her eyebrows went up to her hairline. I could just see her thinking dollar signs, especially when I lugged in the sack of coins.

We took up nine of their twelve machines, and pretty soon the place was humming with wash, rinse and spin cycles. Whenever a machine stopped, either Leon or I would hop over to it, pull out the contents and shove them into a dryer. This was not a ten-minute project. We were there for several hours loading, unloading, drying and folding the best we could, and feeding coins to the machines. We only had one slight mishap. As a machine stopped, Leon grabbed the handle and pulled out a gigantic brassiere. He held it up and said, "Hey, Max, could this belong to one of the kids?" Whereupon a pretty hefty woman walked up to him and yanked it out of his hands, bellowing, "Hey, you big lummox, whatcha think you're doing with that?" Leon shrank to about half his size and said, "Oh, EXCUSE ME, ma'am!, I'm so sorry."

We got the job done, though. I said, "C'mon, Leon, I'm buying us a couple of beers before we go back. Still got about five bucks worth of coins."

I thought we would get a medal for our over-the-top service to the camp and kids, but the only ones interested in our effort were the campers, who could finally get some clothes on. Poor kids looked like little lost Indians wrapped up in blankets.

Chapter 15
Identity, Career and Once Again, Moira

By now virtually everyone in camp knew me. The reason was that I had wheels, a means of transportation, and for staff on a day off, it was important to get out of camp and shake off a tough week with the kids by having a little fun in town or a beach far from camp.

Getting there was a problem for most staff members. Only a few of the Unit Leaders who were older could afford to have a car. Many staff members would ask me for a ride into town. The best way to get back was by hitchhiking. Of course, I would see staff members walking back from town on occasion and would always slow down and ask if they wanted a ride. In this way I became not only well known, but fairly popular.

In looking back on my life, I think the camp driver job was the beginning of my career, although at the time I wasn't able to see it at all. I am, by nature, a quiet person. The wagon had a radio, but a good signal was hard to come by out where the camp was located. So whenever I had passengers who wanted to get to town, I would listen to them talk about their week, the kids they worked with, and eventually the problems they revealed. The wagon had become my traveling office, the ride relatively soothing and comfortable, and I guess, my nature made it easy for people to talk.

At first I just *listened*, but eventually I began to *hear* what everyone was saying. There's a difference between those two words. I found that the male staff mainly complained about authority, and whoever their supervisor happened to be. Their second favorite gripe was about pay. More often the guys talked about sports and occasionally about school, but their favorite topic was girls, or rather certain girl parts. If I had two or more of the male staff with me, I could bet and win that the discussion would be specifically about girls; the biggest "this" or the best "that" and who would indulge in what. Talk would slide off to the Bears and Packers for a while or why the Cubs were so lousy every year, but it always came back to the girls.

I found that it was a lot more interesting to listen to the girls. I think it was because the themes they discussed were so similar. Whereas the male staff rarely broached the subject of their career path, the girls often struggled with it. Most of the guys knew what they wanted to do. School was simply a preparation for future jobs.

On the other hand, the girls agonized about school, what they wanted for themselves, and how to satisfy the expectation of parents who had different ideas about what they should do with their lives. Many of them lamented that they had pressure from parents to become teachers. It was a practical career for a woman, offering easy access to jobs, summers off, and the added benefit of dropping out to have children and go back to teaching later. No one knew back in the 1950's that these limitations on women would start changing in the next decade.

The parents wanted their daughters to get an education, a good job, get married and produce grandchildren. The trouble was that many of the girls wanted something different and felt burdened by all that pressure. It seemed to me that expectations for girls were a lot more demanding than it was for the males.

Kitty, for example, struggled with her mother, who told her to be a teacher and her father, who wanted her to go into science. Kitty's mom was a labor attorney, and from what she said, a very tough woman who thought Kitty should take an easy career route. Kitty, as I knew, was interested in math, and science as well. She thought about engineering, a wild thought for a woman back then.

Phyllis was on a track for social work, and in my way of thinking, had less stress about future marriage and having a family. But still, she fretted about the dual role of motherhood and career.

And Tori, who wanted to be a professional dancer, was getting a lot of static from her family about even being involved in anything related to "show business."

And then there was Moira, who continued to be a mystery for me. I was by now avoiding her whenever possible, and she made that easy for me by being aloof. We never spoke about our relationship. A person couldn't help noticing and watching Moira, if only because of her "over-the-top" behavior. I began to notice changes in Moira not long after we had the second (and last ever) fling in her room.

She had stopped flirting with the male staff, which I took as her concern about how the Professor would evaluate it. But then I noticed other changes. She stopped "making an entrance" whenever she entered a room, whether it was the meeting room on the other side, the mess hall, or in and out of her office. She totally dropped the "Loretta Young" swirl through the door along with the pause so that everyone would see she had arrived; her message, "I'm here, notice me." She just started walking into the room like everyone else.

She was also wearing less jewelry. It wasn't a big difference; I would have missed it if I hadn't been observing her so closely. The first things that went were her suggestive brooches. First to disappear was the one that hung in her cleavage that said, "GO!" She had others that said things like, "Open for Business," or "Special." They were all gone. There were fewer rings and bracelets. Finally, I noticed that her heavy makeup was getting a makeover. There was a lot less lipstick and eye liner.

One morning I walked into the front office to get my assignments for the day. My clipboard, which was either in my mailbox or on the counter with the work and purchase orders, was missing.

"Lee, do you have my clipboard?"

"I think Moira has it in her office, Max. Ask her."

I thought that was odd. I knocked on Moira's door and she said to come in. She was sitting behind her desk, which had been turned so that visitors to her office no longer could see her legs. She was wearing plain jeans, with her blouse buttoned unusually high. Tennis shoes replaced the ridiculous high heels that she'd worn to traverse the camp's sandy roads. Her hair was pulled back into a simple ponytail and she had no makeup on. I thought that was unusual for her.

"Max, you have some errands in town this morning, and I took your clipboard because I wanted to make sure I got a ride in with you."

"Sure, Moira, glad to have you along. What's the occasion?"

"I have an appointment at the beauty shop. When are you leaving?"

"I generally get my clipboard, have breakfast, and leave on the town errands right after that. You okay with that? Be about eight-thirty, quarter to nine, latest."

"Okay, my appointment's at nine-thirty. Should work out just right. You'll wait for me and bring me back. I'm having coffee here; just stop by when you're ready."

"Right, see you shortly."

I didn't think much about our talk. I went to the mess hall and grabbed some breakfast. The French toast looked like it was really limp, but they always had oatmeal. I had some of that with fruit and a cup of coffee. I was sitting with the specialists, who were talking with Harvey and Martha about the raft and kidding them about who misspelled "Friendship." Martha and Harvey blamed each other, but it was all in good humor.

I sat next to Bruce, who asked what I had going for the day. I replied that I would be spending the morning doing errands in town. He reminded me that we'd never found time to check out the canoe rack. There was a big canoe trip coming up this session, and he really wanted to give the rack the once-over before the trip. I told him I'd get it on my worksheet today.

Breakfast over, I went back to the office and found Moira on the porch waiting. She slid into the wagon, and we were off to Walkerville. Moira was quiet as we drove out of the camp. That was all right with me. I was feeling a bit tense to have her along. She made no small talk, and I got the feeling that she just wanted quiet time. I kept still all the way into Walkerville.

When I got to the square, I asked her where the beauty shop was located. She just said that I should park on the square when I was done with my errands and wait for her there. She swept out of the wagon and closed the door without another word. It was odd for her to be so quiet. She didn't yell at me, flirt or argue. I thought something was going on, but couldn't quite grab what it was. She had sort of disappeared into herself. I'd not seen that sort of behavior from her before.

I ambled over to the bakery. The first item on my list was twelve dozen donuts that Lee had ordered for a staff get-together on Wednesday. Next, on to the hardware store for several items that Bob Wheeler wanted, then to the drug store for a few bottles of alcohol, aspirin and calamine lotion for the camp infirmary.

My last errand was (can you guess by now?) the Walkerville Locker for a case of frozen 'beef balls'. I could hear Lee's nervous titter as I once again moved fifty boxes of government surplus butter to get at the beef. I nodded hello to the new bear head next door. It smiled and wished me a good day, then I finished up and hung the heavy parka on its peg.

I figured that I had a little time left before Moira would be done, so I trudged back to the drug store and had a Coke. When I got back to the square I saw Moira sitting on a bench reading a magazine. I tooted the horn, she looked up and I had a mini shock. Her long hair had been cut severely short. It was a man's haircut! It changed her whole persona. She slid into the car and said, "Let's go."

I wasn't sure if I should compliment her new look or simply drive. While I struggled to figure out what to say, she said, "Max, I have something I've been wanting to say to you for a while, but I wasn't sure how to do it."

I got very uncomfortable with that. I didn't know what was coming, but with her I knew it would be a doozy.

"Max, do you remember the day I came up to camp and you took me to that coffee shop? Could we stop there?"

"Sure, Moira, that would be nice." I didn't really mean that, but didn't know what else to say, so I drove to the shop. I pulled into their little lot and saw there were no lights on. "Closed Monday," stated the sign on the door.

"Sorry, Moira, didn't know they weren't open."

"That's all right, Max. Let's just sit here for a bit, okay?"

She wasn't really asking; she was ordering.
So, here it comes, I thought, *whatever it is.* She shifted around in her seat and said, "Max, I have an apology to make to you."

"Moira, there's no need for any apologies, I...."
"Shut up, Max, there *is* a need. For me. So just listen. That day I came up on the train. I, ah....

She paused for a moment, looking for the right words. It made me very tense.

"I, ah, used you— when we got to camp, and then did it again, and it was wrong of me. You were an experiment. I shouldn't have done what I did, and I want you to know that I'm sorry."

"Moira—"

"Shut up. This is very hard for me and I need to tell you more. I need to tell you why I...."

"Moira, you don't have to...."

She screamed and was very upset." MAX, goddammit, I said shut up! why can't you just listen? This is hard enough for me, don't you understand that?"

I think I kept interrupting out of my own anxiety. I didn't know what she wanted to tell me, but I dreaded whatever it might be.

"Max, I like women!" There was a long pause, I kept still now; this was serious stuff she was working on.

"Okay," she went on, "That was the hardest part. I've known this about myself for a long time. It's kept me from having any real relationships with anyone. Have you noticed anything different about me since I came up to camp?"

I didn't know why she shifted gears, but I went with it. "Well, lately I've noticed you've stopped wearing a lot of jewelry, your makeup has become less noticeable, stuff like that. And now, your hair...."

"Max, I know you've been watching me. Women sense these things, and that's part of why I want you to know what's going on. You're a sweet guy, Max. I liked you the minute we met back in the Chicago office. I flirted with you then because I was still testing myself. I knew I liked women, but I tried for a long time to find a guy I could test my feelings out on. Maybe even fall in love with someone and thrash out the struggle I'd been having. I thought you might be the guy. You're younger, and, I thought, sort of pure. Or maybe just naive. So I decided to give you a try. I lost it the day I came up to camp. That damn sailor scared me really badly, and then there you were. You were so sweet and I felt protected. You took care of me. I just thought it was time to, well, you know.

I started to say something but she held up her hand like a traffic cop.

"Just a couple more things. Victoria guessed the truth about me. We've— become...close. And the last thing I need to say is that I will kill you if you say anything about this. Promise me, Max. I was really scared to tell you all this."

Her confession opened up so much that made sense to me now. I knew almost nothing about homosexuality, and certainly didn't know anything about women who might be attracted to both sexes. Her "confession" also explained Victoria's response when I was washing lipstick off my face in the infirmary. I remembered the disappointment in her voice when she realized I'd been with Moira, *"Anyone but Moira, luv"*. I thought Victoria might have had an interest in me. But I was now guessing it was really her disappointment that Moira might not have been a lesbian. I think she somehow knew.

Moira was now very still and sat with her back against the wagon door. She scrutinized me with what I guessed was a lot of apprehension. She was very pale and kept biting her lip. Finally, she reached over and put her hand on my arm. I had all I could do to keep from jumping.

"Max, say something for Christ's sake!"

I opened my arms and said, "Come here, Moira."
She slid across the seat and I hugged her. Then she started crying with her face up against my chest. And damned if I didn't get a stinging sensation in my nose and well up with a lot of tears myself.

"It's okay," I whispered in her ear, "Let it go. I won't say a word about this. We'll be friends and there'll be no more flirting, testing and experimenting. I want you to know that I never felt used. In a lot of ways you did something wonderful for me." She gave a loud sniffle, a loud sort of 'boo hoo' and I thought my shirt would have to go to the laundry. Strange what you think of when the emotions are rolling.

"Max, you don't hate me, do you? I didn't mean to hurt...."
She gasped and another wave of crying came. This one got to me all over again; she was in so much pain that I couldn't hold up, and I started bawling like a baby.

I don't remember how long we sat hugging each other and crying in that wagon. Eventually she sat back, looked at her watch and said, "We have to get back!"

"I know." I felt like a noodle, sort of wobbly inside.

I put the wagon into gear and we drove back to camp. She sat very close to me, but it now felt all right. When we got close to the camp entrance she said, "Pull over and let me out. I'll walk in from here. Don't stop at the office, please, just go past and down to the mess hall or somewhere, okay?"

She pulled the rearview mirror over, a habit she had that bothered me, and looked at her eyes. She thought for a minute and said, "I'm walking into that office and I'm going to bitch about my allergies."

I pulled over and she opened the door and said, "Thanks, Max, for everything." She kissed me on the cheek like a sister would and got out. I pulled into the road, adjusted my rearview mirror, and saw her waving. I stuck my arm out the window, gave her a "thumbs up," tromped on the gas pedal, and rode off into the sunset like a movie cowboy.

I took a deep breath and blew it out. Wow, what an experience! How hard it must have been for tough, sexy Moira to put all that agony and shame out on the table with me. Somehow, I felt that I had helped her, and it made me feel gratified. The sex was an experience I'd never forget, but holding her while she cried, and my own reaction to her pain, I thought, was one of the most beautiful moments I ever had. I took another deep breath and promised myself to keep it all a secret. It was the kind of incredible experience I'd love to share with other people, but that would only serve to turn it into cheap gossip. I knew I'd never do that.

Chapter 16
The Job at Hand

I still had some errands to complete, so I went down to the mess hall to unload the box of 'beef balls' at the kitchen. I never liked keeping frozen food in the wagon for fear it would spoil. After that, I drove out of the camp and took the outside road to the other side. When I got there, I saw Bob Wheeler's jeep outside the meeting room area. This was a bit of luck. I could hand off the hardware that I'd purchased for him, and deliver the twelve dozen donuts for the staff meeting at the same time. I brought the hardware in and found Bob in the kitchen changing a light in a fixture.

"Bob, I got your stuff from the hardware store. You want it now or in the back of the jeep?"

"Stick it on the table, Max, and thanks."

"I also got twelve dozen donuts. Do they go in the refrigerator or where?"

"That's strange, *I* brought twelve dozen donuts. They're on the pantry shelf."

Just then, Larry and Victoria came in carrying boxes of donuts. Victoria said, "Larry brought donuts for the meeting tonight."

I said, "Twelve dozen, I bet."

She said, "Yes, Larry, that's right isn't it — Larry?"

Larry said, "Um."

Bob said, " Larry, you told me to get them and must have forgot. I brought twelve dozen."

And I said, "Me too. Lee had them on a purchase order."

Victoria said, "Hm, that gives us… let's see, four hundred and thirty two donuts."

Larry said, "How about I make some coffee? Anyone want a donut?"

We had some donuts and coffee and a good chuckle, at least Victoria, Bob and I had a good chuckle. Larry was sort of quiet. I gave Victoria her calamine lotion and aspirins and noticed that she didn't look me in the eye as she usually did. I didn't take it personally. I got back in the wagon, drove back to the camp, shot past the front office and went down to the Camp Craft building to find Bruce. Freddy was in the building, holding a clipboard and taking inventory of campout foodstuffs.

"Hey, Freddy, how's it going?"

"Hi, Max. Jesus, they're so dumb!"

"Who's dumb?"

"The nutritionists back in the city who work out the food lists for campouts. Whoever it is knows from nothing. Look, here they specify dried onions to go on a campout when you could easily take fresh sweet onions. They're so much tastier and just as safe. They keep a long time. Then there's the Unit Leaders. What a bunch of dolts. They don't instruct the kids to take off their shoes when they climb into their sleeping bags. So I have to empty sand and all kinds of crap out of them."

"Well, why would anyone want to wear shoes in a sleeping bag anyway?"

"Ah, some of these kids've never been out of the city before. They're always ready to run or fight, and they figure that if they're attacked by wolves they'll have to run for it."

"You're kidding! There are no wolves around here!"

"Hah, like hell I'm kidding."

"Freddy, are you not liking this work? I'm beginning to feel sorry I ever called you about the job."

"Max," he exclaimed with a look of surprise, "I LOVE this job! Whatever gave you that idea?"

"Yeah," I said, "Silly of me. Say, where's Bruce?"

"He's around back cleaning shovels. Those dumb counselors know from borscht about cleaning equipment.
Bunch of schmucks."

"Thanks, Freddy. Say, let me know if you want to send
donuts out with the campers. I know where you can get
a good deal."

I walked around the building and there was Bruce,
cleaning shovels just as Fredy had stated.
"Bruce, you want to work on the canoe rack now, later,
whatever?"

"Hi, Max. Yeah, I'm almost done with this. The rack is
around the other side of the building in a garage. Go
take a look. I'll be there in a minute."

I walked around to the other side of the building. There
was a small garage with the overhead door raised. The
rack was an ugly looking monstrosity. It had one axle
and a two-wheel undercarriage with an iron pipe frame.
Two vertical steel posts stood fore and aft with horizontal
beams welded between them. Four canoes could fit on
each side of the verticals. The rack was loaded with
eight canoes upside-down with their gunnels resting on
the horizontal bars. There were three-foot-high steel
pipes on each corner that had been sawed off at the top,
leaving nasty-looking sharp edges. They looked like
they'd been included as an after-thought for bumper protection. There was a tow bar with a hitch on the end to
hook onto the wagon or a truck. Bruce came around the
corner as I was looking the thing over.

"Max, here's the deal. I want to make sure that the tires are okay. I filled them with air and have been checking for leaks. This rig hasn't had much use, and I want to be sure that we don't have a tire go flat on us somewhere out in the sticks.

My second worry is the rack itself. I need to make sure that the canoes will be secure. So, here's what I want to do. Let's hook the thing to the wagon and take a ride on some good roads and maybe a secondary road, one of the crappy Wisconsin dirt tracks around here. We'll take an air pump in case. Half way out we can check the pressure and also see if the canoes are secure. You got it? Max, are you with me? Looks to me like you're not tracking. Your mind's miles away."

I sort of got it. I was still thinking about sitting with Moira in the wagon, hugging her and the two of us crying. So I snapped out of it and said, "Yeah, I'm with you. Say, what are those pipes for, the ones sticking up? Bumpers or something?"

"Yeah, I don't like them. They should have been finished better, threaded and capped. Someone could get snagged on them. They've got sharp edges. This whole rig is hardly top of the line."

"Okay, we going to test it out now or what?"

"Let's go. We'll be back well before dinner. Can you back the wagon around so we can hitch the rack to it?"

I returned to the wagon and backed it around, watching Bruce as he guided me close to the rack. We hooked the monster to the trailer hitch. Bruce got a tire pump out of the Camp Craft building, and we headed out of camp and onto Route 54. Bruce said, "Let's do about sixty miles an hour first of all. Then we'll head for a secondary road and see how that goes. If we survive, we can stop and check out this pile of scrap.

Bruce was right, I wasn't totally in tune with him. Checking out a canoe rack after listening to Moira's painful explanation of her sexuality and relationship difficulties wasn't a good matchup. I did my best to be in the moment with Bruce. We got out onto the highway. I took the wagon up to sixty miles an hour, and things seemed to be going smoothly.

"Max, how's the thing holding the road? You feeling any sway back there?"

"All good far as I can tell. You ready for a back road yet?"

"Let's keep it on the highway, maybe take it up to seventy for a while."

"You're the boss."

We sailed along without a problem for another half hour and then I said, "So, you think we're good here or what?"

"Yeah, seems fine. Okay, find us a back road and we'll see what she does."

We rode on for another twenty minutes. I saw a county road, slowed up, and made a left turn. We were rolling along in farm country. The road was okay at first, but then we hit some washboard areas and a few potholes that gave the rig a good pummeling.

Bruce said, "See if you can find a place to pull over, and we'll check out how the canoes are doing. You bounced them around pretty good, and if they're still set I'll be satisfied."

There was a turn-out and I pulled off the road.

As we climbed out of the wagon, Bruce said, "Okay, I'm going to climb up and check the canoes on top. You work your way around the bottom group, then we'll test the tires."
He clambered up, and we began by checking the bungee cords that secured the canoes. They seemed all right to me; none of the canoes had appeared to shift since we set out. I had just about finished my go-round when I heard a scraping noise. A sharp yelp from Bruce was followed by a heavy thud. I raced around the rack to find him lying on his back, holding onto his right leg.

"What happened?"

"My foot slipped on a grease spot as I was coming down and I fell. I grabbed that railing to catch myself and the damn thing came loose."

"You okay?"

"Most of me. I think I got caught on one of the bumper poles. Lot of pain in the back of my right leg. Help me up."

I got him sitting upright, then he got his arm around my shoulders and I hauled him to his feet.

He said, "Max, I got to drop my pants so you can take a look, see what the damage is."

He gingerly lowered his jeans, revealing a gouged area on the back of his thigh midway between his knee and hip.

"Bruce, you in much pain?"

"Yeah. Whatt'ya see?"

"Well, there's a gouge about two inches across. The hole looks like raw meat!"

"Bleeding bad?"

"No, sort of oozing though. Tough to look at." I was actually getting nauseated, but I didn't want to add my anxiety to the problem. He asked if I could find something to bind his leg with, and told me to get him to Wallkerville as soon as I could. I found a clean t-shirt from the "lost-and-found" box in the back of the wagon, tore it up and got it around his leg.

"I'll get you to the Walkerville Clinic. I'm almost as well known there as I am at the meat locker. Don't worry!"

By the time we got to the clinic, Bruce's pants leg was drenched with blood, and he seemed to be going into shock. I kept up a steady stream of positive comments to steady my anxiety, and he'd occasionally grunt in affirmation. I was relieved when we got to the clinic.

They immediately rushed him inside for an evaluation. After he'd been in the emergency room for about a half hour, a doctor came out to inform me that Bruce was okay, but would be in a fair amount of pain for a while. The gouge was too wide to close with sutures, instead. the wound would eventually heal by granulating or healing from the perimeter toward the middle. They gave him some injections and painkillers, and instructed me to tell the nurse at camp to keep an eye on him in case there was an infection.
 Twenty minutes later, we stopped at the drugstore to fill his prescription, then we headed back to camp. He was supposed to rest and do nothing to aggravate his wound. I took him to the infirmary, where Victoria fussed around to get him settled in one of the cabins.

I towed the canoe rack back to Camp Craft. I never liked the look of the thing to begin with, and now saw it as evil. I thought to myself, *Just wait, I bet I'll have a nightmare where that damn thing chases me!* Then an image of Crash popped into my head. I remembered what he'd said about my troubles not being over and done with. I wondered if he'd tampered with the canoe rack.

 I climbed up where Bruce had been and looked at the rail that he'd tried to grab. I couldn't tell if the screws holding it were loosened or if Bruce's clutching at the rail pulled them out stripping the threads holding them. I shuddered at the thought that Crash may have been tinkering with the rack, but I couldn't prove it one way or the other.

That night after dinner, I found Kitty leaving the mess hall. I asked if she'd like to get together after the kids were in bed (the request made me feel like an old married man for some reason). I told her what had happened to Bruce. She said she'd meet me on the main road at eight-thirty.

When we met, she said, "Come on, we're going to look in on Bruce. You know where he is?"

"Victoria put him in one of the cabins on the other side; number four, I think."
I liked the fact that she wanted to make sure Bruce was all right. We went to the other side, and I knocked on the door of cabin number four.

"Come on in!" Bruce called. He was really glad to see us. He told us that his leg was sore but he would be okay in a day or two. He said that Victoria was keeping an eagle eye on him. We asked if he needed anything. He informed us that he only wanted his pajamas and toothbrush for now. I said I'd bring it back later.
Bruce said he'd taken something to dull the pain and to help him get to sleep. He looked pretty beat, so after a short visit we left him and started back to the camp.

It was a warm, dry night, and there was a full moon on the ball field. I told Kitty that some of the stuff I'd been through in the last few days had made me on edge. I didn't want to tell her about the experience with Moira, but Bruce's accident and what might have happened during the forest fire had started to haunt me. Even running into Crash at the clinic after my fight with him was on my mind. All of it was piling up. I felt very wound up, and I just wanted to talk to her about it.

It poured out of me, and after a while she put her arms around me and we hugged. I let out a sob, but got control and put my face over her shoulder so that she wouldn't see tears running down my face. Tough sometimes to be tough. She whispered in my ear, "Max, you're a good man," and kissed me on that ear. Then I kissed her back, and we just stood and hugged till the gathering evening dew started to make us soggy. It made everything a lot better.

Chapter 17
Show Time

It was another bright, sunny morning when I came down to the office to pick up my clipboard and get ready for the day. Lee was in her accustomed place, and Moira was drinking coffee in her office with the door open for once, so I waved. She waved back and went back to her files with a sour look on her face.

The daily assignments looked light. I'd had a good night's sleep. Nobody had shot a raccoon. My clipboard was bland. No forest fires, impetigo epidemics, orders for goose feathers, donuts or beef ball orders, which was too bad, since I was getting to be good friends with the bear head. In addition, I would miss my daily work-out schlepping 40 boxes of butter to dig out one small package. Just one measly trip to Walkerville was listed on my daily sheet.

"Lee, it says here I need to make a pickup at the drugstore. What, a prescription? For who?"

"Oh, that's for the Professor. It's something he has to take, I think for high blood pressure. God knows it's probably gone up a hundred points since he got here. He called the pharmacy and gave them your name."

"Okay, and a pickup at the 11:00 am train. Who's that?"

"Mrs. Silverman and child.The Prima Donna violinist is coming to play that concert."

"Sounds like you don't like her very much."

"Who? Mrs. Silverman? She's all right, I guess. Her daughter is another story; a weird duck."

"Bob says she's a real beauty and a great talent."

"Mm-hmm."

Lee said nothing more. I guessed I had to wait and make my own call. I pondered whether to leave for town immediately or head down the main camp road to see if anyone had a requisition for anything. Perhaps there were even staff members who needed a ride. I decided to do that now in order to save multiple trips into town. I had become pretty efficient at the driver's job and really liked it. I jumped into the wagon and took a slow run past Camp Craft. No one was there. On to Arts and Crafts. I saw Martha in front of the building and waved.

"Hi, Martha, what's new?"

"Morning, Max, not much. How's it going?"

"Good. You need any supplies, goose feathers or maybe a ton of chicken wire? I'm heading for town."

"Nope, all good, thanks."

I swung by the waterfront, but it was early and nobody was home. Looked like there was no business to do. I secretly hope that I'd run into Tori, but I didn't see her anywhere.

I glanced at my watch and saw it was still too early to go to town. Then I remembered that Bruce wanted some stuff from his room. I headed over to the older boys' units where he stayed and rummaged around in his dresser for his toothbrush and pajamas, an extra set of underwear and a book that was on his bed. It looked like he had been reading.

I left the main camp, over to the other side, and rapped on the door of cabin four. Victoria called, "Hold on, half a moment." Then she came to the door and told me that she was changing the dressing on Bruce's leg and that I could come in. She whispered, "He's itching to get back to work, but I think he should rest for a few more days. The wound is pretty deep. He handles pain amazingly well. See if you can convince him to take it easy, will you, luv?"

I walked into the cabin and mustered a big smile for my downed buddy. "Hey, Bruce, how's it going?"

"Yeah, okay, thanks, Max. The leg is sore, but it'll be fine. Whatcha got there?"

"Stuff you wanted; toothbrush, pajamas and a book that was on your bed. It looked like you'd been reading it."

"Yeah, great. Put the stuff over here where I can reach it, thanks. Anything new with you and Kitty? Phyllis says that Kitty likes you."

"Did Kitty say that?"

"No, but Phyllis is close to her, and that's what she thinks."
He abruptly changed the subject.

"Max, you know Moira pretty well. Is something weird going on with her? She's looking very different and she isn't hassling the guys anymore."

I preferred not to get into any discussions about Moira, even with Bruce. I figured that one day I'd tell him some of what was going on, but not until we were long out of camp Nowatoma.

"She's working hard because Ken can't be here, and you know what a yutz Larry is."

"Yeah, makes sense."

We shot the breeze for a while. Bruce let me know that he was worried about an overnight canoe trip that was scheduled for one of the older kids' cabins in Kitty's unit.

"It's a three-day, two-night deal involving canoeing down the Wisconsin River to the rapids, a portage around them, and then continuing downstream as far as they can get 'til they call us. It's Mickey's cabin, and Kitty told me that she was going along to make sure things went right."

"So, what are you worried about?"

"Max, you know how I feel about Mickey. She's a disaster, and even with Kitty along to keep watch, I think there could be trouble."

"How do they get to the river?"

"We'll put everything in the big truck. The wagon can tow the canoe rack, which means you'll have to go with them. Some of the kids will ride with you, and the rest will travel on the back of the truck. I'm hoping that I'll be able to oversee the loading and drive the truck. If my leg lets me anyway."

"You'll be fine."

I peeked at my watch. It was time to pick up the prescription at the drug store and get to the train.

"Bruce, I gotta get moving. I'll visit you later. Don't push the leg, okay?"

"Thanks for bringing my things over. Don't worry, Victoria has been great."

I jumped into the wagon and headed onto Route 54. I spotted Fat Fred walking down the road about a half-mile ahead and pulled alongside.

"Hey, Fred, you need a lift?"

"Nah, but thanks, Max. I'm walking because I'm getting too heavy. Trying to get in shape."
He waved; I said, "okay" and stepped on it. Walkerville, next stop.

I went to the drugstore and picked up the prescription for the professor, then turned around and got to the train station with about fifteen minutes to spare. Time hangs when a person's just sitting. I thought about home, and realized I hadn't done my share of letter writing, and made a mental note to write the folks. I thought about Mrs. Silverman coming back, and the different descriptions I'd heard about her daughter Shoshana. Kitty said it was a Hebrew name. Kitty had met her once when she was up visiting the camp, but that was about it. I'd know more soon enough, I figured.

I heard the train coming and eased out of the wagon. By now I knew just where to stand to greet people coming off the train. It pulled in and crunched to a stop, the conductor opened the doors and stepped down to the platform. I realized I was looking forward to matching wits with Mrs. Silverman and meeting her soon-to-be-famous daughter.

People debarked, or whatever the word was. I had been practicing an opening line to use when I met Shoshana; I wanted to be 'cool'. Most of the people had left the train when a girl with short blond hair carrying a musical instrument case in one hand and a suitcase in the other came down the steps.

She slightly resembled Mrs. Silverman, and like her mother, was rather chunky. I moved toward her and said, "Hi, there, I'm Max from the camp, and I bet you're Shoshana, the famous violinist."

She said, "Well, hi, there, Max from the camp, and I bet you're dead wrong. I'm Mary Lou from the UW Marching Band, and if you think a coronet case is for a violin, you're in great need of a music appreciation course!"

"Oh, gee, I'm so sorry! I was supposed to meet someone I never saw before and I guessed wrong. Please accept..."

"Hey, no problem. The name's Baumgarten; Mary Lou, I'm in the Walkerville directory under my dad's name, Herman, only one. If you're from the camp you're okay. My brother washed dishes there before he joined the army. Look me up, we'll have coffee." She started to walk away, then stopped and said, "Oh, and if you're looking for a violinist, there's one sitting in the back of this car. She's sort of nervous-looking and has been hugging a violin case since I got on in Madison. You better go get her, too. She didn't look like she knows where to get off."

"Thanks, Mary Lou, and I'm sorry for being so clumsy."

I scrambled up the steps and glanced at the back of the car. Sure enough, down at the end was a girl about my age, facing toward me, but looking out the window. She was clutching a large black case like it was a life preserver. I hustled down the aisle.
"Shoshana?"

She looked at me like a deer in headlights, and she actually jumped when I called her name. She nodded her head vigorously, eyes wide, blinking wildly and darting around. She said very softly, "Yes."

"Listen, we have to get off. The train will be leaving. This is Walkerville, and I'm Max, from the camp. I came to get you. Let's hurry, okay?"

She bounced up, very frightened. She said, "I fell asleep! My suitcase is up there! Get it!"

She pushed past me and ran to the exit doors. I looked up; a suitcase with gorgeous leather and brass trim was up on the center rack. I pulled it over the edge and it almost sent me through the floor. Another "blacksmith-in-training." adventure.

I heard the conductor shout, "board, all aboard." I got to the door and clomped down the stairs just as the doors slid closed. Shoshana was standing on the platform, still hugging the black case. And then it hit me. "Shoshana, where's your mother? Isn't she on the train? We'll have to go to the next stop and…"

"Mother is driving up."

"Oh, well I was told…"

"I'll explain in the car."

"Sure. Um, did we get all your luggage off?"

"Yes. Mother is bringing the large trunk. Can we go now?"

"Of course. The wagon is over this way."

I pointed. She walked to the car and stood at the passenger door, and made no move to open it. I heaved up her suitcase, duck-walked over and set it down behind the wagon. Then I circled around and opened the door for her. She gave me an odd look that clearly intimated, *"You picked up the suitcase before opening the door for me?"* She got into the wagon and clucked her tongue at the poor service. I dutifully shuffled around to the back of the wagon and schlepped the suitcase in. I wondered what penalty a medieval serf would have received by the Lady of the Manor for such poor service.

"Shoshana, do you want me to park your violin back here?"

"No. And please call me Ahhna." (Said with a very soft 'ahh'.) "I prefer that."

"Right."

I slid into the driver's seat and looked over at her. She had very straight black hair and bangs with the sides cut to her jawline like a Chinese woman's. She possessed Ivory skin, a short, beautiful nose, chiseled, like one on a statue. Her eyes were very large and dark, and she was blessed with very long lashes and a little bow mouth with full lips and high cheekbones. Bob Wheeler was right; she was a beauty and reminded me of those expensive porcelain dolls you glimpsed in upscale shops. She sat stiffly as a storefront mannequin. Her knuckles were white with pressure from clutching on to the violin case. She didn't look anything like Mrs. Silverman, and I wondered if she was adopted. She looked over at me and said, "Are we going?"

"Your mother. I thought…"

She sighed and with some exasperation said, "As I said before, Mother is driving up. She'll be here this afternoon. You're probably wondering why I didn't drive up with her."

"Well, no, I, ah…"

"All right then, since you insist, I'll tell you. Mother's calculating mind reasoned that you would be the likely person to escort me from the train, affording me a greater opportunity to fall in love with you in her absence. This is how she thinks, or better, operates. Mother doesn't approve of the boy I'm dating. This isn't the first of her little ploys to separate us. So, please, just go. No more pressure for further elaboration, all right?"

"Right." I kicked over the engine, popped the wagon into gear and we headed out. I wasn't sure if I should say anything. After all, her mother was a big shot and I was hired help.

We drove in silence for a while. Then she said,"Mother is driving up with her brand new 1960 Cadillac. No one else has one yet; only Mother. She obtains one of the first every year from a contact at General Motors. It sports a new color; Persian Sand. It's as ugly as sin, but she's very proud of it. She doesn't like Lenny."

"Lenny's your boy friend?"

"She maintains that his family has too much money and not enough character. His father is also crude; a commodities broker named Barry Goldman. When you meet him he parrots, 'Hi, Bury Gold, Man,' like it's some kind of scintillating joke." She made a face, like she ate a bad peanut. "Mother hates him."

"She hates Lenny, too?"

"Yes, of course."

" Well" I said, "If Lenny goes into investment work he can say, "Hi, Len' Gold, Man.""

Okay, it was a bad attempt at humor, I admit it, but I was once more intimidated by an odd, good-looking girl; a looker with a very sharp tongue.

She shot a look at me and said, "Mother said that you possess character, no money, and that you're quite humrous. So far I don't see any evidence of that."

Well, that sort of stung. She had no reason to insult me that way. I said, "You don't see the character or the funny?"

"I'm sorry. I act like this when I'm manipulated into one of her schemes."

"So, maybe we can start over. I hear you're a great violinist. What are you playing for the kids?"

"I thought I would play something by Sarasate."

I'd never heard of Sarah Sottay, but wanted to look like I was sophisticated. I hung right in on the conversation.

"Oh, very nice," I commented suavely. "I didn't know there were any female composers." She looked at me as though I'd just landed from Mars.

"What do you mean, female composers?"

"Well, Sarah Sottay sounds like a woman to me." She cracked a smile and then laughed, a short grating choke, as though her laughter mechanism needed 3-in-1 oil.

"It's possible that you are sort of funny. I never thought of his name in that way, most amusing."

I figured I should let that go. I wasn't kidding, but I was sure embarrassed.

"So," She said, "You don't know anything about music."

"Well, I play a little harmonica, some 'sweet potato' and listen to WCKY Cincinnati a lot, the 'Grand Ole Opry' down there. I like Bill Monroe, Flatt and Scruggs, and the Foggy Mountain Boys and especially Lulu Belle and Scottie. I'm a big Blue Grass fan."

She didn't appear to be impressed.

"By 'sweet potato' you mean the ocarina? A peasant instrument."

Like a ball club manager in a losing game, I needed to make a change on the mound.

"So, what will you play for the campers?"

"I'll play Zigeunerweisen, of course, 'Gypsy aires' in English. I surmise that the group will enjoy it. I have to talk with Richard about whatever else. We've played that piece enough so we can just run through it."

I needed another change from the bullpen. I was playing sixteen-inch sand lot softball here against the National League.

"So, I heard from Bob Wheeler at the camp that you play a Guarneri." I pointed to the black case she was still squeezing. "Is that it?"

"Oh, God, no, it's my junker, but it's still a good violin. I only play the Guarneri at real concerts. This is violin by Eugenio Degani, made in1875. Italian maker, very good."

"I guess with a name like that he'd have to be either a violin maker or a designer of women's sunglasses."

Grate-choke-smile. Then she tensed up on me and said, "It wolfs on the G-string but it has a very sweet tone and rich low notes."

I had no clue what she was talking about. Just then there was a loud buzzing noise on my left, and a guy wearing a cape, black mask and a large floppy black hat came roaring up next to us on a motorcycle. He casually cut me off and gave me the finger. I yelled, "Hey, it's El Dédo, and this is the first time I've seen him! WOW!" I blew my horn and waved.
Shoshana became very frightened.

"Will he hurt us?"

"No, please don't worry. He's just a local nut."

"Are there bees at camp? Last time I was here there were bees. I'm afraid of them."

"Hey, no need to be afraid of bees. They die if they sting you so they don't go after you unless you really are bothering their hive. Now wasps, that's another story. You can really get a bunch of…"

She gasped, and I realized that she had a lot of intense fears.

"But don't worry, no one is much bothered by them."

"I'm afraid of spiders, too. I have arachnophobia."

"Well, we have a couple of spiders, but they stay in their webs and catch hornets and wasps." I was trying like hell to calm her fears. I was beginning to think it might take a bucket of anti- anxiety pills.

"I didn't want to come up here. Mother doesn't miss a chance to show me off. Do you know what her plan for me is? I'm supposed to play the Beethoven Violin Concerto at Carnegie Hall in New York with the New York Philharmonic, no less. Then I will abandon the stage for a bit, marry well, produce twins so that she can show them off to her friends at the club, nurse them, and finally return for a fabulous world tour to wild acclaim."

I looked over and thought that the twins would be sending out for milk soon as they were able, but I didn't say it. She was a beauty, all right, but lacked some heft up front.

 Instead I said, "I met your mom; she's pretty smart. Do you ever get a chance to talk things over with her, or is there only one way?"

"It's my fault too, sometimes. I don't stick up for myself enough. Dad knows we have tension, and he also sticks up for me. Mother isn't totally negative; she just gets obsessed with an idea and we have to go along. For ex-

298

ample-- you. She doesn't care that you aren't from money. She said you were dependable and trustworthy."

That made me feel like an ad for a bank or life insurance.

"So, what's your verdict?"

"I don't think that you'll have to worry about a love affair with me. What's your name again, Marty?"

"Max."
I felt some relief that I didn't have to fret about a relationship with her, like I had a say in anything anyway. We drove on in silence. She looked straight ahead as though she was alone in the wagon. Then she turned to me and said, "Mother told me an unusual story about a calf that made a mess in a car. Is that really true?"

"Sure is. Why we're sitting in it."

Another wrong thing to say. She tensed up and hugged Eugenio tighter. I think she held her breath the rest of the way to camp, probably so that she wouldn't inhale any germs. I drove her over to the other side, and there in front of cabin two was a very long 1960 maroonish Cadillac, or "Persian Sand," no less, if you read the hype from Detroit.

I pulled up beside it and got out. Shoshana made no move to open her door giving me no choice but to walk around the car and open it for her. I wondered if she would start calling me 'Jeeves'. As she exited the wagon, the door to the cabin flew open and out sprang Mrs. Silverman like a jack-in-the-box.

"Oh, Sweetie, you're here! Hello, Max. Have the two of you been talking?"

Despite the fact that the violin case was still in 'Ahhna's' clutches, Mrs. Silverman gave her a massive hug. I figured that Eugenio got more of the hug's benefit than Ahhna. Then it was my turn.

"Oh, Max, so good to see you again!" I got a hug and a very sloppy kiss on the ear along with a long ''mmmm'' that sounded like she'd had a climax.

"Max, get the trunk out of my car like a good fellow, okay?"

"Yes, mom— ma'am— I mean. Ma'am."

She used a key to open the trunk that was huge, but had barely enough space for the footlocker inside. The brass tag on it declared that it was the "hernia model deluxe." I dragged it out, and Mrs. Silverman pointed to the cabin. As you know, I lift weights, but the trunk gave me a run for my money. I hauled it in with Mrs. S. close behind, spewing directions like a director of stevedores, as to where she wanted it. After I sweated the thing into four different positions, she decided that the first one was best.

"Well, I said, "I guess I'll leave you ladies to catch up. Have more errands to run. Lunch is at noon and it's almost time. Can I take you over?

Mrs. Silverman said, "No, thank you, Max. I've ordered lunch from a caterer in town. There will be enough for you, too. We're having lobster bisque and Cornish Hen with a pear and goat cheese salad. Oh, and a beautiful bottle of Puilly-Fuissé, a lovely French white burgundy. I got that for you, Shoshana."

I said, "Gee, I think the camp lunch is macaroni and cheese, my favorite. Sure you won't come over?"

Mrs. Silverman demurred, I guess the word would be, and so I got the hell out of there and drove back to the camp. I decided that the Silverman family was way too much for me. I wondered about Shoshana's dad, the surgeon, and how he managed with these two women. Maybe long hours in surgery. It certainly would be a lot more fun cutting people up than being cut up between those two. I'd thought at first that Mrs. Silverman liked me the first time we met. I realized it was more about herself and me than about my suitability for her daughter. She lives to control.

The mess hall was full by the time I arrived. I saw Richard Merrens and went over to tell him that Shoshana was on the other side with the Mrs.

A shadow crossed his face when I mentioned Mrs. Silverman, but he said, "Oh, super. I'll go over soon as I'm finished and we'll discuss what to play."

"I think you'll be playing "Secondary Bison" by Sarah somebody. That's what Shoshana told me."

301

He looked at me with a blank expression at first, then he registered a look of recognition and said, "Okay, thanks, Max. A great piece for the kids."

I sat with the specialists and shoveled in a large bowl of macaroni and cheese. I wondered how the lobster bisque tasted and if the wine was properly chilled.

Chapter 18
A Concert and Surprises

A day or two went by without too much excitement for a change. Bruce developed an infection in his wound. I took him to the Walkerville Clinic where they were able to give him a course of antibiotics. His leg remained sore, but he wasn't complaining about it. Larry was overseeing Camp Craft, and Freddy was bitching about his style.

The day before the violin concert I was having lunch at the mess hall when Lee came to the staff table where I was eating and said, "Max, I need you. Something's come up. Step outside for a minute, okay?"

It was unusual to see Lee in the mess hall. She was always working and ate lunch at her desk. I put down my tuna salad sandwich, with one bite missing and followed her outside.

"What's going on, Lee? Why the secrecy? You could have told me what you needed while I ate."

"Trouble between Mrs. Silverman and Shoshana is what."

"So, what do you want with me? I'm a social worker now? You got a staff full of them."

"Don't go getting sarcastic with me! I've had enough of a bad morning with those women!"

Lee was always even-tempered. Something had riled her up badly.

"Okay, so what's going on with the ladies? You want to go up to the office and talk?"

"Sorry, Max. That's more like it. No, Mrs. Silverman is at the office talking with Moira and Larry about the concert. Something must have gone on with her daughter, though. She's very tense and is giving everyone a tough time."

"Well, what can I do about it?"

"Shoshana needs some repairs on her violin and has to get to Port Edwards, since they have the closest violin maker in these parts. There's a music store in Walk-erville, but they just sell stuff. Shoshana needs an expert to work on her violin. To top it off, Mrs. Silverman thought she had brought her good violin up for the con-cert. When she found out Shoshana brought her 'junker,' as she calls it, all hell broke loose. You've got to take her there."

"Take her where, to Port Edwards? That's really quite a drive. Can't I just take the violin there myself?"

"No, she has to go along to make sure the work is done to her satisfaction."

" So, I have to go with her? She can't just take that big Cadillac and go by herself?"

"Come on, Max, she doesn't know her way around here. And anyway, what happened to our happy road warrior who's always shuttling the lookers on the staff to town and yakking about the freedom of the highway? Suddenly you got cold feet to spend a half day with Miss Icicle?"

Wow, she really let me have it! I didn't know she was keeping track of who rode with me. She pegged me good. I'd never seen Lee get so hot under the collar and sarcastic. All the same, she had a point. Mrs. Silverman was all lightness and charm with me, but I thought she was a hard case on others. Lee was just taking her frustrations out on me rather than Mrs. S. I already had a good dose of Shoshana when I met her at the train, and "Miss Icicle" was a good fit for a name.

I put my hands on Lee's shoulders and attempted a little pacification. "Hey, calm down, I'll get the thing fixed, no need to go off like a bomb!"

"I'm sorry, Max, I didn't mean to take it out on you. It's been so keyed up since the two of them got up here.

Mrs. Silverman has been firing orders at Moira and Larry all morning, taking her anger out on all of us. I never saw her like that."

"Okay, I get the picture. What do I have to do?"

"Shoshana is waiting for you on the other side. Mrs. Silverman told me to call her and figure out how to get the fiddle where it has to go. Neither of them is any fun to work with. Shoshana is acting as bitchy as her mother. I'm not sure why, okay? Just get her to the violin shop in Port Edwards. It's on the corner of fifth and Sherman. Right downtown. If she hasn't had lunch, buy it for her. Do whatever you have to and settle her down. Here's some money; I figure you'll need it. These people expect to be taken care of. Get receipts if you buy her anything."

Lee handed me an envelope with some cash, turned around and started walking back toward the office. I caught up to her, slipped an arm around her waist and said, "Hang tight, Lee. I'll get things straightened out."

I jumped into the wagon, my feelings mixed. I was both the hero off to save a damsel in distress, and the coward who feared a pretty face hiding a razor tongue. I drove much more slowly to the other side. I was so used to the roads by now that I could really move on them. My sluggish progress told me just how much I wanted to be with 'Aaahnaa'.

I pulled up and parked. Shoshana was standing in front of her cabin, clutching the violin case containing "Eugenio, her junker violin" to her chest. Made, she told me, in the eighteen-seventies. I wondered how many people had caressed, held and played on that old piece of wood. I wondered if it possessed a soul and a memory. I wondered if there was a way out of driving to Port Edwards with this neurotic girl who was plagued with every sort of fear. I put on a smile I didn't feel and stepped out of the wagon.

"Hi, Aaahnaa," I said. I hoped I got the intonation correct. "I hear you're having a violin problem. What's going on?"

"My sound post is out of position."

I had no idea what a sound post was, or what position it would be in. I thought I'd try a little humor. "So, what position does it play, short stop or third base?" I thought that it was a hilarious line.

"God, don't you know anything? And you're not funny, you know. This is serious!"

I never saw such a look of frustration on anyone's face. Her lips compressed and her cheeks were angry red blotches. Her back was ramrod stiff, her eyes blazed with anger. Her fingers were white with the pressure of grasping the violin case. I didn't understand how what I'd said triggered all that, but I knew that it had ignited something.

"We have to go to Port Edwards. There's a violinmaker there. I've talked with him and he can fix the problem. Can we get started?"

I opened the door to the wagon and she entered, still clutching the violin case to her chest.

"Be more comfortable if you put the case in the back seat," I said as cheerily as I could. She shook her head, I said, "Right," and we got rolling. I wondered if she used the damned thing as some sort of protective armor. I headed east on Route 13 toward Port Edwards.

We rode quiet for about ten minutes; then she said in a weird flat voice, like a robot, "The sound post is a small piece of wood that fits inside the violin. Its placement is key to the sound the instrument makes. It's not where I want it. You need a small tool to correct the position. *AND I'M TIRED OF YOUR BAD JOKES AND UPBEAT MANNER. YOU'VE BEEN ON MY CASE SINCE I GOT HERE! WHY CAN'T YOU JUST LEAVE ME ALONE AND RUN SOMEONE ELSE'S LIFE FOR A CHANGE? YOU'RE A ROTTEN BITCH AND A TERRIBLE PER-SON AND I HATE YOU!*"

She started pounding on the dashboard with her fists and stamping her feet. The violin case tumbled down beneath her feet. Then she started shaking, and I wondered if she was going to have a seizure or something.

She scared the crap out of me. I almost did a "Marilyn Monroe" right there in the wagon. I thought she'd gone around the bend for sure, and I had no idea what to do. Then it came to me. It wasn't me she was screaming at; it was her mother. I mean, heck, I'm not a "bitch." The kid was shaking it loose because we were out of Mrs. Silverman's control for a while. It was a full- blown tantrum like kids pull in supermarkets when they can't get a candy bar they want. This kid needed the Professor, not me.

"Hang on, Aaahnaa." I saw a forest preserve entrance up ahead and pulled off into the parking lot. There were only a few cars with some tourists heading off on the trail for a hike. I cut the engine, put the car in first gear, and pulled up the emergency brake. Shoshana didn't have much gas left in her. She went sort of limp and stared out of the windshield at nothing. Her face was blotchy red. She covered her face with her hands and started to sob.

I waited. It took a while for her to get her composure and, just as I thought she was getting it together, she flew across the seat and started screaming and hitting me with open hands. I was so startled it took me a moment to react. I blocked her hands reflexively, and nearly hit her with an overhand right to the kisser. I mean, she was wide open; no sense of guard at all. Instead, I tied her up in a clinch and held her tight. I wondered if the dream I'd had in which I was at a boxing match was somehow a psychic glimpse of the future! She squirmed for a bit, but then went limp again and cried softly against my chest. It took a while for her to gain control, then,

"I'm all right now, Marty."

"Max."

"Um, Max."

"You sure?"

She nodded, her head still buried against me. I eased up my grip, hoping she was done with the wild swings. I was conscious of some pain on my cheek. I glanced at the rear view mirror. She'd caught me with a nail; there was a scratch that seeped blood. Nothing much to be concerned about. She straightened up and moved away. Her face was a mess, her hair all tousled, eyes puffy.

We sat quietly while she got her breath under control and composed herself. After a bit I said,
"If it would help, would you like to hike a little way on the trail here? There's a stream that runs nearby. It's real pretty. Wild flowers, birds."
She sat looking at me for a few moments, then nodded her head.

"We can hide the violin under a tarp. I don't think anyone would break into a car up here."

"The violin is with Victoria, the nurse, back at the cabins. The case is empty."

"What? Well, how? I mean, why? Aren't we supposed to...."

"It was a ruse to get away from my mother. She's been harping about everything since I arrived at camp. I couldn't stand it any longer. I had to escape, so I lied about the sound post. I took the case as a cover. She can materialize anytime show up when you least expect it. She's always watching. We don't trust each other. I'm sorry I attacked you. Is your face...."

"Yeah, I'm fine, no problem. You're pretty quick."

"Yes, my staccato is excellent, especially my up-bow staccato. Marty, do you know anything about how violinists are trained? Do you know that I sometimes practice seven or eight hours a day? Do you know what it's like to be chained by your mother to an instrument that you've come to hate? I haven't had any fun in years. My boyfriend, Lenny, is the only thing in my life that's real or joyful. That's why my mother detests him. She's afraid he's going to take me away from her."

"I thought you— I thought the violin was, you know, the main thing in your life."

"It IS, Marty, it IS!"

"Max. But you just said you're chained to it and hate it."

"I hate that my mother *chains* me to it. Look, some people wear charm bracelets. You're acquainted with them, right?"

"Well, sure, I..."

"My mother has a full-size, real-life charm bracelet. She's shackled me to it so that she can boast to her friends that she has a daughter who's a prodigy and will soon be world-renowned. My dad's also fastened to it; he's a brilliant surgeon. Her organizations are chained to it; they fawn over her great work. My older brother is manacled to it; he's at Harvard law. You want more? Okay, the building we live in is bound to it; she's manipulating the powers-that-be to grant it historical status.

You'll be attached to it too, if she gets her way! You getting it yet?"

"Yeah, I got it. You're rebelling against your mother by taking everything out on yourself. You want to both play violin and dump it because your mother wants to brag about your playing and being famous and you don't want her to have that pleasure. Is that close?"

She opened her mouth, then closed it. Then I prompted, "Let's go for that walk."

I slid out of the wagon and she still sat motionless. I forgot to do my chauffeur bit. I came around to her side wondering if I was the chauffeur or the shrink, Jeeves or Sigmund. Something told me to just keep my mouth shut. We walked down the path toward the stream, then along the bank. A warm breeze mussed our hair. There were wildflowers all around, with some ducks poking their heads down in the stream for lunch. I hadn't finished mine.

She said, "I've always admired ducks."

"Why's that?"

"They're so accomplished."

I looked at her puzzled.

"Can you swim, walk on land AND fly? Being accomplished, that's what she wants for me, so she can flaunt it to the world. It's what she lives for. It's what I crave for myself too, but I hate giving it to her."

"So, who's suffering?"

"Both of us, I guess."

"You hungry?"

"Famished, I haven't eaten anything all day."

"Well, I'm no duck, I can't dunk for lunch, but I got a pocket full of cash. Whaddya say we run away to Port Edwards and I'll buy us the best meal we can find?"

So, that's what we did. I found a supper club that was open, a pretty upscale place. I let Shoshana go in first, because she was much better dressed than I was. She was also much better at talking to the wait staff and letting them know she was totally comfortable and in her element. She ordered wine, and though we were underage, no questions were asked. I was uncomfortable in such a fancy setting, but she was relaxed, and I could tell she was in her stomping grounds there. It helped settle her down. So did the wine. I drank just a little because I was driving. I really wanted a beer, but was too intimidated by the place to ask. She ordered a lot of stuff I'd never heard of; Oysters Rockefeller, blue points, and Cornish Hen, which turned out to be a tiny chicken with not much meat on it. Wasn't bad, though.

We killed almost two hours there. She talked about her lessons in London, master classes with brilliant musicians from all over, and how she expected to get into Juilliard or maybe the Curtis Institute. I never heard of those places, but from the way she talked about them I figured they were special. She talked about her father a little. She didn't see much of him because of his hours at the hospital, but he seemed very special to her. She didn't ask anything about me, and I said very little. I knew she just needed to talk.

I blew everything Lee had given me on that meal, plus all that I had in my pocket. Shoshana had to leave the tip. I made sure to take a copy of the check, and we left. Shoshana was a bit high when we got back into the wagon. She seemed loose and relaxed for the first time since I met her.

"Marty...."

"Um, Max."

"Yes, Max, thank you so much for understanding and taking care of me. I loved our walk by the stream, and the lunch was divine. I'm sorry we got off to such a bad start. You're really quite a decent person. Now, take me back to camp. I must practice."

It sounded to me that she had cleared the deck, at least for a while. I fired up the wagon and headed back. Mostly we were quiet on the way. I was trying to put her distraught thinking into some kind of order in my own mind. Her only comment during the ride back was on the beauty of the woods and farms we passed. We got back to the other side, I went through my chauffeur routine, and her mother sprang out of the bushes to greet us.

"Oh, honey, how did it go in Port Edwards? Is the violin all right?"

"Yes, mom, he did a great job. I have a bit of a headache. I'm going to ask Victoria for some aspirin." She took the empty case and walked to the infirmary. Smooth.

Mrs. Silverman jabbed an elbow in my ribs and said in a conspiratorial voice, "So, Max, how did the trip go? Say, is that a scratch on your face?" She was grinning like the Cheshire Cat. I bet she thought that Shoshana and I maybe had had some wild sex on the trip, or were at least getting to know each other really well. She was sort of right and sort of wrong. I thought, *no charm bracelet for me, lady.*

"Oh, yeah, I got snagged on a low bush when we parked in Port Edwards. We had a good trip. Everything worked out fine, Mrs. Silverman. By the way, Shoshana told me that your husband is a great surgeon. What's his first name? You never know when you'll need a great doctor."

"Oh, sure, Max, it's Marty. Marty Silverman, M.D."

I'm a psychic. I knew his name would be Marty.

The concert by Richard and Shoshana was planned for seven P.M. on a Tuesday evening. Mrs. Silverman coached the staff about the proper etiquette for a serious classical music concert, and she asked the staff members to teach the campers. She thought that proper behavior at a concert was something all children should know. I attended her training session and learned a lot. I never knew it was bad form to applaud between movements, for example, and that one was expected to stifle

a cough and not rattle the program notes. This was so different than blue grass concerts. I had a recording where Lester Flatt called to his steel guitar man, *"Say, let me hear you play that one more time, Brother Oswald!"*
I bet you would never hear Heifetz say anything like that to Emanuel Bray in the middle of a chamber piece.

Campers were asked to wear white clothes for the concert. They were told they were in for something special, therefore, their behavior should be the best. There was a buzz of excitement in the mess hall that night.

Shoshana and Richard Merrens were offstage in the kitchen until everyone was seated. The mess hall tables had been folded and put against a wall and the chairs were in "concert audience formation."

The Professor stood on a slightly raised wooden platform that was a makeshift stage for the occasion. Somehow Bob Wheeler and the kitchen boys had moved the grand piano that had been in the corner of the mess hall up on it.

The Professor called everyone to order and said, "Ladies and gentlemen, we have a very special treat for all of you this evening. We have a virtuoso violinist, Miss Shoshana Silverman, who will be accompanied by our very own Richard Merrens, counselor in Unit Seven. The violinist is the daughter of Mrs. Barbara Silverman, Treasurer of the Camp Board of Directors. Mrs. Silverman, please stand."

She stood and waved and got some applause. Then the Professor said, "And I have another great surprise for you this evening. Let me introduce Mr. Ken Greenman."

And darned if Mr. G. didn't walk in from the kitchen looking hale and hearty and twenty pounds lighter than he did the last time I saw him. He waved to the crowd and got a standing ovation from the staff. We were truly surprised and happy to see him.

He came to the platform and said, " Hello, everyone. I'm so pleased to be back with you again. I've missed you and being here at camp. I'm doing well and I want to thank those of you who called and sent cards to me while I was out ill. And now let me introduce Miss Shoshana Silverman and her accompanist, Richard Merrens. They are playing Zigeunerweisen by Sarasate and several other pieces."

Richard and Shoshana walked in to applause. He was wearing a black sweater and slacks. She had a gorgeous black silk gown, off the shoulder. She had a black ribbon around her neck that had sparkly stones or maybe even diamonds in it. Richard played a note on the piano and she tuned the violin just a bit, and then they played.

I'm no expert on classical music, but I thought their performance was amazing and so did everyone in the room. They took several bows. Shoshana was a different person up there. Beautiful, gracious, smiling, bowing, blowing kisses and mouthing "thank you's" to the audience. She was utterly unlike the frightened, phobic nervous wreck I brought from the train. I thought that there had to be two of her. I later learned that she possessed what's called "stage presence."

Mrs. Silverman stepped up to the stage, kissed her daughter with a grand flourish and gave her a bouquet of roses, kissed Richard, and then sat down. The performance was a real hit with everyone. I was grateful that it went off so well and amazed that nothing crazy happened for a change.

The crowd broke up quickly; it was getting late for the kids. I went up to Mr. G. and said, "Ken, I'm so happy you're back! I want to apologize that I didn't write you."

He replied, "Not to worry, Max, I've been keeping tabs on the camp. The Professor tells me that you've done a great job here. He also said that your friends have all done well. The summer's almost over and I'm hoping you'll all come back next year. I know some things haven't gone well, but your group has really come through with flying colors. And, hey, now you know all about impetigo, too!"

He slapped me on the back and we had a good chuckle. Then he started working the room, saying hello to many staffers that waited to wish him well.

I ambled back to the tent and got a great night's sleep. Next morning I learned that Mrs. Silverman and Shoshana had already left for Chicago. What more could you ask?

Chapter 19
My Longest Day

Toward the end of each session the older campers got the chance to try out their camping and water skills with a canoe trip that lasted several days. A cabin or two would pack up their gear and we would take them out to a river where they would paddle downstream and camp out for two nights. The kids would get a chance to build fires, cook, put up tents, sleep out of doors, and try their hand at "roughing it" in the wild. Generally, the trips went off without a hitch. Safety precautions were strictly enforced; kids and staff wore life jackets in the canoes, and had to pass tests on their canoeing and swimming skills.

Bruce had done a good job teaching fire-starting, choosing the right wood, cooking skills, rope handling and knot tying, using hatchets and knives safely, even anticipating weather conditions.

The Waterfront Team also did a great job teaching canoeing and safety on the water. The kids had to be able to capsize a canoe, get it righted, and climb back inside. They taught gunneling, the art of standing on the gunwales of the canoe and pumping their legs to propel it. The campers were well prepared, and looked forward to these outings. They came back to camp dirty and exhausted, but pleased with themselves because they had "bested the wilderness."

The last outing of the summer was scheduled for Mickey's cabin. She was now in Kitty's unit with the older girls. Kitty had worked long and hard getting Mickey and her girls ready for the trip. There were ten campers, Mickey, and for good measure, Kitty, who were set to go on the excursion.

On the morning of the trip I backed up the wagon and hitched the canoe rack to it. I pulled into the parking area so that the big truck could back in and load at the Camp Craft Building. Bruce was still not able to work. His leg was giving him trouble, and he had gone into Chicago to have it examined. Freddy was handling the food and Larry was overseeing the equipment loading with Leon and Michael Jenner. I checked the wagon and the canoe hitch and decided to go to a nearby gas station to fill up the tank and put a quart of oil in the crankcase.

When I got back, I grabbed a roll and a cup of coffee and went to check on the loading process. I noticed that Larry had piled up the tents, blanket rolls and a lot of utensils all across the bed of the truck. This meant that the campers would be riding very high in the back of the truck. Their weight would make the truck top-heavy.

I walked over and said, "Hey, Larry, the kids are going to be sitting pretty high up back there. Why not line the sides of the rack with the tents and put the blanket rolls down on the truck bed? That way the kids will be resting on softer stuff and lower down too."

He said, "Max, I don't need you to second guess me."

"Yeah, but Larry, the truck is going to be top-heavy and the kids will be up in a stiff wind as they travel."

"Max, keep your adolescent attitude to yourself. I know what I'm doing."

So I shut up. I shouldn't have, but I did. Kitty, Mickey and the campers came down the main road singing, and it was easy to see how happy and excited they were. They carried their pillows, had jackets tied around their waists with pockets filled with snack bars. They were smeared with sun tan lotion and cocoa butter, and all wore floppy hats to prevent sunburn. Kitty was leading the singing.

Mickey sang too, but I could tell her heart wasn't in this. She was not, as my mother would have said, "from the pioneers." The summer had been tough on her. I hadn't seen much of her lately, and she looked tired and thin. There were dark puffy patches under her eyes. Too much necking in the woods at night, I thought. I shrugged and went back to the wagon to review the trip on my Wisconsin map. Another half-hour passed before everything was organized. The campers were chattering and arguing about who would get to ride in the truck, a big thing for them.

Kitty and three of the girls got into the wagon with me. Mickey and the rest of the girls climbed aboard the truck. Larry was driving and Leon sat in the shotgun position. I smiled to myself when I thought of that. I wondered if Larry remembered it was Leon who shot the raccoon. He scurried away so quickly that I didn't think it registered with him who was holding it. Bob Wheeler probably puzzled it out from hearing the story. It bothered me that Larry was driving. The truck was an old model, probably from the early 1950's, had no power steering, and the brakes were nothing to write home about. I'd driven it once and found it hard and unwieldy to handle. My driving was a hell of a lot better than Larry's. It also bothered me that Larry was so harsh when I tried to tell him about the truck being overloaded and top-heavy. Was I being an adolescent? I didn't think so.

Kitty sat next to me, and the three girls sat in the back. The rest of the wagon contained some equipment and a couple of coolers with food. I scrutinized the instructions that Lee had given me. We were headed for the Wisconsin River, up near Stevens Point. I had to travel east to get to the river, then head north to the drop-off point.

The day was bright and clear, and the temperature was fairly cool this early. The campers gave a cheer and the truck started to move out. I gave it a bit of space and started the wagon's engine. We were off, and the girls started another song. I let go of my anger at Larry's harsh words, put on my sunglasses, and decided to enjoy the ride and the company.

We headed east on highway 54. The road was good and the traffic light. Kitty started to say something and then thought better of it. Probably, I thought, something about Mickey. I wanted to say something about Larry, but decided not to because of the campers.

The singing kept up. We were making good time; Larry was holding a pretty good pace in the truck. I settled in, swung my visor down, and enjoyed the drive. About an hour away from camp, we came to the top of a hill. We were in the midst of a lot of rolling country.

From the top of the hill I could see the truck about a half-mile ahead as it approached a fork in the road. It was hard to determine the fork from the main road because of the bright sunlight. It looked like the main road went around to the right and went behind a copse of trees. The fork went straight ahead. I had nearly reached the bottom of the hill when I saw the truck attempt to make a very sharp turn to stay with the main road. I saw it skid around the curve out of sight. As I got closer, I saw that the road did go right, and the fork went straight ahead. The fork was a smaller gravel road. The gravel shined brightly in the sunlight, and that made seeing the correct direction difficult. I had to brake hard to stay with the road. There was a lot of gravel in the intersection that caused skidding. It was a dangerous intersection. I was glad that I'd slowed up.

 We came around the bend and I caught sight of the truck about a hundred yards ahead. It had slid off the road, rolled down the left side embankment, and had come to rest upside down. The wheels were still spin-ning, and billows of dust and smoke obscured the wreckage.

Kitty spotted it too. She gasped and said, "Max, look!"

"Yeah, I see it. This doesn't look good. Kitty, stay in the wagon, don't get out, and don't let the kids leave either."

I pulled onto the right shoulder, shut down the engine and scrambled out. I raced over to the truck. There was dead silence. I was gripped by fear, and thought every-one was dead. The truck was wedged against a utility pole, and wires wires were down. I didn't know if they were phone or power lines. I looked into the cab; the truck's engine was still running. Larry was jammed up-side down in the driver's seat and was very still. I saw Leon struggling to heave himself upright and yelled, "Leon, shut off the goddam engine!"

Then I heard weak cries from the back of the truck, girls moaning for their mothers and screaming for help. That was the best indication so far. At least some were alive.

"Leon, for chrissakes, cut the ignition!"

I could make out that he was in shock and not respond-ing. Then I smelled gas and spotted a leak in the tank. That sent a jolt of fear through me, and I started to pull on the driver's side door. It was wedged closed from the impact.

I screamed, *"Leon, kick on the door! You gotta get out of there!"*

It was fortunate that Leon had been the passenger. His size and strength made the difference between minor injury and a total disaster. He managed to get himself oriented and used his legs to land a desperate smash on the driver's door. It blew open and knocked me back. Larry flopped limply like out like a sack of potatoes, and Leon slid out next, nearly falling on him. It struck me as funny, but I was too frightened to laugh. I wasn't sure if Larry was alive or dead. Leon was still in shock and kept muttering, "I'm alive, Max, I'm alive."

The cries from the campers grew louder. I went to the back end of the truck and looked in. The campers who had been riding high up were sprawled on the ground, covered by tents, pots, utensils and blanket rolls. I began dragging them out, trying not to hurt anyone in case they had injuries. I wished Bruce had been there, as I knew nothing about first aid. The kids were banged up, bleeding, frightened out of their wits and crying. I counted all seven and positioned them against the embankment with their feet elevated. Somehow I remembered that when a person's in shock, getting blood up to the head was good. Anyway, I hoped it was that way around and not the head that should be elevated. I wasn't thinking clearly.

Leon yelled, "Hey, there's gas leaking and it's heading for those wires! I think that's dangerous!"

Then I remembered that Mickey was still somewhere in the back of the truck!
I started to burrow my way into the equipment like a mole. She had been riding up at the front of the truck bed, and the gas tank was just ahead of her behind the cab.

I screamed, *"Mickey! Are you all right? Mickey, I'm coming for you!"*

"Max, I can't move!" Her voice was very weak.

"Hang on, I'm coming!" I crawled along the ground, shoving aside all kinds of junk. Something snagged my shirt and it ripped. Leon yelled to me that the gas was gushing out faster, and I doubled my efforts. I saw feet, one with a shoe and the other without. I crawled alongside of her, pushing debris out of my path, and finally got to her. She had a gash on her forehead, some bruises, and her face was white.

"Mickey, come on, we have to get out of here!"

"I can't move!"

"Where's it hurt?"

"It's my shoulder! And something is pinning me, my sweatshirt is stuck!"

I crawled practically on top of her and saw that her sweatshirt was pinned to the ground by one of the vertical posts of the rack. She screamed in pain as I jostled her.

I yelled, "Leon! Can you get your back under the truck bed and lift it up a little?"

He scrabbled around for a purchase. I heard him grunting with effort, but the truck was wedged tight and he couldn't budge it. I heard a 'pop' and knew the gas had caught fire. We would be roasted alive if I didn't get us out. And then I did something that boggled my mind. To this day I'll never understand how I was able to pull it off. I got both hands on Mickey's sweatshirt and ripped it apart like it was tissue paper.

"Mickey, put your arms around my neck! I *know* it hurts! Do it anyway!"

I got my right arm under her and used my left to inch my way backwards, pulling her along behind me. We got

into the open just as the truck exploded. Mickey passed
out. I dragged myself to my feet and hauled her away
from the back of the truck.

 I sat on the ground gasping for breath when a voice
next to my ear grated, "Got some trouble here, son?
Name's Arty Swenson. Looks like you might need a
hand."

He was an angel in an odd form; a grizzled farmer sitting
in an ancient Dodge coupe. He wore a dirty tee shirt and
Oshkosh B'Gosh overalls. He was chewing on a weed
that drooped from his mouth.

"You sure everyone's out of that thing?", he said. I nodded. "Right, then get in my car. I'll take you to my place
and we'll call the State Police, get an ambulance. Okay,
son?"

I crawled up the embankment and said, "Thank you, sir.
Just let me tell my people what's going on."

I trotted down the road to the wagon, Kitty had opened
the windows down and was looking out at me with fear
on her face.

"Max?"

"Kitty, the kids are pretty much all right. Larry is out cold;
I'm not sure what's wrong. I think he hurt his head.
Leon's in shock. Mickey's hurt, probably not too bad.
That guy in the Dodge is a local farmer. He'll take me to
his house and we'll call for help. Maybe you can keep an
eye on the gang over on the embankment. Stay away

from the truck. I think it's just going to burn, but I don't know for sure. I'll be back with help as soon as I can."

I trotted back to the Dodge and we sped to Arty Swenson's house. It wasn't far. We pulled up to a plain white frame farmhouse with a small front yard. The house was old, but well kept. Geraniums drowsed in pots on the windowsill, a white picket fence corralled a small shepherd dog in the yard that was frantically wagging its tail. A woman that I guessed was Mrs. Swenson gazed out of a kitchen window. She was a thin woman with graying hair pulled back in a bun. When she opened the door Arty said, "Ma, got a problem down on 54. Kid here was in an accident, got to make some calls."

He went to a candlestick phone like the one my grandmother had, flicked the gizmo that held the earpiece a couple of times and waited. "Yeah, Maude, I'm fine, how're you, how's Harold? Uh-huh, still on the booze, shame."

"Listen, Maude, truck went over near the gravel road out ta' 54. Wish to hell the County'd put up a sign there. 'Bout the third time last couple months someone missed that turn and wound up in the ditch. No, nobody dead, I don't think. One guy stretched out, maybe out cold. Yeah, the usual. Call Port Edwards, get 'em going." I got a kid with me; says he's from the camp. I'll take him back there. His name? Yeah, wait, I'll put him on. Here, son, she wants some information."

I took the phone. "Yes ma'am? Yes, okay, I'm Max Lewis. I drive for Camp Nowatoma. There were seven campers and a counselor in the back of the truck, along with two in the cab. One of them may be badly hurt. Yes, that's right, please send ambulances and police, maybe firemen. The truck is burning; wires are down. They hit a pole. Yes, okay, thanks."

I thanked Arty and Mrs. Swenson; then he took me back to the truck. We'd been gone about twenty minutes. About ten more minutes after we returned we were suddenly surrounded by a cyclone of action. Several ambulances, State Police cars, and a fire truck showed up. There was a bustle of activity with the ambulance guys looking first at Larry, who was still unconscious, then Mickey, who they said had a broken collarbone and a probable concussion. The rest of the kids had various bruises and cuts, but thankfully most were in reasonable shape, having just been shaken up.

One of the ambulance attendants came over to me and drawled, "You Max? That little blonde wants you to go with her in the ambulance."

I asked where we were headed and told him to give me a minute. I walked over to Kitty and told her we were going to Port Edwards Hospital.

"Can you handle the wagon?"

"My license is at home. Is that all right?"

"Yeah, just drive carefully. Follow the ambulance, but if you lose them, just go to Port Edwards. Can you read a map?"

"Hey, I'm a science-math major!"

"Yeah, okay, I forgot. Sorry." *Geez,* I thought, *what a time to get huffy about her IQ!*

"Shouldn't be too hard to find the hospital. Mickey wants company."

"Okay, Max, see you there. Is this thing hard to drive with the canoe rack on it?"

"Just go slow, you'll be okay. Don't get into a situation where you have to back up; that's a bitch.

Oh, by the way, can you handle a stick shift?"

"Hey, I'm a...."

"OKAY! Sheesh!" I crawled into the back of the ambulance. Mickey was strapped down flat on her back with blankets over her. She was as pale as a ghost. The ambulance medics had cleaned and bandaged the gash on her head. I held her hand and it was like ice.

"Max, thanks for getting me out of there. I was terrified. You keep showing up when I'm in trouble. I haven't been so nice to you. I'm sorry."

"It's okay, Mickey. Just rest. We're headed for the hospital and you'll be fine, just relax."

She closed her eyes. I'd never been in an ambulance before. We were moving like crazy with the siren wailing. I think Mickey conked out. I sat scrunched up next to

her, holding her hand. I was wishing that she loved me--
or maybe that I didn't love her.

I don't know how long it took to get to the hospital. I worried about Kitty finding it and driving the wagon trailing
that damn canoe rack that I now believed had a curse
on it.

We got to the emergency room. The ambulance attendants delicately unloaded Mickey and wheeled her inside. I figured Larry must be in another ambulance.

I was standing by the ambulance when a nurse grabbed
my arm and barked, "Okay, you're next."

"No, I'm all right. Take care of everyone else, I'm fine."

The nurse said, "No, you're not fine! You're in shock,
and look! You're bleeding. You've been shot! Come this
way."

I looked down to where she was pointing and saw blood
on my jeans. I was wearing the ones that I had on when
Leon shot at the raccoon. There were pellet holes in the
leg. The bandage underneath must have come off and
the wound opened from crawling on the ground.

"No-no! I'm okay, I am!"

She looked at me closely and said, "You're sure? I've
seen pellet holes like that before and you're bleeding"

"Yes, I'm fine, honest. Just an old wound from being shot at when my friend missed a raccoon that was eating Michael's potato chips. Nothing at all."

She gave me an odd look and pointed. "There's a rest room. Go in there and clean yourself up."

This was the third time I'd been banished to a bathroom to clean myself up. The first time was the time I nearly got roasted in a forest fire and I looked like Al Jolson doing "Mammy." The second was after Moira and I, well, you know, and *that* wasn't so bad except that I looked like Mad Magazine's Alfred E. Neuman smeared with lipstick on the Valentine's Day issue. And now number three. I wondered how I'd look this time. I didn't count the time I got shot in the leg.

I opened the restroom door and flicked on the light. The guy in the mirror was a stranger. My hair was wild, matted with dirt and brush from crawling under the rubble on the truck. My shirt was torn, filthy, and had a lot of blood splattered over it. Wasn't mine, it was from everyone else. But my face was the worst. I looked like an old man! My eyes were bloodshot from smoke and gas fumes, and my skin looked like it was covered in dirt and flour, snow white with dark patches. No wonder the nurse wanted to pull me in for assistance.

I washed up as best I could, poured cold water on my hair and tried to comb it with my fingers. I scrubbed my face and tried hot water to get the blood moving. Then I just braced myself on the sink for about five minutes, stared at my image into the mirror, and had absolutely nothing going through my mind.

Then I said out loud, "Okay, Max, lets find out how everyone else is doing and get the kids back to camp."

I straightened my jeans, tightened my belt, and went looking for the nurse. I didn't see her, but I found a supervising nurse, told her who I was, and got an update. They wanted to hold Mickey overnight for observation. Same with Larry, who'd had a bad crack on the head from the windshield. He had a concussion, maybe a skull fracture, and a sore neck that needed x-rays. The kids were pretty much unhurt, shaken but not seriously injured. Leon had suffered contusions and had a sore back, and they wanted to keep him for a while also.

Someone had called the camp, and Mr. G., Bob Wheeler and Moira were on the way. I thanked the nurse and shuffled outside to the parking lot. The wagon with canoe rack was double-parked with Kitty behind the wheel. She had a smug smile on her face.

"See, what'd I tell you? I got here, no problem. Jesus, Max, you look like shit!"

Hearing her words, the campers tried to choke back their laughter, but couldn't keep it in. There were now six of them stuffed inside the wagon, four on the back seat and two in the rear luggage space. The rest were still being examined.

Kitty queried, "Max, you want to drive?"

I shook my head. She gave me a worried look and said, "Wow, you're not you!"

She drove back to camp with a heavy foot on the accelerator. I felt the blood rushing into my face several times, but only commented once when we did a curve and the canoe rack fishtailed. I gulped, "Please, a little less juice on the turns."

"Okay."

And that was it. I sighed in relief as Kitty pulled into the camp parking lot and killed the engine. I went into the office where Lee was making calls to parents and reassuring them that all was well. She looked at me and said, "Max, you look like you went through the mill. How're you doing?"

"Another day at the office."

"Was it bad?"

"Yeah, I'll tell you later. I think I need to lay down, very tired."

So, that was the day. I went back to the tent and lay down, closed my eyes and slept. It was about four in the afternoon. When I woke up it was ten A.M. the following day. I was sore, stiff and groggy. The accident seemed like a dream. I was filthy and smelled of sweat, my clothes stuck to me and my leg throbbed. A hot shower and a change of clothes did some good.

I went down to the mess hall since it was between meals and quiet there. The cooks hadn't yet come in for the noon meal. Bob was in his office, and he got up and motioned me to come in.

"Max, I heard the whole story from Kitty. You did a great job. We could have had a real disaster there. Ken and Moira spent the afternoon at the hospital. Everyone will be all right except for Larry. They're still trying to figure out the extent of his injuries. I'm very proud of the job you did."

Well, that made me feel a lot better. Praise from Bob meant a great deal to me. I thanked him and then used the extension in the kitchen to call home. I had to make sure the folks knew I was all right. They had already heard from Margie that I was okay, but they were glad to hear from me just the same.

The wagon was in the parking lot with the canoe rack still attached. I didn't want to touch the damned thing. It looked evil and dark.

Chapter 20
The End in Sight

It was now near the end of the summer. Things had settled down to a boring routine, which was all right with me. I'd had enough excitement. Staff members started thinking about the coming fall, worrying about next semester, getting applications done, registering for classes, and looking forward to going home. I had not yet learned to think ahead like that, and for me the focus was on working through the remainder of the season. I was at lunch when one of the kitchen boys came over to my table with a message. Moira had called the kitchen and asked that I come down to the office. I finished up lunch and walked down. Lee was out, and Moira was in her office with the door open. I walked on in.

She had taken to wearing a lot of black clothes. That day she had on a black silk shirt that was tailored for a woman, but looked masculine. It sported French cuffs that seemed out of place. She wore black slacks, no make up, and her newly short hair was styled with a side part and pompadour.

"Sit down, Max. How're you doing?" All business. I missed her Loretta Young routine a lot.

"Hey, fine, Moira." I wanted to add, 'how they hangin,'" but I didn't have the nerve. I sat down. She shuffled some papers, then eyed me for a moment. It was unsettling.

"Max, you have a run to make this afternoon to the four o'clock train. Someone is going back to Chicago. It needs to be done quietly; nobody has to know."

"Who?"

"It's Mickey. I just fired her."

"But why, Moira? The summer is almost over."

"Max, ordinarily I wouldn't discuss a staff termination with anyone, but this whole deal with Mickey has been a mess from the start. I know that you know, so we don't have to play games and you don't have to deny anything.

Mickey faked her application from the start and hoodwinked Larry, who couldn't see past her slick smile and dreamy eyes. I messed up my review and didn't check her out effectively. My fault. After the accident I had to go through her file for questions about workman's comp, who pays for the hospital, stuff like that. I got suspicious, and started making calls. She's not enrolled at the school listed on her application, and the reference letters were faked, a serious enough issue by itself. She forged letters and signatures from professors who never heard of her. I believe you knew each other in Chicago. I bet she suckered you into not saying anything. Her record as a counselor has been dismal, except that she did better working with Katz. You want to say anything so far?"

I shook my head. Moira missed her calling; she should be working for the FBI. She went right on.

"Larry blocked my move to can her early in the summer. That business with you and Crash getting into a fight because of her was bad enough. But then there was the dreadful way she handled her campout and lied about Bruce and you. She just isn't the right material for us. You want more?"

"No, it's plenty. I'm sorry, Moira. She asked me not to even acknowledge that we knew each other. I had a thing for her and...."

"It's okay, Max. Listen, you and I have had our ups and downs...."

I said, "Yeah, a couple of times!" and couldn't help smiling at that. She cracked a smile in return.

"Close the door."

I threw up my hands up in mock horror and said, "Oh, no! Again?"

She laughed and said, "No, I'm a new man—, person, I mean person!"
And we laughed until tears came down.

"Moira, I don't have the right words, but I hope we'll always be friends. We have a special relationship, I hope you agree."

"Max, you're a super guy. Come here; just a hug, I need one."
And we hugged like brother and sister. Or maybe a couple of brothers. Who the hell knew anymore?

So that was it. What should have happened before the summer was coming down now. I killed a few hours down at the beach, just looking at the water and thinking about the summer. I looked at my watch; it said nearly three o'clock, ordinarily too early to leave to make the four o'clock train, but I wanted to get Mickey out of the camp and out of my life. I walked back to the mess hall and slid into the wagon and drove down to the older girls' unit. I saw a few stragglers strolling toward the beach for an afternoon swim and figured it was a good time to get Mickey out of there with nobody around.

I went up the three steps to her cabin and knocked.

"Yes?"

"Mickey, it's me, can I come in?"

"Okay, Max."

There was a suitcase on the bed and a duffel bag on the floor, all packed. Nothing left in the room of her personal effects. She sat on the bed with her hands in her lap, looking at the floor.

"I came to take you to the train."

"I know. Moira told me you would."

"Mickey, I'm sorry it ended like this."

"Not your fault, Max."

"You ready?" She just nodded. She never took her eyes off the floor. I took the suitcase, hefted the duffel strap across my shoulder, and stowed them in the wagon. She came down the stairs with a wooden walk and didn't turn around to look at the cabin. She got into the car, and I pulled out for Walkerville.

The drive to the station was in silence. Mickey gazed out of the side window the whole time. I kind of hoped she would talk to me, but nothing was said. At the station, I retrieved her baggage and placed it on the platform. It was still early for the train, and I asked if she wanted company while she waited.

"No, I'm all right, Max, you don't have to wait. The conductor will help me with the bags."

"Goodbye, Mickey. Safe trip." No response, not a thanks or a goodbye.

I got into the wagon and pulled out of the parking lot. The last I saw of her was the receding image in my rearview mirror. And then I was on the road back to camp. As I drove, I started to feel a weight lifting off of me. My summer should have been a fun time. Mickey's presence was unexpected, and now I felt how unwelcome it had been. She'd nearly gotten me killed a couple of times. It caused me to become secretive and dishonest, and it caused me pain to watch her constant flirting with so many of the guys-- even a drip like Crash Kelly-- while shunning me. What was I holding on for? Whatever it was I felt it slipping away, like when someone gets a stomach bug and feels miserable, weak and nauseous, then senses his body healing and getting stronger. I figured that I was getting over Miss Mickey, and that it was all right. Maybe that particular bout was over done. I glanced at my watch. The train had probably made its stop and she was gone. I was pretty sure, forever. Then again you never know.

Chapter 21
Getting Back to Reality

The summer came to an end. The campers gathered at the beach for the final closing program, and this time Harvey and Martha managed to spell "Friendship" correctly. The next morning initiated the chaos of the campers packing up for home, the farewells as the buses pulled in to transport them to the train, some girls crying, some singing, and some hugging their counselors. The boys were slapping each other on the back, and experiencing the joy that the end of a good time brings.

And then the camp was still. You could hear birds singing in the trees as they settled down for the night. You could hear individual screen doors creak as they closed without shouts and laughter to cover the sounds. The ball field was empty, the mess hall uncommonly quiet at meal times. Slowly those staff members who owned cars packed up and said goodbyes after breakfast. I took others into town to take the train home. We were soon down to the specialists and some other staff who could work extra time to put the camp in the end of season mothballs.

The pier on the beach was dismantled. The Camp Craft building had its heavy window shutters closed for the winter, the same for the Arts and Crafts building. The bathhouses were also closed and the pipes drained. The kitchen boys and I took down the tents and moved into camper cabins that were much more comfortable. It was nice to have walls, doors and windows with screens. And two light bulbs, real luxury.

The administrative staff continued to work in the office and type up reports, pay bills and notify vendors that the camp was closing for the season. Ken was back in his office. I learned that Lee was also his secretary in Chicago. She'd been the one who was out on a break when Moira and I went to see him. Larry had been released from the hospital and was doing all right. Moira let me know that he might not be back next season. She wouldn't say anything more. She continued a relationship with Victoria.

Bruce was accepted to the University of Illinois and entered a pre-med program. He and Freddy went back to Chicago on the train. Kitty and I stayed on to help put the camp to bed for the winter. She had come up early and earned extra cash for school at both ends of the summer. We were among the last there. The local kitchen boys came in to work each day to close up the mess hall and kitchen. The cooks and assistants were down to just a skeleton crew. Bob Wheeler was overseeing the entire operation.

A couple of days before Kitty was scheduled to leave, I told her about the trip I had taken to Port Edwards with Shoshana including my first experience at a fancy supper club.

"Kitty, since you're leaving in just a couple of days, I want to take you to a supper club and celebrate the whole summer. I'm ready for a great dinner. I'm so tired of tuna and macaroni that I can't look at it any more. Bob Wheeler told me about a place near here called Michelson's. He raved that it's just great, not terribly fancy, but the best cooking from here to Madison. Let's go there tomorrow night and honor the end of camp with some food and drink. It's been some experience for me. What do you say?"

"Sounds terrific, Max. I've had it with camp food, too. I think it would be great to get out of here and let someone else serve us for a bit. What time tomorrow?"

"Ah, let's say six-thirty. That way we'll be good and hungry when we finally eat."

"Okay, I want you to pick me up at my cabin. I'm going to have a big surprise for you."

I couldn't imagine what she had in mind. I got myself cleaned up the next afternoon. Showered, shampooed and shaved as closely as I could. I pulled out my one good shirt and gray slacks that were a bit wrinkled, buffed up my shoes, doused myself with aftershave and stuck a peppermint in my mouth.
    I walked down to the front office at about six twenty-five and drove through the camp to the older girls' units. Everything was so unnaturally still now. The campers were all gone, even most of the staff. I pulled up to Kitty's cabin and tooted the horn with a ''shave-and-a-haircut'' rhythm. And waited.

    I must have sat there for another ten minutes before the cabin door opened, and I caught my breath. The big surprise was Kitty. She was wearing high heels and a Chinese-styled emerald- green silk dress with a slit up the side. She had on a pearl necklace. Her red hair was down, blown full out, and she had makeup on for the first time since I'd known her. She was gorgeous!

"You like?" She said as she slipped into the wagon.

"Oh, I like! Kitty, you're beautiful!"

She smiled leaned over, and kissed my cheek. "A girl
has to get fixed up once in a while, makes us feel better.
Let's go, I'm starving."

I had trouble keeping my eyes on the road. It was like
being in a limo with a movie star. I knew Kitty was a pretty girl, but I had become used to her without makeup,
wearing old jeans, and with her hair in pigtails, frizzy
from humidity. She was a knockout. I felt so proud just to
be in the same car with her.

 When we got to Michelson's, I parked the wagon,
jumped out, and opened the door for her. When she
stood I realized that with her high heels she was at least
as tall as I am. I let her lead the way into the restaurant,
figuring she would make a much better impression than I
would. We were seated at a small table in a quiet area
with not much more than candlelight. There was a musician playing a guitar softly in a corner. The waiter asked
if we would like drinks. I nodded to Kitty, who selected a
vodka Martini, dry, with extra olives. I chose beer. We
went the whole route, ordering salads and the
Chateaubriand for two. The food lived up to Bob Wheeler's description.

After a couple of hours, I paid the tab (it was more than I
expected, and worth every penny). We walked out arm-
in-arm, well-fed, and floated into the wagon to begin the
drive back to camp. About a half mile from camp on
Highway 34, I saw two police cars across the road with a
blocking sawhorse between them. They had their flash-

ing lights illuminated. Several local policemen and a couple of state troopers stood watch around the cars.

Kitty said, "What's going on, an accident?"

"Not sure." I brought us to a stop, and an officer strode to my side window. His pistol was out and he rested the barrel on my windowsill. That made me nervous. He looked around the inside of the wagon, especially at the back.

"Howdy, folks, where you headed and what's under that tarp?"

" We work at the camp up the road a bit, officer. We're just heading back for the night. You want me to pull the tarp back?"

"Yep. You look a little spiffy to be working at a summer camp."

"End-of-season celebration. We just had dinner at Michelson's."

I craned around and whipped the tarp back. There were a few cardboard boxes, a coil of rope and some other junk. The officer nodded and told us to proceed slowly through the space between the two police cars. He nodded to the others, and they began pulling the blocker away.

"What's the trouble, officer? An accident?"

"Nah, there was a smash-and-grab at a jewelry store in
Walkerville. Some guy grabbed a bunch of watches. Not
much, but an off-duty trooper was passing and they
traded shots. Trooper went down, got a graze wound on
the head. We want that bastard. We caught sight of him
leaving town and followed him up around here, where
we lost him. There are other road blocks in the area; we
got it sealed up pretty good. You two watch yourselves,
It'd be best to go to the camp and stay there tonight."

That explained the drawn gun. "Thanks, officer, we'll
take that advice."

I went through the roadblock slowly as requested. I
didn't want to make any quick moves. I thought the police were jumpy and, without question, so was I. We got
back to the camp and I parked the wagon at the office.
Kitty seemed tense.

"You okay?"

"Yes, but that cop scared me. I couldn't take my eyes off
his gun. Why'd he keep it on the windowsill like that? It
was pointing right at me!"
I slipped my arm around her waist and said, "We're
okay. He was probably scared, too."

We walked down the road. Kitty said, "Max, they've
closed the bathhouse closest to my cabin. I need a
powder room. Wait for me. I'll just duck into the mess
hall, okay?"

Kitty went into the mess hall, and I sat down on the
bench outside. I'd spent a lot of time on that bench trying

to sort out various problems, waiting for Mickey to finish talking to Bob Wheeler after my fight with Crash, and grabbing quick snacks between trips. I was tired from the heavy food we'd eaten and was feeling mellow. Time slipped by. I started to wonder where Kitty was. Reminded me of when Moira disappeared into the bathroom at the coffee shop for a half an hour. *What is it with women and bathrooms?* I pondered. I started to reminisce about Moira and all we went through together. Then a voice snarled through the window behind the bench.

"Hello, Asshole, come on in here. I got a proposition you can't refuse."

It was Crash! I jumped off the bench, turned around, and saw him standing behind the window. He had an arm around Kitty's neck and a gun in her side.

"Max, do what he says. He's got a gun!"

I walked around the corner to the main door of the mess hall and walked slowly inside.

"Well, well, my old pal Max, and Miss Katz, too. What a nice reunion."

It didn't take a genius to figure out what was going on, who had robbed the jewelry store and had traded shots with the trooper. I tried to keep cool and play dumb.

"What do you want, Crash? Put down the gun, okay. Someone could get hurt."

Kitty struggled, and he tightened his grip on her neck. She grimaced and squirmed.

"I'm in a bit of trouble and you're going to get me out of here. I'm running from the cops. They're after me, but I'm not the one they want, okay. I didn't do anything."

"How did you get here? There are roadblocks everywhere. We just came through."

"Ah, those dummies. I know the roads around here better than they ever will. I lost them by going down back roads. My car's parked on the other side; they'll never find it. But they'll know it if they see it. I was spotted. I can't use it. I came to get the wagon, and what great luck! I got the wagon, you with the keys, and Miss Katz here, so the three of us can drive right through the road-blocks. I'll be happy to drop you off a couple of miles down the road. You two will be in the front, and I'll be flat on the wagon bed, right behind Miss Katz's back with my gun against her seat, okay? Come on."

Kitty hissed, "I smell gas." She kept wriggling, and Crash tightened his grip again. I hadn't believed anything Crash had said. He was a natural-born liar. I knew he wouldn't let us go. We could identify him. Abruptly I also smelled gas. Something was really wrong.

"Crash, there's gas coming from the kitchen. Let me go check on it and we'll help you out, okay?"

"No, we're going now. I turned on the gas. My little surprise goodbye to Camp Nowatoma and all the jerks I had to deal with here. Come on!"

The stink of gas was getting stronger, and I dreaded that the place would erupt. Crash's turning on the gas proved to me that he was crazy, that he carried out the robbery and shot the trooper. Trusting him would get us killed. If we left with him in the wagon we were as good as dead.

Kitty moaned. Between Crash's strangle hold and the increasing gas fumes she was getting sick. Her knees buckled and she sagged against Crash. He lost his balance momentarily, and I reacted without thinking. I stepped forward and slammed my fist down on his gun arm with everything I had. The gun dropped and skittered along the floor. He let go of Kitty. She dropped like a sack of potatoes and sprawled on the ground, unmoving. I swung and missed Crash's nose. My fist caught him on the right ear. He wrapped one arm around me and reached into his back pocket with his other hand. I figured on a knife. We struggled, both off balance. I slipped and went down hard. He came at me with a long kitchen meat knife. Kitty muscled herself up to a sitting position, stuck one long beautiful leg out, and tripped him. The knife went flying, and he fell on top of me. He landed with his forearm thrusting into my neck. I was already winded from the fall and started to lose consciousness.

As I started to pass out, I heard Kitty screaming…"YOU LOUSY SON OF A BITCH, YOU RUINED MY DRESS AND PEARLS!"

I saw a yellow flash in the dark and heard a sickening crunch. Crash collapsed on top of me. Kitty was standing over us, holding one of the heavy maple chairs. She raised it again, and I squeaked, "Stop, for god's sake! You'll kill him if he isn't already dead!"

"My pearls," she cried. "They were my Grandma Fannie's! My mom will kill me. That bastard!"

I rolled Crash off of me. I didn't know if he was dead, but he sure was out cold.

"THE GAS!" Breathing like an old steam engine, I ran into the kitchen.

Kitty was screaming, "Max, don't turn on any lights! A spark will blow the place up!"

It was dim in the kitchen. I knew my way around even with the lights off. I twisted off the burners, and then opened the windows and doors. I stumbled back into the mess hall, and together we dragged Crash outside. There was a phone in the mess hall, but I didn't know if using it would be safe. I staggered my way to the office. I found my key, pushed inside, and called the operator.

In minutes later we were no longer alone. Flashing lights, fire trucks, police cars and an ambulance for Crash who was still unconscious. We had to answer a lot of questions. All in all, it went pretty well. The police had their man. It was about two in the morning by the time everything got straightened out. Kitty and I started walking back to her cabin. She was shaking and crying about the dress and the pearls. She still wasn't sure whether she had killed Crash.

"Max, did I kill him? Don't tell me I'm a murderer, please."

"He was alive when they put him in the ambulance. The medic told me he was breathing."

"I didn't want to kill him. Something went off in my head. Oh, I don't feel so good. The Martini made me woozy, and when he got his arm around me, he choked off my breath. He stank, Max. Like cigarets and alcohol. And the gas in the mess hall... oh, god, it was awful. Max, I don't feel so good. I think I'm gonna..."

She fell against me, gagged a couple of times, and threw up twenty-five dollars worth of Chateaubriand on my good shirt and shoes.

"Max...."

"I know, sweetie, you don't feel so good." I got an arm around her and kept her walking toward her cabin.

"Grandma Fannie's pearls, Max...."

"Kitty, I'll go pick them up at first light tomorrow. You can get them restrung when you get home. Grandma Fannie will never know."

"My dress!"

She had me there. I can do a lot of things, but I'm no tailor. I got her into the cabin. She asked me to unzip her dress. Any other time, I thought, wow. Not this time, though. I got her into bed and went to my cabin. The celebration didn't go as planned. It beat getting killed, though.

Crash lived. He got five to ten years for his night of robbery, shooting, and terror. The judge gave him the maximum sentence. He would have received a heck of a lot more if the mess hall had blown up or if the trooper had died.

Kitty left the next day as planned. I took her to the train and handed her a small paper bag with Grandma Fannie's pearls safe inside. It took me two hours of crawling around on the mess hall floor to find them all. I put them in the little bag my dad gave me that still held the unused condoms. Kitty looked into the bag and started to laugh when she spotted them. We hugged and kissed. It was a sad goodbye for us. And then she was gone.

A few days later, Bob Wheeler took me to the train station. My first time away from home had been much more than a summer job. It had been filled with experiences and people I would never forget. I went there as a boy and came back a man. When I stepped off the train, the ambience back in Chicago had a different look. I knew it was I who had changed.

Epilogue

Twenty-five years later, the unsophisticated boy had become a man. Now grey at the temples and heavier at the waist, I was married to a wonderful woman, and had two beautiful children. I had knocked around at college for a while. My first year at school after the summer camp experience had been pretty much wasted drinking coffee and flirting with girls in the school library, the lounge, the cafeteria, on the stairways, in the hallways and the sidewalk outside. I liked girls.

I thought at first I would be an engineer, then an architect, a criminologist, or a history teacher. Finally I took the Professor's advice and tried a psychology course. I never looked back.

I was now working for the social service agency that had first hired me to be an employee of Camp Nowatoma. The agency had become large and successful, due primarily to a new generation of executives who had the usual degrees in social work or psychology, but who were also skilled politicians, expert at raising funds, and had a solid business sense. They were people who looked at a flaw in the budget the same way a surgeon looked at a tumor.

The old guard had died off or retired. I had worked my way up from an entry position to Director of Family Services, and I oversaw a good-sized department of family therapists, wrote grant proposals and spent a fair amount of time educating board members and even legislators about programs and community service needs. The organization grew and prospered and met a wide range of client requirements.

Mrs. Silverman had come and gone as Board President. We became good friends, but I always thought she was irked that Shoshana and I didn't get together. Her daughter was now on the board. She spent little time working for the agency. Shoshana married the boy her mother disapproved of, had one son, not twins, and divorced. It wasn't Mrs. Silverman's grand strategy, but Shoshana's career made up for a lot.

Whenever she was in town we had lunch as old friends. It always amazed me that when we got together I saw an unhappy, anxious, phobic person who always appeared frightened. She jumped each time the waiter asked if everything was all right. Whenever I saw her perform, it appeared that another personality inhabited her body. She became effervescent and charmed audiences with her wide smile and graceful bows. She appeared to be a different person altogether. Her playing was spectacular.

I lost track of many of the camp staff from those past years. I'd heard that Bob Wheeler had died of cancer when he was eighty. Ken had retired and moved to Florida. He'd call me every so often, and we would talk about "the old days" and chuckle bout Marilyn Monroe befouling the wagon.

Moira and Victoria became a couple and moved to San Francisco, where their lifestyle was acceptable. Bruce Marshall became a physician, and after serving in Viet Nam, opened a successful family practice in Los Angeles. We're still in touch. Now and then I would hear from somebody who'd worked at camp and we'd dust off our memories about the good times we'd had. Kitty and I traded letters for a few years. She completed her degree in physics and then changed direction. She entered medical school and became a pediatrician; she'd always loved children. The last letter I got from her stated that

353

she was pregnant and had married one of her professors.

At a quarter-century camp had faded to a fond, long-
past memory. One morning I was in the office early as
usual and began my day by filling a pipe, a habit I've
since quit. The phone rang, and because the reception
staff hadn't arrived, I answered it.
"
Hello, Dr. Lewis here."

"Max, it's Mickey. How are you, Max? It's been a long
time."

"Mickey, I'm so surprised to hear from you? How are
you?"

"I'm fine, Max. I wonder if I could come to see you—at
your office. Would you give me some time?"

"Oh, I'd love to see you again, Mickey. Sure, let me look
at my calendar."

I checked my schedule and gave her the first open date.
She wanted to come early in the morning, and didn't
mention why she wanted to see me. I was pretty sure I
knew. I figured that she had a problem. It was the only
reason that people called me at work.

I thought I had our meeting figured, how it would go. We
would catch up on our lives and share some memories
of times past. She would then fill me in on whatever was
troubling her. I'd suggest someone with whom she

could work. I would explain that it wouldn't be proper for me to work with her given our history together.

I really did relish hearing from her and was burning with curiosity about how her life had gone. I had no romantic feelings for her; I had let those go a long time back. I thought that I understood her and more importantly, myself. It would just be two old friends reminiscing with no loose emotional ends.

I was in my office early on the day of her appointment. None of the reception or professional staff had come in as yet. I heard the elevator doors open down the hall and went out to greet her. She looked terrific. She had kept that beautiful figure. The eyes were less "dreamy" but no less arresting. She'd seen a lot with those eyes. I thought they showed some grueling experiences. Her skin was still flawless except for tiny crow's-feet at the corners of her eyes that lent character. We hugged. I wanted to keep it short. She clung on long enough to make me feel uncomfortable.

It was a bizarre encounter that didn't go the way I thought it would. We spent too long chatting about the past, and it finally struck me that Mickey was flirting with me, all smiles and warmth with a touch of seductive-ness. I became ill-at-ease and found myself retreating to a more reserved and more "clinical" mode, quietly ob-serving rather than participating in the conversation. I wasn't quite sure what she wanted. It didn't appear to be help with a problem.

Eventually she simply stopped the effort to engage me and said, "You don't mess around, do you?"

There could have been several possibilities to her meaning, but only one made sense. She wanted to renew our
relationship. I simply shook my head. No argument to
stick in my throat this time, no bridge, no regrets.

She took the rejection without emotion, thanked me for
my time, and restated that it was so good to see me. We
said our goodbyes with no talk of "getting together some
time." I watched her walk down the hall, press for the
elevator and walk in, as always, without a look behind
her. I never saw her again.

About a year-and-a half after our meeting, one of the
social caseworkers stopped by my office. His name was
Jerry Solomon. He was one of those pompous types
who wore a small beard in the style of Sigmund Freud.
He usually wore a suit with vest and sported a gold
watch chain across his belly. I wondered why he didn't
part his hair in the middle, wear a monocle, and finish
the job.
"Max, you got a couple of minutes?"

"Step right in, Jerry, no waiting. You want your vest
pressed?" He didn't catch the attempt at humor, and I
didn't much care.

"You know a woman named," he consulted a manila
case file in his hand, "Mrs. Robert Simons?"

"No, rings no bell, why?"

"I was working with her for the past month or so. She
was hospitalized and I was trying to track down her former husband. She's about forty-two, had a mastectomy

a couple of years back. She was married to this guy Simons who's a commodity trader. He was very successful, but made some bad trades. That and the two of
them were blowing money like there was no tomorrow.
Sank the fiscal ship. Okay, so the money's gone, Mrs.
Simons gets diagnosed with breast cancer, and he bails
on her, divorces her and leaves her high and dry. She
gets depressed; apparently her looks are the most important thing to her. Her surgeon had outlined a course
of chemo and she neglected it. The cancer spread and
she winds up at Evanston Hospital. They called us in. I
got the case and went to see her. She told me she
knows you. Asked me to tell you she's there. Said she
wanted to talk to you."

"Yeah, okay, Jerry, but I don't know her."

"She said to tell you her name's Mickey."

"Oh, god, I do know her! What room's she in? I'll go visit!
She's where, at Evanston?"

"Max, she died last Friday."

" She— Jerry! Why the hell didn't you tell me?"

"Confidentiality. You know the rules."

"What the fuck are you talking about? I'm a colleague.
I've supervised you on cases!"

"Yeah, but Max, you knew her personally and that...." I
grabbed him by his out-of-date lapels, pulled him out of
his chair, and slammed him against a wall.

"You dumb son of a bitch, you sorry bastard— the woman is dying and asking for me and you don't tell me? Get the hell out of here!"

And with that I shoved him out of my office and fell into my swivel chair, stunned. Mickey was gone! Her death gnawed at me for a long time. It had nothing to do with the love I'd had for her; that was long ago put away. Two things haunted me, and still do. The first is that when someone is dying and asks for you, it's a solemn duty to go. I had ultimately failed to be there when Mickey needed me.
The second thing, of course, was what she wanted to tell me. I had lost that forever.

The End